TANGLED AT FIRST Sight

Once Upon a Romance
Book 6

LAURIE LECLAIR

DEDICATION

To the many wonderful people who love and support me. Thank you. I am so blessed to have you in my life.

And to my husband, Jim. Words can never come close to how grateful and humbled I am to have you by my side. Thanks, babe, for loving and supporting me and my dreams for all these years.

CHAPTER 1

"Earth to Paige. Earth to Paige!"

Paige Sumner heard her name and the snapping of fingers in front of her. She stilled, and then jerked her head up from her drawing. "Dolly. I didn't realize you were here."

"The whole building coulda tumbled down around you and you wouldn't have noticed, honey." The funny, sweet lady was right, of course. Waving her hand, she said, "Enough with that. You come help with the drinks and we'll join the rest of them in King's Café." Lowering her voice, she said, "Big news. B-I-G!"

She gulped hard. *Why am I invited? I'm just an employee.* Forlornly, she looked at her drawing again and back at the blank wall in this chamber. She was just getting into the ideas for the knight mural—castles, horses, a dragon, knights in shining armor. It would be a great addition to the café. The little princess room was a smash hit. Now, the King family had asked her to do the mural for the all-boy room to balance it out.

"Hurry. Time's a wastin'."

Smiling, Paige rose from the bare floor. She gave a lingering glance to the drawing and the room, and then a lusty sigh before she followed the perky older woman. Dolly was still talking and chuckling. "Special drink… coming up…"

Does she always talk to herself? Paige made her way down the hall and into the huge restaurant kitchen screaming stainless-steel everything.

The hearty laughter from the overwhelming King family gathering rushed to her from the main dining area. She gulped hard at the thought of the noisy grandkids playing, grandparents cooing at the babies, and adults conversing. Dodging the crowd when she first arrived seemed the best defense. Now, she'd have to at least make an appearance. "I don't belong here," she whispered.

"Just take in that tray of drinks for me, will ya, honey? I've gotta grab these babies out of the oven before they burn." The metal clanged as she took out the baking sheets. "New recipe. Marcus, Stu, and I did the buffet. Gotta have taste testers for our new recipes. We're putting together a cookbook for King's. Ain't that somethin'?"

Paige murmured and grabbed for the tray. *One good deed, and then I'm back to drawing.*

The tray was big and cumbersome. *A restaurant tray with at least ten glasses. Figures!* Backing out of the room, she went unnoticed. She tiptoed away, turned, and promptly ran into someone. Reaching out, Dolly grabbed for the tray to help steady them. Lemonade sloshed over the sides and splashed on the metal.

"But, how did you get from there to here?" Paige wondered how the woman had moved so fast. *It was like something out of the movies. The woman moved at lightning speed.*

"Well, I'll be a monkey's uncle," Dolly exclaimed. "I was just checking on the crowd and boom, you're under my feet. You scared me half to death, Paigey. Come and help me tidy up."

Paige grimaced at the nickname the King family cook had bestowed on her and the idea of hanging around. But, she did cause this mess, so her manners won out. "I'll be glad to." *Well, not really*, she thought as twin boys banged through the doors and rushed into the kitchen.

"Slow them steps down, Pete and Repeat." Dolly winked at her. "Love them two little rascals."

"Yes ma'am," they called out in unison. They scrambled in and rummaged for something, and then, just as quickly, dashed back out again.

"My, this place is Grand Central Station if you ask me. But, I love it." She giggled.

Smiling at the likeable lady, she followed her back into the big modern kitchen with every known stainless-steel appliance gleaming. The wonderful aroma of chocolate made her moan. "This could be straight out of one of those design magazines Priscilla loves so much.

Now I know why you like to use this as your test kitchen and bake all those goodies to send to the store for us."

Dolly patted her hips. "Honey, you can't keep a good girl down. If you know what I mean?"

Hurriedly, Paige wiped down the outside of the glasses while Dolly cleaned off the tray.

"You can't fool me. You were trying to sneak out. No, don't you go denying it. I can tell just by your cheeks turning pink."

Heat stung her. *Caught!* Shrugging, she said, "I'm an only child. I'm not used to a lot of people." *That much was true.*

She burst out laughing. "Well, get used to it and fast. You're the next big thing at King's, so you're going to get noticed."

Her throat went dry—well even drier than it was. Shaking her head, she said, "No. No way. Not me."

"Uh huh. Yes, you."

This time a chill went over her. All she wanted was a normal, boring life. *Was that asking too much?* At twenty-seven, she'd had enough drama and attention to last her a lifetime. Normal, was her adopted mantra this last year.

Going against her parents' wishes, she'd found a roommate and moved into an apartment. They were still overprotective and dropped by or called several times a day. Truth be told, they'd smothered her, but she didn't have the heart to come right out and tell them: *Mom,*

Dad, I need my own space and you need to find something else to focus on now. Or, in other words, get a life.

They'd been through so much pain because of her. She couldn't hurt them again.

Slowly, she struck out to do the things she'd never been allowed to do before. It was liberating and scary all at the same time.

Normal was nice. Normal was just where she wanted to stay.

However, her recent nine-to-five job had turned against her when Charlotte King, the owner of King's, spotted her drawings one day. From one artist to another, they'd hit it off and soon Paige found herself designing dresses instead of selling them.

She loved to design and thought she'd hide in a room all by herself. It had worked. Until recently.

Ditching get-togethers and ducking out of the spotlight had worked fine. Until now…

"Ah, Dolly. I'm not sure what you mean." Fear trickled down her spine.

"You, silly. You're the next hit at King's. I can't wait to see that blush wedding dress you just designed." Lowering her voice, she whispered, "Charlie wants you to model it for the promo ads. My, that long, long blonde hair of yours…How long is it, honey? You never did answer that one?"

Um…over four feet, when I take it down or out of the braid.

"And your beau-tee-ful big blue eyes..." She sighed wistfully.

This was the first she heard of the plan. "She... never said anything."

"Oops!" She chuckled. "I let the cat out of the bag, didn't I? Never you mind what I say."

How could she forget something like that? Her picture splayed across newspapers. Again! No, not this time.

"You take this tray to the family, will ya? No ditching us, either, hear me? I gotta check on the whoopie pies. My first time making this kind of whoopie, if you know what I mean."

She chuckled with the lady. Dolly kept talking and laughing as Paige picked up the tray. She tread lightly out of the room and to the large double swinging doors. Glancing around, she spotted a table to set the heavy tray down on before she made her getaway.

Male voices grew louder, making her heart jump to her throat. She froze. Someone, maybe Dolly, would come and find her here, ready to bolt. Then she'd never get away.

There was only one thing to do.

Balancing the tray in her hand, she scurried to the door and shoved it open. It shoved back. The force propelled her backwards. She stumbled, the glasses clinking together, and then she righted herself. Going back again, she pushed forward. *Charge!*

Before she could get there, the door swung inward.

She saw a chest—wide and in her face—covered in a denim shirt just before she plowed into it. *Now I know what it's like running into a brick wall.*

"Wow!" Gulping, she looked up and into startling warm chocolate-brown eyes. She tried to draw back, but her hair was snagged on him. *Somewhere.* She didn't dare look any lower.

"Wow, yourself," he said, looking at her and then to her long, thick braid draped over her shoulder and now part of it tangled in the buttons on his shirt. "Here, let me," he offered, gently extracting the silky, long strands.

"Jay, I told you she was pretty," the man-boy beside him said.

"That she is, brother, that she is…" He whispered the last, his voice low.

It tugged at her. Something crashed and fell, hitting the pit of her belly. Finally, she dragged her attention away from Mr. Rock Hard Sexy and turned to the guy beside him. "Hey, I know you. Danny, what are you doing here?" Her breakroom buddy stood with that sweet, goofy grin of his. He shoved his glasses back up on his nose.

"I know you, too. Fancy meeting you here. Paige, this is my baby brother. Jay, this is my friend from King's, Paige. Now shake hands." He eyed them closely.

Reluctantly, Paige rebalanced the tray and did as he said. *Baby brother?* The guy was taller by at least six inches and broader. Sexy Jay took her hand and held it in his large grasp. She let out a gasp at the strong, yet gentle touch. Pinpricks raced up her arm.

Paige grew warm, very warm. Tugging her hand and her gaze away, she shoved the drink tray at him. Thankfully, he grabbed it and held it easily in his big hands. “Help yourself. And while you’re at it, you can pass them around.” She tilted her head to the voices coming from the dining area. “I’m outta here.”

“Uh…” He stuttered. “Your shirt. Wet T-shirt contest kinda wet.” His gaze flickered over her damp shirt and met her eyes. His lopsided grin made her weak-kneed. “If you’re going for that look, no problem. But, I’m not sure if you’re into public partial nudity.”

Jerking her gaze to the front of her white shirt, Paige groaned at the large wet spot and how it seeped to her bra, making everything particularly transparent. Quickly, she repositioned her braid to cover the right one and crossed her arms over her chest and covered herself.

Could you die of embarrassment? Was there some kind of study done? Like how it begins with the whooshing heat and continues until there’s nothing but ashes left? ’Cause she could feel the heat blasting through her cheeks at the moment and the rest of her was on fire. *Is this the answer to the great mystery of spontaneous combustion?*

She tried to glimpse a peek over his broad shoulder. “I gotta go.” *But where to, looking like this?*

***

Jay Whitfield sucked in a sharp breath. "Is it something I said?" His lips twitched when his question stopped her short. The bright pink in her cheeks was still there and she couldn't look him in the eye.

At least she smiled. "I'm not a people person."

"Well, Jay is. Aren't you, Jay?" Danny elbowed him. "Everyone loves him."

"That's not entirely true." He took pity on the poor girl and handed Danny the tray, Jay shucked off his denim shirt, revealing the black T-shirt he wore underneath, and held it out to her. God, it was a shame to cover her up. He'd glanced and swallowed hard. She was incredible. But he wasn't a dog. *Never was, never had been. Not his style.*

There, she looked up and held his stare. It was hard to breathe. Reaching out, she took the offered shirt. "Thanks. I owe you." Hurriedly, she jerked it on, pulling the long braid out. The fabric hung down to her knees on her petite body. She gathered the edges, bunched it up, and tied the tails together low on her sexy hips. *Skintight jeans and sexy sandals. Was it getting hotter in here?*

"Come on, bro, don't be selling yourself short, now. Here, you can show Paige around."

"No. I'm good." Jay cringed at his brother's interference and took the tray of drinks back. How many times did he have to tell this one and the other two, his job was taking care of them? Ever since their dad had died when they were just kids and then their mother when Jay had turned eighteen, he had taken over as the sole caregiver to his older, mentally challenged brother and his two younger ones. They were always trying to fix him up, telling him he needed a life. *He had one, thank you very much.*

"Again? Paigey. Tsk Tsk!" The older woman came up behind her and slipped her arm through hers. "I'm glued to you now, honey."

Paige groaned out loud. "Oh, the suffering."

Jay and his brother chuckled.

"Oh my, it's you! It can't be. You're even bigger and handsomer in person." The older woman waved her hand. "Come in and set those drinks down."

"In person?" Paige whispered to the woman.

"Yeah, don't you know who you're flirting with?"

"I wasn't flirting," she said, looking at him under her long lashes.

"Yeah, right. If you say so." His brother chimed in.

"Danny, I thought you were my friend?' To Dolly, she said, "It's the hair. Everyone stares at the hair." Under her breath, she asked, "Who is he?" But Jay heard her.

"I'm Dolly, by the way. You two hunks come on in."

"Not family. So who?"

Holding the tray prevented him from sticking out his hand again. "I'm—"

"Oh, no you don't, handsome. This one is trying to bolt. Let's keep her curious and she'll hang out for a while."

Jay read the debate chasing over her beautiful features. Her eyes clouded over, yet took him in.

He grew warm, feeling her gaze travel over his face, and then his shoulders, his biceps, and skimmed the rest of him. The blood in his veins buzzed. Jay swallowed. *No one had ever made him this hot with just one look. No one.* "See enough?"

There it was again; that battle going on in her shone in those crystal-clear blue eyes. She shrugged nonchalantly.

"Oh, come on, you want to know," Jay's brother pressed, grinning from ear-to-ear.

Someone burst through the doors. "Shake a leg, will ya?" A voice from behind him caught his attention.

"Girls, where have you been? You're missing all the fun—" The colorful guy stopped in mid-sentence when he halted beside Dolly. His jaw dropped for a second. "O-M-G! Well, I rephrase that. You two were having all the fun. Hello, gorgeous." *He did a great Streisand impersonation.*

Jay's brother said, "Thank you, Rico. I got all the looks in the family."

They chuckled in unison.

"Who do we have here?"

Dolly elbowed him. "It's a surprise, Rico. Paige was going to duck out on us. So now she's gotta stay and find out."

He smacked Paige on the arm. "Quit doing that, girl. Admit it. You can't hide anymore."

"Not with the two of you breathing down my neck," she muttered, defeated. But there was a smile in her voice.

CHAPTER 2

What in the world is going on? Paige sat tense in her chair. *And guess who they'd sat next to her?* Of all people, the handsome mystery guy and her former breakroom friend, Danny. Too bad she'd never gotten his last name. He'd started working a few weeks ago, in the stockroom. He'd helped her with a vending machine when her drink had gotten stuck. Her *former* hero.

"Don't think I won't hold this against you," she said, leaning around hot guy to tell Danny.

"You're funny, Paige. One day, you'll thank me."

The food was delicious. In spite of being anxious of the crowd and the mystery guy, Paige polished off her food samples. On a nearby sheet, she rated the dishes—appetizers, salads, main meals, dessert. Maybe she needed another bite or two. *Just to help out, of course.* She glanced down at his plate. "You gonna finish that quiche?"

"Help yourself." He shifted his arm and laid it along the back of her chair.

His scent, warm and musky, filled her nostrils. The heat from his arm seared her back. She eyed him under her lashes. “Food. That’s all I want.” Her tummy grumbled. *Starving.*

He chuckled. “Sounds like you haven’t eaten in a week.”

Whoosh! Heat blasted her face. It was something she’d dealt with for years now. Side effects of her treatment. But she wouldn’t tell him that. “Like a cat, you know. I purr when I’m hungry.” *Oh, fudge, that came out all breathy and sexy.*

“I thought they only purred when they’re happy… and satisfied.” His husky voice whispered in her ear.

She shivered.

“If I could have everyone’s attention please,” Charlotte King called out as she stood before them. The dull roar eased and the room hushed.

Thank you, Charlie, for saving my butt. Quickly, she grabbed the quiche off his plate and bit into it. She moaned softly.

Jay sucked in a sharp breath.

In mid-chew, Paige glanced at him. His eyes were on hers, and then his gaze dropped to her mouth. She must have crumbs there. Scrubbing her lips with her fingers, she swore she read disappointment in his eyes. Turning away, she popped the rest into her mouth and quickly finished it off. She’d never let a hot gaze detour her from food.

“Thank you all for coming today. Although most of

you didn't have a choice, did you?" Charlie looked at her family. "Dolly threatened and Eddie rounded you up." Everyone chuckled.

"Griff," she nodded to the man she'd hired to run the store and now her brother-in-law, "and I have some exciting news to share with all of you. But, first, we want to welcome our guests. Rico, you're part of the family, and, even if you weren't, there'd be no need to introduce you since you're one of a kind and everyone loves you."

"Of course I am," he agreed, much to everyone's delight. He fluffed his hair. "I make an impression."

"Indeed you do," Griff, sitting nearby, said.

Rico stuck his tongue out at Griff. "Smarty pants."

"That's our Rico," Charlie offered. "Now, back to business. I'd like you to meet our rising bright star, Paige Sumner. Paige, stand up so everyone can see you."

She froze. She slid down in her chair. *Didn't work.* All eyes focused on her. She forced a polite smile and waved off Charlie. *No thanks.*

"Take your bow," Jay said, coaxing her.

"Thanks, I'm good," she said for everyone's ears. To Jay, she said, "Mind your beeswax, will ya?"

Before she could get anything else out, Dolly was by her side and tugging her chair back. "No getting outta this one, Paigey. Go on up there." The woman half pulled and half dragged her out of her chair and up beside Charlie.

Her boss touched her arm. "Everyone, this is Paige Sumner, our newest wedding dress designer. She's incredibly talented."

"Hear, hear!" Francine King Goode, the wedding dress buyer for King's and Charlie's stepsister, cheered. "Exquisite designs!"

"Gorg!" Rico, King's wedding coordinator, chimed in, clapping louder than the rest. "Swoon worthy!"

Charlie nodded to her sister and Rico, and then continued. "You have seen her artistic work in the princess room here at the café. Well, she's now working on the mural for the knight room opening soon."

Paige wanted to simply die, quick and fast. Her cheeks burned and she could barely look at the people clapping. She let her gaze skim the thirty plus family members and sunk inwardly a little more.

She wanted *out* of the spotlight, not *into* it. *Once was more than enough. And for all the wrong reasons.*

Bravely, she glanced at Jay. His grin made her breath catch. She caught the slight nod he gave her and the tension in her eased a bit.

"We—Griff, Francie, Rico, and myself—have decided Paige should get her own wedding line dress label at King's…"

A thousand bees buzzed in her ears. She missed the rest of the speech; her mind crashed. *No, I must be hearing it wrong. No can do! Safe. Boring. Hidden away. That's what she longed for.*

"Okie dokie, got the contracts all done," Peg, the

executive assistant to Griff, said, tapping on her clipboard.

"Paige? Honey, you've gone white on me." Charlie put her arm around Paige and hugged her to her side. "I know. It's a surprise. But, really, you're tops. Take some time to let it sink in." To the family, Charlie said, "We'll give Paige here some breathing room. Right, honey? The King family can take a bit to get used to."

On shaky legs and to more applause, Paige made it back to her chair. Jay stood and helped her sit down. "Impressive, Ms. Sumner."

Her tight smile made her face ache. "What, the red face or the white one?" *I'm talented like that.*

His chuckle warmed the cold places in her and she began to feel again. *Not a good sign when it was Mr. Rock Hard Sexy doing it to you.*

"Marcus, would you like to tell us your news before I go any further?" Charlie asked.

"Sure thing." He kissed his wife and baby girl before moving to Charlie's side. He nodded to Jay and said, "We have two more guests. King's own, Danny, who started in the stockroom a few weeks ago. He's amazing at organizing things and, if he's willing, I can use him to help organize Stu and my restaurant storerooms."

"I'm your guy," Danny said, grinning from ear-to-ear.

Jay pat his brother on the shoulder. "Great job, buddy."

"My new side business." Danny rubbed his hands

together.

Paige chuckled.

"Now, the guy sitting next to him is his brother, Jay Whitfield. Jay, if you don't already know, is a former Dallas Cowboys tight end—"

"Oh, shut the front door," Rico exclaimed. "Tight end?! I call dibs!"

Paige stilled and then slowly turned to the man sitting at her side. She blinked once and then again as she stared at him. *Why hadn't she realized it before now?* He was known for his quick moves and fast legs. *The great Jay Whitfield! Her father would flip if he knew she'd met him, never mind sat beside him.*

"Surprise!"

"You…*the* Jay—" She gulped hard. Something inside her crashed and burned. He was incredible on the field. His college and pro records could fill a book. His name alone would stop traffic, never mind his gorgeous face, warm brown eyes, and wavy shoulder length hair. He made men—look at Rico now—and women swoon. Kids looked up to him. His charity work was legendary. He was just as at ease off the football field as he was on. And people adored him.

He made the papers slightly less now that he'd retired due to several concussions. But he'd been rumored to be working on some exciting new things to be announced soon. It was only a matter of time before he hit the Dallas headlines again.

"You look mad for some reason," he whispered to

her.

"Congratulations on being a god," she muttered, turning away from him. For some reason it hurt. He hadn't said a thing. And why should he; he was a stranger to her. But, she should have known he was special, should have sensed he was famous and in the limelight…

Where the heck was her radar when she needed it the most?

***

He couldn't figure her out. One minute, they're joking and the next, she's looking at him as if he'd grown a horn in the middle of his head.

"Jay?" Marcus asked.

His brother jabbed him in the side with an elbow. "They want to know if you're gay."

Jerking his head back to focus on Marcus, he said, "What?"

"Rico wants to know what side you play on."

Looking across the many tables packed with the King family, he caught the man's wide eyes and big, hopeful smile. Jay shook his head. "Sorry, bud, not my type."

He pressed the back of his hand to his forehead. "Why? Just tell me why all the good ones are straight?"

Jay chuckled and the others joined him. Even Paige let out a puff. *Was it a laugh or a snort? Why should he even care?*

"Your true love is out there, Rico." Under his breath, Marcus said, "Somewhere. Hopefully he'll show up soon and help us all out."

"I heard that," Rico said. "And I used to like you, too."

Marcus grinned. "No hard feelings, Rico. It's just you need to get—"

"Hey, not in front of the children," Dolly chimed in.

"A man." Marcus finished and shook his head. "What did you think I was going to say, Dolly?"

The older woman blushed. "Mr. G., you don't fool me. I know what you were thinking."

He winked at her and the pink turned to red. There was a lot of ribbing from the other family members.

Jay smiled. The close-knit family made him realize he was making the right move for his brothers and himself. This wasn't so much a world-renowned department store as it was a family business that happened to be very, very successful.

Marcus held up his hands to quiet them. "Okay, folks, back to more news. Jay, Stu, and I are in serious talks, which is code for it's a go, to open a sports bar and grill in the city."

"What?"

"I'll be damned…"

"Yes…"

Cheers went up and congratulations went around. All but Paige reacted. Well, she did, but not in a good way.

“Is it the bar and grill or just me you don’t like?” Jay asked. *Why should it matter to him?*

Finally, she turned to him. “It’ll be a smash hit.” She shrugged. “If that’s the sort of thing you like.”

He recalled her reaction to being called up beside Charlotte King—her cringing at the request, her reluctance to take a bow. “Don’t you like success?”

“Love it,” she said tightly. “For other people.” She shoved back her chair.

Jay stopped her. “He’s not finished. You have to stay for the rest of it.” *No wonder Dolly had to warn him she was a flight risk.*

“Not only that, but there’s more,” Charlie said. She nodded in his direction. “Jay has agreed to an exclusive deal with King’s Department Store. He will have his own line with us. So we’ll have two new lines we’ll be promoting in the next few months: Jay’s brand and products and Paige’s wedding dress line.”

“No, she just didn’t say that, did she?” Paige muttered, jerking her head to look at him.

“Yep.” Jay smiled with satisfaction at her stunned expression. “You and me, Paige.”

***

Paige’s heart plunged to her belly. *No. No can do.* It was bad enough with the thought of her line, but him, too? The King’s campaigns were legendary. *Smart. Hip. And pure genius.*

Now with Jay added to the mix, there was no getting out of being noticed, especially if they promoted them back to back or side by side. *Whatever! She couldn't go there.*

"There's more," Charlie continued. "Alex, Griff, Shane, do you want to join me?"

Gulping hard, Paige couldn't imagine why Charlie called her husband, Alex, the head honcho at King's, and Paige's roommate's new fiancé to join her. *Oh, what next? Is they sky falling yet?*

Glancing over at her roommate on the other side of the room, Paige got the shrugging shoulders look of defeat. Evelyn knew something, but wasn't telling. *Some roommate Ev was! She was glad she was moving out soon. Well, not really, but seriously, what else could go wrong?*

Charlie took a deep breath. He husband, Alexander Royale, of *the* Royale Enterprises, squeezed his wife's hand. "Griff reworked King's five-year and ten-year business plans. We have far exceeded any of our expectations since I've become owner. So we're moving up our plans and getting to work on…Rico, drum roll, please."

He tapped the table.

"King's just bought the vacant building next door." She nodded to the other end of the café, on the opposite side of where King's stood. "Royale Enterprises agreed to help with the exterior design and Shane Weston here of *the* Weston Construction has signed on for the interior construction…"

"And Priscilla is doing the interior design," Francie chimed in, hugging her sister sitting next to her. "And I'll be in the mix…a little." She held up her finger and forefinger an inch apart.

"Of what, honey?" Dolly asked, gripping her husband, Edward's, hand so hard it looked like all the blood had been clamped off his hand. "You know, Eddie, don't you?"

"Yep." He grinned widely.

The grandparents murmured, looking around. Alex's grandfather smiled, most likely in on the deal since he founded Royale Enterprises eons ago.

"I'll just tell you." Charlie threw up her hands. "King's is expanding. We're going to have the new building totally devoted to wedding gowns. Our own Charmings Wedding Boutique in its own building!"

Gasps of delight sprinkled the air. Paige's breath caught and held. *How wonderful! How exciting!*

Then realization hit hard. *More fuss. More attention. More press. Her own line would be in the spotlight.*

At one time, long ago, she'd have loved it. Now, it didn't fit into her new normal.

Her heart squeezed in her chest.

It was just too bad she'd never be a part of it.

CHAPTER 3

Jay Whitfield toured the new King's building. Demolition was slated for next week.

He shook his head, wondering how they'd do it all. There were decades of ugly paint plastered to the walls, the rooms were small and claustrophobic, wires hung from the punched-out ceiling, and dust swirled in the air.

Rubbing his hand on his unshaven jaw, he said, "Man, Marcus, you sure this is going to work?" He hoped they'd find a building soon, but, if it was in this much disrepair it would take months to fix it into the sports bar they'd envisioned.

"No problem, buddy." His cell phone rang. "Hey, I've got to get this one. Marcus Goode here…" He walked away to continue the conversation.

Time was of the essence. Jay had his two younger brothers applying for graduate schools. Law school and medical school weren't cheap nowadays. He wanted a steady income to take care of them. Most of his NFL earnings were wrapped up too tight. No one, especially Jay, thought he'd be literally and figuratively knocked out of the game this soon.

Six years was just too early to end a career. But, he had his brothers to think about. He was supposed to take care of them, not the other way around. So he did what he had to do and retired.

Now he wandered the dim, tiny rooms. Somehow, he felt sorry for the forgotten time capsules. How could people work in these offices? Cramped so tight? Bottled up?

He shivered. How was he going to make a life for his brothers and himself? He'd invested wisely, but he hadn't accounted for this unexpected turn of events.

Offers to speak in other cities flooded in. How could he leave his brothers on their own for many days and nights? So he nixed the speaking engagements to only a few and only ones close by.

Product endorsements requests filled his emails and clogged his voicemail. He didn't want to promote just anything.

Then he'd run into his buddies Marcus and Stu from years before. Catching up on old times, they'd dreamed up the sports bar idea. His name and their restaurant experience combined seemed the perfect merger. Plus, it was in the city that had made them all who they were. *Perfect!*

His brother, Danny, couldn't speak highly enough of his new job and King's Department Store. When Jay realized Marcus was married to one of the sisters, he dug into the history more. He liked the new generation taking over and what they were doing.

The next logical step was to ask Marcus for an introduction. That was only a week ago. Now, he was on his way to sign the contracts with Charlie. His lawyer would meet him in less than an hour.

He had time to kill, so Marcus yanked him to see the new building. But it wasn't new. It was old and decrepit. And needed a lot of TLC.

"Yo, Jay!"

"Over here," he called out to Marcus. He met him in the narrow hallway.

"That was my realtor. He's got a couple of properties he's scoping out for the sports bar."

Jay led the way out of the aisle and into a bigger room. The windows were grimy, but there was a little more light coming through. "Tell me it's not this bad."

"Not so far. But we have to be open to anything in our prime location."

Smiling, he said, "Yeah, you and Stu drummed that into my head. Location. Location…"

"Location," Paige finished.

Jay twisted around. He'd recognize that voice anywhere. He gulped hard. "Paige," he barely got her name out. "Nice to see you." *Petite. Sexy.* His heart beat faster. *And I'm not even doing the hundred-yard dash, but it feels like it.*

She folded her arms. "Can't say the same. Hey,

Marcus. I didn't realize you both were here."

Marcus brushed a hand through his hair, looking from Jay to Paige and back to Jay again. "Something I should know?"

"Nothing," Paige said. "Nada."

The air thickened. *Yeah, right! If you felt nothing then you'd be able to look me in the eye right now.* "Don't ask me." Jay shrugged. "She's Danny's break buddy" She did return his denim shirt via Danny days ago. Every time he went to wash it, he couldn't bring himself to erase the combined scents of lemonade and her. "But she can't stand the sight of me."

He swore she turned pink and then white. *There she goes again.*

Her braid hung over her shoulder and nearly reached her knees. She ran her fingers over it, and then, when she realized he was staring, she stuffed her hands in the back pockets of her skinny jeans. "You have a complex."

"Me? I'm good. It's you. The success thing and all."

She snorted.

"Here's my guy," Francie said, rushing into the room and being swept up into Marcus's arms. "God, I missed you."

"Me, too." He brushed her hair off her cheek and kissed her.

Paige cleared her throat. The couple kept kissing. *Wow!* Jay looked away.

"I don't know about you, but I'm outta here," Paige

declared.

"I'll join you," Jay said, following her. "Sometimes your disappearing act makes sense."

"I don't disappear." She ducked her head as she walked under a low hanging cobweb. "I dodge—"

"Uncomfortable situations," he finished. *Like now.* She was trying to rush ahead of him.

"Now that's just..." she sputtered, coming up short when she faced another wall. Turning to her right, she moved away and down the hall.

"It's true, Paige Sumner. Admit it." She moved quickly. *Maybe she should sign up for the team. They could use a star running back. Oh, yeah, she hated that kind of thing.*

"Fat chance." She stopped in front of a tall window. Picking up a nearby rag, she swiped at the dirt on the window, making a circle to see out of. "Nice view."

Jay came up behind her. "Mmm..." *Was he talking about the skyline or her?* Paige was wearing skintight jeans, a bright blue top that ended just below her hips, and matching sandals. *Sexy.* She didn't try hard at all. A little mascara and lip gloss, but nothing else as far as he could tell. It came natural. And she smelled like a mixture of roses and oranges. He moaned softly.

Pulling back, she looked up at him. "You okay? Indigestion or something? Heartburn? What's that, heartbreak of psoriasis?"

"None of the above. You, on the other hand, have an insatiable appetite." *His mind went there*. He skirted the sexual meaning. He recalled the buffet the other day with delicious food. She'd filled her plate three times before Charlie began and Paige had gobbled down his quiche. "Tapeworm?"

"I call it the pit."

"Of despair?" He smiled. *God, she was not only hot as hell, but cute and funny, too.*

She jabbed him on the arm. "Feeding the beast. You know, throwing food in the pit for the beast to consume." Her delicate skin turned pink again.

His gut tightened. *Sexy was too mild a word for what she had.*

"That's why I agreed to meet with Francie and Marcus to discuss some of the plans for this place." She grinned. "Free lunch at his and Stu's bar and grill. Today's special is double cheeseburger and all-you-can-eat fries."

"Of course, you couldn't turn it down." His voice softened of its own accord.

The air crackled. Her smile faded. He heard her gulp hard. That crystal blue-eyed gaze fixated on his eyes, looking, searching. There was layer upon layer of emotions there.

What was she thinking?

"Jay," she whispered. Her glance dropped to his lips. "I want normal. Humdrum."

His gut clenched. *Could a look make your lips throb? I think it just did.* His blood pulsed in his neck. Her stare looked there. It picked up speed.

Her eyes flickered, and then she closed them briefly. Opening them again, she glanced at his chest. Tentatively, she reached out. With just her fingertips, she brushed the thin cloth of his white shirt. *Fire!* He sucked in a sharp breath. *Why her? Why this? Why now?*

"Your heart," she whispered. "It's pounding."

Among other things.

"Hard."

If you only knew.

"It's scary."

To me, too.

She placed her palm on his chest. Heat seared him. He swore he stopped breathing altogether. "You don't talk much."

"And you talk too much." He lowered his head.

Paige tilted hers up. "Are you going to kiss me?"

"Only if you stop talking," he murmured, his lips a hairsbreadth away from hers.

"For crying out loud, just do it!" Francie's voice rang through the air.

Paige jerked away from him. Jay straightened up and groaned. *Of all the luck!*

***

"Really? Francie, did you have to make a big deal out of it?" Paige headed toward the door.

"There she goes again, running for the exit!" Jay

called out.

Paige stopped in her tracks and whirled around. *She did do that a lot lately, didn't she?* "I suppose you're not embarrassed or anything, are you?"

At the moment, his face looked flushed. "Embarrassed is a little mild, don't you think?"

What was he trying to say? Horrified? Mortified, maybe?

"Look, my bad. Okay?" Francie held up her phone. "But, seriously, you two are hot. H-O-T, as Rico would say. Here, I took a picture."

"You didn't?" Paige, Jay, and Marcus, coming into the room, asked at the same time.

Francie had the good grace to wince. "Sorry. But you two would be perfect together…in an ad campaign, that is. See for yourself." She held out her cell phone.

Paige reached for it, but Jay got there quicker. He held it and they both looked at an image of what could only be described as a ridiculously perfect picture of them with their heads close and their mouths even closer.

"His dark hair, tanned skin. Your long blonde hair, pale skin. Her mouth raised to yours…"

Marcus snuck a peek. He clapped Jay on the back. "She's right, brother. Great ad material."

"No," Paige said, shaking her head and backing away.

"Yes," Jay said, fixing her with a keen stare. "That's the only way I'll do an ad for King's. You and me."

"Hell, no!"

CHAPTER 4

Paige sat facing a firing squad. *At least that's what it felt like.* Jay sat beside her. In her boss's office, Griffin James sat behind his desk and stared, first at Jay, her, and then the cell phone picture. Over and over, he looked at all three.

Invisible squirm. He was intimidating on a good day. *But this was off the charts.*

Charlie stood over Griff's left shoulder and Peg leaned over his right shoulder, doing the same. Marcus and Francie were there, standing slightly back, but still eyeing them closely.

"What did we miss?" Priscilla King James rushed in with Rico on her heels.

"Yeah, what did we miss? Francie called the troops, so it's gotta be importante," Rico said, clapping his hands. "I just love when that happens."

"You guys are the bomb. Look at all that hair. Together!" Peg offered. "Pickles and pancakes, we hit the jackpot with the two of them." She nodded to Paige and Jay. "Sorry, sweeties, but when you got it, you got it."

She liked Peg Newbury Rhodes, really she did, but at the moment she wished the woman would pipe down about how spectacular she and Jay looked together.

"Pickles and pancakes?" Jay asked her under his breath.

"You'll get used to it," she said. "Well, maybe."

"What are we going to do about this?" Griff caught and held her gaze.

"Forget you ever saw it?" she asked hopefully. His scowl seemed to deepen. His wife reached out and touched his arm. He visibly relaxed.

"I have an idea." Jay shifted in his chair, gaining everyone's attention.

Well, he did make an impressive figure whether sitting, standing, or doing nothing. If she hadn't felt it for herself, she'd always wonder about his pecs. *Divine, as Rico would say.*

"It's a…compromise."

Griff sat forward, placing his elbows on the desk and clasping his hands. "You're not backing out of the deal, are you, Whitfield?"

"Of course not. My handshake is as good as my word, James."

He tossed Griff's last name back to him. Griff actually smiled. *Well, if you can call the corner of his lip moving slightly upward a smile, that was.*

"Paige." The way Jay said her name made her

insides melt.

She felt his heated stare on her. Slowly, she turned her head to look at him. *Wrong move, sweetheart. You melted into one big aching puddle.*

"I want you to be in the ads with me." His voice was soft and hypnotic.

Closing her eyes, she asked, "Is that your idea of a compromise?" *Slay me with your eyes? Your voice?*

He chuckled. Her heart jumped.

Dang, he hit the spot.

"Your hair. Your eyes. They can use me all they want." He cleared his throat, and then turned back to the watchful eyes of their audience. "No nudity, understand?"

"We're not that kind of store, Jay," Charlie said. "Family first. Values. Respect."

He nodded. "Good. I knew that. But just to cover my bases." He glanced down at his watch. "My lawyer is late."

"Your idea?" Paige prompted, none too gently.

"They use only your beautiful hair. Your gorgeous eyes. Just parts of you show, so you can," he leaned close and whispered, "disappear right in front of everyone's eyes."

"Holy space cadets! Futuristic stuff? Magician act? Or John Cena you can't see me, stuff?" Peg held up her hand and moved it back and forth in front of her face.

Jay eased back in his chair and chuckled. "Very inventive, Peg."

Gulping hard, Paige glanced at him. His offer *was* unique.

"I love it! L-O-V-E!" Rico exclaimed, coming around the desk and hugging Paige and smoothing her long braid. He seemed to purr. "But, honey, if you ever, ever decide to whack this thing off," he picked up the heavy rope-like braid, "I'm your man."

As if she'd sacrifice years of, well, becoming normal again. She stiffened. He gripped her harder still. Finally, Paige relaxed and he released her. "I didn't say I'd do it." *Either the ad or the hair chopping part.*

"You'll get a model's fee, of course." Griff named a five-figure sum. "To begin with."

"There's more available in the budget for certain ads and campaigns," Charlie added.

"Big ones." Peg nodded. "I see the checks."

Trying to swallow, it got stuck in Paige's throat. Her breath stayed trapped in her lungs and her eyes watered. "How much again?" she whispered, sucking in air.

"You heard, honey." Rico raised his hand. "Pick me! Me, me next. I'll do it for half the price and twice the exposure."

Paige Sumner gripped the arm of her chair. She wanted a normal, boring, nine-to-five job. She'd gotten what she'd asked for, along with the measly wages to go with it. Some weeks she could barely scrap two pennies together.

Her roommate, Evelyn, met and was engaged to Shane Weston and ready to move out. So until she found someone else, Paige had double the expenses to contend with in the near future. *Like tomorrow or the next day, maybe. It wouldn't be long before Ev moved all her stuff out.*

Going to her parents was out of the question. They'd sacrificed for her. *Blood, sweet, and tears.* They'd drained their life savings, mortgaged their house, and lost nearly everything they had to save her years ago.

They'd keep her in their house and smothered her with love if she'd let them. But she had to break away for their sakes, as well as hers.

Once she explained her part in the wedding dresses, they beamed with pride. Her designs earned more. And every now and then she could take her folks out to a special dinner.

"That's a lot of money," she said. Swiftly, she calculated a few ads' pay and realized she could even help them get another house or condo. Her father would love one on the golf course. He hadn't played in years; his two jobs consumed his time and there was little money left over for luxuries at the end of the month.

"Is that a yes?" Jay asked.

Slowly, she turned to him. His stare did strange things to her. And it wasn't just the beast in her belly making her feel like this. *Weak. Hot. Tingly.*

Melt!

***

"Jay, buddy, you didn't make a deal without me, did you?" His younger brother, Max, asked him later that night. "Man, I was cornered by Coach. He wants me to reconsider law school and go for the pros."

Something deep down hurt. "You're not thinking about it, are you?"

He waved him off, and then resumed setting his side of the table while Jay took care of the other side. "No, that's not me. I love the game. I've had good times. But I'm scrawny compared to you. And I don't have the heart for it."

At six foot? Thin, compact body, but scrawny?

"What's this?" Jonathan placed the salad on the table. He was the intense one. "Keep your head down and in the books, brother."

"Who's older here?" Jay asked, looking around in wonder. They usually surprised him at least once a day. But there was a well of pride beaming in him at how they'd turned out. *Good job, Mom!*

"Me. That's who." Danny grinned as he carried in the mashed potatoes and corn.

They chuckled. "Right again." Jay shook his head, grateful he had his brothers by his side. Soon the younger ones would be off to grad school. *God, he'd miss them*. But, it was their dream and he had to make sure they lived them.

"Steak, coming up," Jonathan called, going back for the main course. "Don't start talking without me this time."

A few minutes later, Danny said grace as they clutched hands. "Thank you for the grub. Bless Mom and Dad. Don't be mad at me, Mom, for breaking your dish this morning. Make Max and Jonathan stop snoring. They're shaking the house again." That got a chuckle; it was the truth. "Keep Jay outta my hair, okay?" He grinned. "And bring me a girlfriend—"

"Hey, when did this become part of grace?" Jay asked, frowning at his brother. He'd never mentioned a girlfriend before. *Was there someone special in his life?* "To be continued. Finish the blessing."

"See. He's so bossy. Alright. I'm finishing. Thanks again for the good eats. Over the lips, past the gums, look out stomach, here it comes. Amen."

"Amen," Jay and his younger brothers said in unison. "Now, do you want to discuss this girl?"

"Ha, ha! You didn't let me end it. Bring me a girlfriend for *Jay*." He winked, spooning a heap of mashed potatoes on his plate. "Pass the corn, please."

"Me?" Jay stilled. They'd never made it a secret they wanted him to be happy. Football had been it. Until his unexpected early retirement. But this?

"Yep. I think Paige likes you."

His heart stilled. *What did he see?* If only they'd gotten a load of that cell phone picture, they'd never let him hear the end of it. Luck was on his side when Max never showed up for the meeting.

"Who's Paige?" the younger two brothers asked together. Most people mistook them for twins. At only eleven months apart, they might as well have been. *They look and act the same. Even think the same.*

"The girl at work I told you about. She's nice." At their puzzled looks, he said, "You know, the one I take a break with every once in a while. She draws. I talk. It works for both of us. Long, long, long hair—"

"Oh, the hair girl."

Jay cringed. "She's more than just about her hair, guys." *She's so much more…complicated and fascinating and hot as all get-out.*

"He does like her." Max pointed a finger at him.

"I invited her over," Danny said, grinning from ear-to-ear.

"What? When?" Jay nearly fell off his chair. *Paige here?*

"Tonight."

He closed his eyes and shook his head. "She said no, right?" *He had that to be grateful for; no telling what his brothers would say or ask her.*

"Nope, she said yes. She'll be here in an hour."

He dropped his fork. It hit his plate with a clatter.

Jay wished he could swear, loud and long. But, he'd banned it for his brothers and himself years ago.

Ah, fudge!

***

Jay met Paige at the door. "Of all the times you decided not to back out, this had to be one of them?"

Her skinny jeans hugged her in all the right places. The silky button-down blouse she wore, minty green, remained him of the first time he met her. The lemonade had splashed on her, making the white blouse sheer. He'd never, ever forget the image. *Was it getting hotter in here?*

"Do you want me to leave?" She held a bakery box. *Her shield? Armor?*

The scent of chocolate and strawberries made his mouth water. *Or it could be her that was making him thirsty?* He dropped his gaze to her mouth. *So close to her lips today, yet so far.* Shaking his head, he said, "And disappoint Danny?"

"Paige, don't believe a word Jay says." Danny stuck out his tongue at his brother. Offering his arm, he said, "Please, come meet our brothers."

"There's more of you?" She giggled, hooking her arm through her friend's.

That sound did strange things to Jay's blood. All his nerve endings hummed. *Why is this happening to me? With her?*

"Only two," Danny said. "But I'm the best-looking one."

They laughed. Jay closed the door and trailed behind them, feeling left out of their little tête-à-tête . He was mesmerized by her long braid, wondering how her hair would feel between his fingers.

Looking over her shoulder, she met Jay's gaze. Her eyes were soft and vulnerable. Her smile wobbled.

He sucked in a sharp breath, realizing how difficult this was for her. His resistance melted away. Going to her side, he leaned over and said, “We’re civilized. Mostly.”

“I’m not so sure about you,” she said under her breath, making him laugh.

“Just you wait and see,” he warned.

Her slight shiver said a great deal.

A poker of desire shafted through him. Jay moaned. *Why her?*

***

Paige sat looking from one brother, to the next, and the next, and the last one. All were different, except for the last two, yet they had similar mannerisms. Their hair, various shades of brown; eyes, brown, yet different hues, fit the brother mode. Three out of four had the same builds and heights. Jay stood out, taller and broader than the others. And much longer hair.

Fascinating.

The two younger ones scarfed down the chocolate cake with chocolate frosting and decorated with fresh strawberries. Danny lingered over his, obviously enjoying each bite. And Jay popped a strawberry in his mouth, stared at her, and licked his lips.

Silent groan.

“So good.” Max inhaled. “More?” He looked at Jay.

“Help yourself, brother.” Jay sunk back in a chair

across from hers.

The simple stone, ranch-style home was not what she expected for a bachelor pad of four men. For one, it was neat and tidy. The large screen TV did take up a big portion of one wall, but, nothing else screamed party town or man cave. There were a few pictures scattered on the fireplace mantel.

"Like it?" Max smiled slyly. "Jay has no imagination when it comes to being single."

"He's more like our dad," Jonathan piped up. "In a good way."

"Yeah, we lost him young. Some lowlife repeat offender…Dad was killed trying to buy us some milk. I was only five." Max shrugged.

Her heart ached. She peeked at Jay. His face was shadowed. And he wouldn't look at her.

"That's why I'm going to be a lawyer. I was going to go for just a cop, but Jay here talked me into doing more with my life."

"Always interfering," Danny said with a huge, dramatic sigh.

She grinned at her buddy and he smiled back.

Jay covered his eyes. "Take your shots, guys."

"He's a pest when it comes to homework. In a good way." Max winked. *The more outgoing brother.*

"And he makes us do the dishes. And pick up our socks and underwear," Danny added for good measure. "But in a good way."

Paige smiled. In spite of their tragic loss, they

seemed like healthy, well-adjusted young men. *In a good way.*

"And we all have to work. No freebies here." Jonathan nudged his brother's arm. "Max and I are in college. But we have part-time jobs."

Max leaned forward. "That's us, in a nutshell. Well, except we lost our mom. Jay was a teenager, but he rounded us up and," he spread his arms wide, "here we are. So, Paige, what's with the hair?"

Her middle clenched. She lifted a hand to smooth down her braid. "I like it?" she half asked, half answered.

"It's kinda neat. How long is it? Did you ever let it down? How long does it take you to wash and dry it?"

"Wait, how much shampoo do you go through a month?" Jonathan's eyebrows came together. *The curious brother.*

Jay sat up, now resting his elbows on his knees. "Hey, guys, this might be a little too personal for Paige."

How could he tell? Somehow he'd sensed it. She shot Jay a tight, but grateful smile.

She heard him suck in a sharp breath. *Wibbly wobbly knees and I'm not even standing.*

Never having to face such direct questions before, Paige thought it might shut down the interrogation if she'd just answer them. Plus, it would keep her mind off Jay staring at her. *As if!* "It's over four feet long. It takes half a day to wash and dry it. I keep it in a braid ninety-seven percent of the time. And I go through three bottles of shampoo a month."

"No way," they said in unison. *Forks suspended in mid-air and mouths hanging open. Yep, I get that sometimes. Stares. Gawking. But this wasn't the hurtful type.*

"And four bottles of conditioner. But who's counting?" She grinned at their stunned looks. *Kinda like them, the brothers Whitfield. Just sayin' And Jay is gorg, as Rico would say.*

"Oh, man, that's cool and a drag at the same time," Jonathan said, shaking his head.

"By the way, he's our retro brother. He's going to medical school. He wants to be a surgeon." Jay beamed with pride.

Silent gulp. A future doctor? But she couldn't hold it against him. He wanted to help people. Most did. They just gave her the willies now.

Jonathan shrugged. "For Mom. You know…" He couldn't finish.

"No way," Paige said, liking the brothers' straightforward approach, even if she wasn't used to it. *Daunting yet with a hint of refreshing honesty.*

"Scared yet?" Jay challenged. A smile lurked in his eyes.

"Not so much of them. You, yeah," she said, with a little more truth than she realized. *Shaky on the insides.*

He raised his eyebrows. "Really? I'm the harmless one."

Max snorted. "Heartbreaker is more like it. Why, we've had girls swooning all over him for years."

Jay's smile vanished. His eyes were cool and his face froze.

"But," Jonathan glanced at Jay and rushed on, "he never led them on. Not our Jay. No way he'd ever do that. He was up front with all of them. We came first—"

"Still do." The words shot out of Jay.

Paige relaxed for the first time since he almost kissed her. "That's a good thing. It's an honorable thing." She had no need to worry he'd push things further with her. That was the one and only reason she'd agreed to come tonight. She had to make him understand the ads were business and there was nothing between him and her. *Yeah, right, tell that to your flip-flopping belly. And you can't blame it on the beast this time, either.*

A momentary lapse. Caught on camera.

Smoking hot with a capital H.

Quit that, she scolded.

Now she didn't have to bother explaining to Jay or defending her position. *What a relief!* So why did she have this pang of regret lancing through her heart right now?

CHAPTER 5

Jay hummed. He actually *hummed* as Rico dusted him with some kind of product. *Shimmery powder?!*

"Oh, swoon. You make my toes curl, you hunk of man, you!" Rico exclaimed.

Eying him, Jay said, "Don't you have a boyfriend or something?"

"Moi?" Rico batted his long, false eyelashes. "I could if I wanted one. But—" He stopped himself. "Why, you know anyone?" He poked his bicep with a forefinger. "Anyone like you, Adonis?"

He shrugged. "A couple of workout buddies, maybe. I'll ask around. But no drama, okay?" That was one thing he didn't want or need in his life.

Rico placed his hands on his hips. "Not my circus. Not my monkeys."

Grinning, Jay said, "Ditto for me, too." His house still wasn't the same since Paige was there. He'd had all he could do to stop his brothers' questions once she departed the other night. They harped on him every chance they could get. *What part of no didn't they understand?*

Jay had to take care of them. He had to finish raising them the way his mother wanted him to. The custody papers were a formality, because he'd have rather died than lose them. He fought hard, worked even harder, and kept them and him out of trouble. They were so close to getting the youngest ones into good colleges and so close to living the dream his mom had for all four of her boys.

No distractions. Period.

And Paige Sumner was one big distraction to him. His thoughts centered on her more and more. It felt like he had a million butterflies flapping in his belly right now waiting for her to arrive.

On the outside he may look calm and cool. *And shimmery.* But on the inside he was a mass of contained anticipation. He hadn't seen or heard from her since she left his home. His nerves jumped at the mention of her name. *Paige. Why are you doing this to me?*

Looking around, he saw Peg, with her mighty clipboard, whispering to the guy in charge. He threw up his hands and then pointed to the clock. *Was Paige ditching the shoot? Ditching him?*

"You are H1 to the max," Rico was saying, going around to his back and dusting more powder on his shoulders.

"Whatever that means," Jay mumbled.

"H-O-T! My, my, what shoulders you have. I could

scale them like a mountain."

Half naked, Jay looked over his shoulder. "Don't get any ideas, Rico."

"Just sayin'. It's not like anyone hasn't told you that before, right?" He tsked under his breath.

"Finished? 'Cause I am." His good mood was rapidly disappearing. Every few seconds he scanned the room only to find the same people roaming about—photographer, lighting people, hair, makeup, production, wardrobe staff.

No Paige. He had this horrible sinking sensation in his gut now. *Maybe Peg and that French photographer had been discussing her whereabouts.*

"Have you seen Paige?" Jay's muscles tensed.

"Nope. Nada. And I so wanted to get my fingers into that luscious hair of hers, too."

"Who wouldn't?" Jay moaned under his breath, fantasizing about how soft and silky it would be against his skin.

"You like?" Rico chirped, coming back around to his front and searching for missed spots. "I may be able to help you out. You know, you get me a hot date and I'll get info on sweet Paige. Deal?"

Intrigued, Jay raised an eyebrow. "What kind of info?" Granted, he didn't know much about her, other than she liked to disappear. *Quiet, yes. Timid, no.* Family? Boyfriends? He clenched his jaw at the last thought.

"I know she lives with Evelyn, my assistant at the

moment. Ev is engaged to hunky Shane Weston—"

"Of Weston Construction, right?"

"Got it. But Ev and Shane are trying to make a baby, so it's only a matter of time before she moves in with him. Wedding or no wedding first, understand?"

"And Paige?"

"On the hunt for a roommate, I hear. Asking around. Nice place, too."

"You've been there?" *What was it like?*

"Party at Ev's, oh yeah! She and I are like that." He crossed his fingers together and held them in front of Jay. "Paige, not so much." He leaned closer. "But I've seen her room. O-M-G! Total masterpiece!"

"Master—"

"Piece de resistance. Divine. Colors and fabrics and comfy, oh my!" He pressed his hand against his lips and giggled. "She is an artist. And it shows."

Jay could only imagine the space. "An artist? I thought she drew wedding dresses. Gowns. Or whatever." *Or was it wedding dress designer?*

"Hotty, that's only the tip of the iceberg. Why, she's doing the mural for King's Café. Knights and castles." He sighed.

It struck him then. *The café. Where they met.* "Show me?"

"Now? But we're getting ready for a photo shoot." He turned his wrist, checking the big face of his watch. "In two minutes."

"It can wait."

"It's Sunday. The café is closed."

"But you can get us in there, can't you?"

He stepped back to take in Jay. "If you're serious about getting me a blind date with one of your friends. It's a deal?" He stuck out his hand.

Jay shook it, realizing he'd have to follow through on it now. "Deal. Now to the castle," he said with a smile in his voice. He had a wild hunch that Paige may be there.

***

Leaning back on her haunches, Paige eyed her work. The gray for the castle was just the right shade now. The shading cinched it. "Finally," she said, a slight smugness in her voice. "I knew it was there. I just had to find it."

Invisible pat on the back.

She giggled at herself.

There was a commotion behind her. *Footsteps?* She twisted around.

"Paige!"

"Jay?! What are you doing here? Rico?" Jay led the pack as Rico, Peg, and several other people followed. But it was Jay who grabbed and held her attention. Shirtless, barefoot, in jeans. *Melt at his feet, why don't you?* "You…sparkle," she said lamely, allowing her gaze to travel over his muscular torso. *Bingo, he just won the part of her knight in the mural.*

"I *shimmer*," he corrected. "Did you forget?"

Paige frowned, and then took in the others filling the arched entryway.

"Holy mother of all that's beautiful, Paige!" Peg swept in, clutching her clipboard to her chest. Stopping in the middle of the room, the assistant looked up and twirled. "It's fan-King-tastic! Has Charlie seen it yet?"

"W-O-W!" Rico half squealed, half shrieked. He grabbed Peg and swung her arms as they danced. "It's off the charts!"

Gulping hard, Paige backed up a step. "It's only half done." *Could they please just go now?* She glimpsed at Jay.

His eyes met and held hers. *Shiver me timbers! Thrill alert!*

Jay slowly walked into the room. Looking up, he brushed his long, wavy hair back and held his head. "Paige." His voice was filled with wonder. He spun around, taking it all in. "Castle…"

"What's all the fuss, guys?" Charlie asked. "Coming through. Excuse me." She nudged her way into the room. She stopped in her tracks when she caught a glimpse of the artwork on the walls.

"It's not finished." *Duh!* Paige looked up to this woman who had reinvented King's Department Store. She didn't want Charlie to see it until it was completed.

"Paige Sumner, you are a genius," Charlie said, smiling widely.

What did I do?

"Peg, buddy ol' pal, clipboard please." Charlie waited for the assistant to hand it over.

"But…but. Boss, I don't go anywhere without it."

"Okay, just turn to a clean page, hold it out, and let me borrow your pencil."

In a short time with sparse strokes, Charlie drew. "New vision of ad campaign coming right up, guys."

Jay was still awestruck by the walls and Paige was still awestruck by him. *Was it smoldering hot in here?*

"Charlie, zee vision waz complete already." Andre, the French photographer Paige had met at another shoot stepped forward.

Photo shoot? That's where I was supposed to be today! "I forgot," she whispered.

Turning to face her, Jay smiled. "Figures. At least you didn't disappear altogether on me."

Another melt. Soon I'll evaporate or combust!

"Voila, my friend!" Charlie exclaimed, ripping off the piece of paper. She handed it to the Frenchman and began to give instructions. "Bring the equipment here—lights, cameras, screens—you name it."

"Here?" Paige cringed at the break in her voice. Still holding the paintbrush in her hand, she waved to the half-complete walls. "There's more work to be done."

Charlie zeroed in on her and strolled to where she stood. Touching her shoulders, she said, "Paige, you are the canvas. You and Jay. He is the star of our new ad campaign, Knight In Shining Armor." Lightly, she brushed back a strand of Paige's hair. "Your hair will be his armor."

Gulping hard, she asked, "My hair?"

A sinking sensation filled the pit of her belly, crowding out the beast.

Oh no. What had she gotten herself into?

CHAPTER 6

In a nude bodysuit and her hair freshly styled and hanging down her back and to her knees, Paige stood a few inches from Jay's naked chest.

"Now touch it. Run your fingers through it, Jay," someone from the production crew called out.

Paige steeled herself. Never before had she allowed anyone to be this close to her, touch her braid, never mind run their fingers through her hair. It was *her* shield, *her* armor from sickness and the world.

"Are you all right? You're shaking?" Jay's soft questions sent arrows piercing her fragile heart.

Her lip trembled. She bit it to keep it steady.

"Hold onto me," he whispered and then he placed her icy fingers on his bare sides.

They sucked in a sharp breath together. "Sorry," she mumbled. "Cold hands…" His skin was warm to the touch. Visions of vapors rising from them floated through her mind. *Steam.*

Was that a tremor she felt?

"Be gentle," he said with a grin in his voice.

She giggled, releasing some nervous tension. "I'll try."

If possible, he stepped even closer, so his body brushed hers. Another sharp intake of breath from both of them rent the air.

"Look up at me," he whispered.

It was difficult to pull her gaze from all the hard muscles and glistening skin. Slowly, she lifted her stare higher and higher—skin wrapped around sinewy muscles; defined, chiseled, collarbone; hair skimming his broad shoulders; pulse hammering at the base of his long neck; Adam's apple; strong jaw; nice chin; high cheekbones; and *gulp*, those eyes that penetrated to her soul.

He saw things. Knew things. No one else bothered to see.

His lip tugged at the corner and it seemed as if her heart answered with its own tug. "Jay," she whispered. "I wouldn't be doing this if it were anyone else but you." He wanted to care for his brothers. That hit a tender spot in her.

"I know. Thank you." He touched her arms, drawing his hands up as his fingertips danced along her skin.

His gentleness surprised her. As an athlete, he'd been exposed to demanding plays and brutal hits. Being one of four brothers, she was certain there had been tussles and roughhousing. But with her, his light touch and almost awe-like reverence shook her.

He brushed the backs of his knuckles over her cheek. "I'm going to touch you now." The minute he sank both his hands in her hair, she clutched his sides.

A breath hissed out of him. "Soft." His dreamy voice calmed her nerves. She relaxed her grip on him.

Warning! He just entered the danger zone!

In the back of Paige's mind, she heard the shutter click repeatedly. Otherwise, there was only Jay's breathing mingled with hers.

Jay cupped her face, tracing his thumbs along her jaw. "Beautiful," he whispered a second before he lowered his head.

Of their own accord, her eyelids fluttered shut. She waited. His lips were feather soft against hers, stroking and coaxing.

Her gasp was whisked away. It was she who deepened the kiss, touching his tongue with hers. His moan vibrated through her.

Melt! And double melt!

***

Jay Whitfield imagined he'd died and gone to heaven. Her sweet taste and soft skin nearly sent him over the edge of reason.

With his back to the painted wall with the half-complete castle on it and Paige facing him with her long, flowing hair released from confinement, he pictured what the camera and all the eerily silent people were seeing now.

"It's better than porn," Rico whispered loudly.

There were a few chuckles and some murmurs of agreement.

"Wonderment!" the French photographer, Andre, added.

She grew bolder, hotter and there was nothing more he wanted than his desire to continue. However, if it did, he'd surely embarrass them both. With a great deal of reluctance, he pulled away. "Paige," he half said, half breathed. *I want you!*

By slow degrees, she focused on him, his retreat. *Funny,* she *should have this down to an art.*

There, her tension returned in full force. She clamped her eyes shut and curled her fingers. The slight movement along his sides made him shiver.

Paige leaned her forehead against his chest. Jay sucked in a sharp breath and brushed his lips against her temple. He fanned his fingers out and pushed them through her long, silky soft hair. His moan couldn't be tempered.

"Is it over?" she asked under her breath.

Not by a long shot, sweetheart. Not by a long shot.

***

Her knees still shook every time she thought of yesterday's photo shoot, but Paige shoved that aside to work on the wedding dress draped over the mannequin.

Visions of Jay, shirtless and in the last-minute change to black skin tight pants, sprang into her mind again. He was the knight to her fair maiden.

Perfect advertising for King's. Not so perfect outcome for me, though.

A sleepless night coupled with a heap of berating herself still could not erase that incredible kiss.

Shaking her head, she forced herself back to the task at hand. *Mr. Jay Whitfield, his sexy highness, would just have to wait.* She had less than an hour to make the necessary adjustments to the gown.

"She promised to lose ten pounds, not gain more," Francie said, holding pins out to Paige. "I was more than happy to order a bigger size, but she insisted."

"We can fix this, right?" Paige saw the defeat in Francie's face.

"Why didn't she just agree? It would have been much easier."

Snap out of it, Francie! "We can't go back…" She trailed off, thinking she should be taking her own advice. "Do you have another skirt? We can keep the top portion to fit her snug curves, but the bottom… there's no material left to work with."

"Genius, Paige. But you already know that, don't you? Charlie told us about the photo shoot with you and Jay. And Rico put his two cents in, too."

Gulping hard, she asked, "Us? Who us?"

"No time. I'll go get that skirt. I know the perfect match."

Us? How many people knew and how fast would word spread?

Her heart sunk to her toes.

***

"Jay, did you see them yet?" Marcus Goode showed him another property for a possible location for the new sports bar. This was by far the best out of the ones they'd viewed. *Location. Size. Affordable. Already demolished to the bare bones*. It had all the qualities they were looking for.

"What did I see or not see yet?" He stifled a yawn and rubbed a hand over his eyes. With his brothers' questions peppering him when he got home and Paige floating in and out of his very vivid, very hot dreams, he'd been hard pressed to get a couple hours' shut-eye.

"The pictures from the photo shoot, of course." His cell phone rang. "My mother's calling." He answered, "Mom, everything alright? Isaac getting ready for the big domino tournament tomorrow."

Stunned, Jay watched as Marcus walked away, still talking on the phone. Who else had seen those pictures? How good or bad were they anyway?

It was one thing signing on for the project and another thing being in the middle of an entire new campaign conjured up at the last minute. Charlie had had an epiphany after seeing Paige's castle rendition.

He'd gotten caught up in the enthusiasm, liking the

idea. But in the cold light of day, he had second thoughts.

The brothers would see it. What would they say?

Max had read, scanned, and dissected the contract, finally giving approval. The Kings were fair and decent people. Still, it was his reputation, his family's honor that would be judged.

And Paige would be, too.

***

It was difficult to look at her. It practically hurt.

Something wonderful and scary had happened between them yesterday. He couldn't explain it, didn't dare try, but he couldn't ignore it either.

It pulsed in the air. People stared. He couldn't take his eyes off her.

And Paige had tolerated the attention until she was at a breaking point. Then she ducked out, yet again.

It was becoming a very bad habit of hers.

Jay stood a few feet away, watching as she hand carried the large garment bag for the beaming lady. *Blushing bride?*

His chest grew tight at the sight of her. "Paige?"

She stopped abruptly, her long braid swinging. "Jay? What are you doing here?"

"I have something to show you."

"Here?" Both she and the bride asked.

At his nod, Paige called over an assistant. "Could

you please help Ms. Tatum out to her car with her dress? Thanks. I owe you." She made her goodbyes to the lady and drew near. "Jay?"

"How are you?"

Couldn't he come up with anything better than that?

Her shrug and glance over her shoulder told him a great deal. "Planning a getaway?" Pink edged into her cheeks, making him smile. "I'll walk you back." He tapped the envelope in his hand. "There's something you should see."

She of few words shot him a look.

It didn't take a great deal to twist Marcus's arm to get him to put in the call for him. In less than an hour, Marcus led him to King's executive offices, where Jay was allowed to view the photos.

Smoking hot.

But would Paige think the same?

"What's up, hotshot?" Rico said as they entered the black and hot pink Charmings wedding boutique. "Got anyone for me yet?"

"It slipped my mind, buddy. Here, got a pen?" After Rico handed over a pad and pen, Jay scribbled down an address. "My gym. Meet me there tomorrow. Six sharp."

"P.M.?"

Chuckling, Jay said, "A.M. You can see for yourself."

"Beefcake? Yummy! Paige, you can come, too. After all, you and Jay are practically slaying dragons together.

It'll be fun." There was doubt lingering in the air. "Right?"

"Of course." Turning to Paige, he shook his head and winced. "You game?"

"I don't do workouts." She pointed to the envelope he clasped. "Is that for me? What, may I ask, do you have there?"

He gauged her features. She gave nothing away. *How would she react?* There was only one way to find out. "You bolted out of the café so fast after the shoot. I tried to catch up with you…" He was making a mess of things. Jay shoved the envelope at her. "Proofs. Of us."

"Let me see, too!" Rico came around the desk.

Paige, to avoid him, stepped closer to Jay. Her perfume teased him. He inhaled and thought he'd died and gone to heaven. *Roses, definitely. Oranges, too?* She was petite and would fit snugly against his side. Jay wished he could take her long braid and slowly undo it, feeling the silky texture again. He nearly moaned.

Instead, he put his hand on her waist. *To protect her, of course. And to keep her steady. Or was it to keep her from running again?*

She shot Rico a guarded look he didn't see, but at least she didn't shove Jay aside. Gingerly, she undid the clasp and pulled out the glossy prints. Her gasp shot right through him.

Good or bad?

"Oh la la," Rico exclaimed, leaning his head nearer as she flipped through the small stack. "Go back. I want to take them all in, one at a time."

Surprisingly, she didn't protest. After she scanned each one intently, she handed them off to Rico.

"O-M-G! I love the way you're looking down at her, Jay, and you can only see part of your face, part of your oh-so-muscular biceps, your dark hair, Paige's long, gorgeous blonde hair, and your bare feet, nothing else." He started fanning himself. "Hot flash. Emphasis on the hot!"

Paige remained quiet, until the last one. "Oh…"

Was that a good oh or a bad oh?

"My…God…"

"Shut the front door, kiddos! Look at the way his big hands are in your hair and your lips are touching. Fire leaps off this pic! I've got to call someone—maybe a fireman to put out the flames! We've got another hit on our hands."

Her hands shook, and then her body.

"Peg! That's who I'll call." He squeezed Paige and squealed with delight. Then Rico reached out and embraced them both to him, squishing Paige. Just as abruptly, he let go and rushed around the desk to grab the phone. He punched in the numbers. "Come on, come on, please pick up—"

"King's—"

Rico shrieked. "Pegster. The pictures. Jay. Paige…."

He talked in abbreviated phrases, somehow conveying what he meant; Peg's answers satisfied him.

"King's Knight In Shining Armor Campaign!" Rico

threw kisses their way. “Combustible!”

“Jay.” Paige’s voice sounded tiny and weak. “I think I’m going to be sick.”

CHAPTER 7

Facing her parents across the table at King's Café, Paige smiled weakly. "I've got some news."

She only talked to them a few hundred times a day and still she hadn't gotten up the nerve to tell them about the ads. Paige didn't want to upset them. Now, she had no choice. The ads would hit this week.

"Oh, have you tasted this soup, sweetie, to die—" Her mother stopped in mid-sentence. "Divine. Potatoes are tender, cheese is melting, and…" She slurped up another spoonful. "Delish!" she said, then patted her blonde hair. It was the same shade as Paige's.

Only Mom's was out of a bottle now. She'd done wonders getting the beautician to match it perfectly.

"Alice." Her father scowled at her mother. Turning back to his salad, he stabbed a piece of cucumber. "Don't mind your mother, dear, she's still overly sensitive."

Seven long years had passed and still they were tiptoeing around her and the elephant in the room.

Avoid. Deny. Run. She played well with it, too. *The running part, at least that's what Jay thought. Oh, Jay, swoon!*

Paige ran her hand down her braid. Her parents stilled, watching her. She dropped her hand. "My news, remember?"

"This place is so beautiful, honey." Her mother gazed around in wonder, licking a drop of soup off her ruby red lips. "King's Café. I love the colorful chairs against the black painted wood. Elegant." She scraped her spoon on the bottom of the china, causing a screech and dragged up the last of the potato soup and shoveled it down.

"Food is out of this world, too. You sure we can afford this, honey?" Her father's brows came together. His dark hair seemed peppered with more gray lately. "This might be too rich for our blood—" He groaned as her mother whacked him. Jerking to his wife, he asked, "What? What did I say?" He rubbed his arm. "Still can give me a wallop."

"Marty, you said the b word," she said out of the side of her mouth. "B-l-o-o-d. Icxnay on the oodblay."

Didn't they realize she could spell? Or translate Pig Latin?

Dawning chased across her father's face. "Look," he pointed. "Aren't they cute?" Three little girls in silky beaded gowns and with their hair up and tiaras in place stood near the private princess room. They giggled into their white gloved hands.

"Adorable," her mother said. "Oh, honey, you have to get one of those dresses. You'd be the belle of the ball."

"Mom. I'm twenty-seven, not seven." Paige clamped down on her exasperation.

"You'll always be my little girl." Her dad wiped his eyes with the edge of his cloth napkin.

She gulped hard. "Thanks, Daddy." *Would they ever let her grow up?*

"This is the perfect time to talk about this." Her mother dropped the spoon. It clattered. She licked her finger, making loud smacking noises. "We miss you so much. Come back home to us, honey. Your daddy will fix your bike and we can go riding around the neighborhood like we used to."

"The good ol' days," her father agreed.

Okay, I've just been reduced to six years old now. Reminiscing about her infant stage would come next.

"Remember when she took her first step?" Her mother pressed her hands to her heart. "She scared me to death—"

Her mother and father jerked their gazes to her, eyes wide.

"I didn't mean anything by it, Paige."

Silent beat. "I'm good, guys. Healthy as a horse." Well maybe she had the occasional stomach issues, but they weren't going to find out she still had side effects from her treatments.

The color came back into her mother's cheeks. Paige

sighed inwardly.

Her father patted his wife's hand. "I'll borrow a truck. We can have you moved back and tucked away in your room by the weekend. What do you say, honey?"

"You're moving, Paige?" Jay's voice came from somewhere behind her.

Whipping around, she felt the color drain from her face. "Jay, what are you doing here?"

***

Jay stopped by King's Café to hand deliver the signed contracts to Marcus. The sports bar wasn't just a dream anymore. It was a reality.

His brothers were going to meet him so they could celebrate. Yeah, the Whitfield brothers just put another gold star on their charts for their mom to smile about. *This is for you, Mom.* And Jay was another step closer to seeing their dreams come true.

A nest egg for Danny, a livelihood for me, and tuition for Max and Jonathan.

Now, he eyed Paige's stunned features. "Interrupting?" He swore if she could, she'd bolt.

"As I live and breathe! Jay Whitfield, tight end for the Dallas Cowboys." The older man's mouth opened and closed. "I'm a huge fan." He felt his front shirt pocket. "A pen? Paper? Autograph?"

"*Former* tight end," Jay corrected. It didn't hurt to admit it anymore. Football was his past. His present and future focus was on giving his brothers a better life, financially and every other way. "Sure thing, Mr….?" He looked to Paige. "Sumner, is it?" He guessed.

"You know him, Paige?" the older woman asked. Most likely her mother.

"Sorta," Paige said. "That was part of my news."

"News? You didn't tell us about any news."

***

"I was trying to do just that…" It wasn't worth it to rehash their ongoing exchanges whenever they got together. They dodged anything that might upset the cart. Paige tried to keep them tethered to the real world.

"You haven't told them yet?" Jay gazed at her long and hard.

Wilt. Melt. Splat!

The man was dangerous.

Her heart thumped in her chest. "Nope. You could always help me out."

"Then you'd owe me. Big time."

She didn't like the sound of that. But, with what she had to deal with, he may be the buffer.

Jay slipped into the chair beside hers, slipping an arm around the back of her chair. He grinned from ear-to-ear, trailing his hands over her back. She shivered.

"Oh, my," her mother said. Her shrewd eyes took in a great deal. She nudged her husband's arm. "Look, they look so cute, blonde hair and pale skin and oh so dark—pale against dark."

Cute? That word was a death knell to a guy. So why did she care about that? She had dresses to design, a castle to finish, and hide in front of or behind him in the ads. She'd be virtually invisible. Her hair would be the star. *Gulp!*

"The news, Mom and Dad," Paige prompted. "Jay, meet Marty and Alice Sumner. So, Jay here will tell you all about it, won't you?"

"What's my prize?" He dropped his gaze to her lips and then looked into her eyes.

Double gulp! "I'll…paint something for you?" *Maybe?*

"A room?"

"Waitress," her father called out. "What was her name again? Anyway, I need a pen and piece of paper, so Jay can give me an autograph. Oh, this is great. My daughter knows a football legend. Hey, buddy, can you get me into a game?"

Paige wanted to *dash,* not crawl, under the table and wait for her parents to go—her mom on to her Wednesday afternoon appointment to do the nails of the rich and even richer and her dad to his second shift job at the factory.

"Don't worry, Mr. Sumner, I'll get you an autograph before we leave," Jay offered. His smile didn't seem forced or phony, something Paige was grateful for.

"Thanks," she whispered.

"My prize just got bigger," he mumbled under his

breath.

"Two rooms?"

"Kids' stuff. Murals."

"What kind?" Her curiosity piqued. His brothers were kinda old for that sort of thing.

"Charity stuff. Hospitals."

Her insides turned over. A numb sensation shot down the side of her head. *Stroke? Please, strike me, so I can slither away.*

"My brothers and I are going to start a charity in honor of our mom." Pride pulsed from him.

"Go-good. Nice." *Were her lips blue?* She couldn't feel them move.

"Cancer research."

A deafening silence roared in her ears. *Cancer?!* His mother died. She had cancer. He'd never told her. Why should he? They barely knew each other.

Her father and mother opened and closed their mouths, like guppies. *They did that whenever the C word was mentioned.* Her mother recovered first.

"Paige, honey, tell us your news," her mother said, changing the subject as she gazed from Jay to her and back again. "Oh my GAWD, you're engaged!" She pressed her hands to her cheeks. "Marty, can you believe it?!"

Her father slammed a hand to his chest. "Jay Whitfield's gonna be my son-in-law?! Oh, I'm in football heaven." He reached out and grabbed Jay's hand and shook it. "Welcome to the family, son. We have a guest house. Full of junk right now. Not so great, but we'll fix it up. The landlord said we could any time. You and Paige will love it there, right, honey? Just until we can put on an addition to the house. The landlord said we could…if we pay. No problem, right, honey?"

"Married?" his brothers asked, coming up behind them.

"No, no. It's not that. Nothing like that." Paige held up her hands to stop them. She whipped her head around to gaze at Jay for help.

His slack jaw and wide eyes told her everything she needed to know. The bottom of her stomach dropped.

He hates me.

CHAPTER 8

"Married? Man, Jay, why didn't you tell us?" Jonathan asked. He brushed a hand through his hair. All three of his brothers looked stunned.

"That's because I'm not." He grit his teeth and glared at Paige. Jay smoothed his features and turned to her parents. "Mr. and Mrs. Sumner, I hate to disappoint you, but it's not like that. Paige and I hardly know each other, barely just met, in fact…" His voice trailed off as he recalled the photo shoot. Something slammed into him at the memory of her, the feel of her silky hair, the touch of her skin against his, her sweet breath hitching, the softness of her lips…

Shaking his head, Jay dragged himself back to the moment and the devastated look on Mr. Sumner's face. Mrs. Sumner now was dabbing her eyes with a tissue.

"Ah, man, I would've liked Paige for a sister-in-law," Danny said.

"Honey, it's not a baby, is it? You're not in the family way, are you?" Her mother half stood, half leaned across the table and felt Paige's tummy.

Paige cringed and gingerly removed her mother's hand. "No, Mom. You can sit back down. We're attracting a lot of attention." She slunk down in her chair.

He knew that look, knew she wanted to bolt. As his brothers grabbed chairs and came closer, Jay said, "Now that you know the worst isn't taking place—"

"The worst? Is that what you think of marrying me?" Paige muttered under her breath.

Trying to ignore her question, Jay continued, "Our news won't be nearly as upsetting. You see, Paige and I are in a King's ad together. It's a tie-in with the King's theme. You know, royalty, princesses, right? Well..." He shrugged his shoulder. "I portray a knight and Paige is the fair maiden princess."

Five blank looks stared back at him.

"Help would be appreciated right about now," he whispered to her.

She touched her braid, smoothing it.

"Rapunzel?" Max asked, scratching his head.

"No," Paige shrieked, sitting up straighter. "I mean, no," she said softer.

"It kinda is," Jay corrected. "You don't see Paige at all, except for her hair."

"Like Lady Godiva? You're naked?" Jonathan's mouth hung open. "You, too, Jay?"

Her mother openly wept now. "Oh, Paige. How could you?"

***

Shell-shocked, Jay stood in the middle of King's Department store. Customers milled by, some did a double take, some shot him a look, and others muttered under their breath, saying he should move out of the way. All walked away, following the marble floor paths to their shopping destination. "Where did it all go wrong? Lunch with my brothers, that was it. Easy, peasy."

"Stop talking to yourself, Whitfield," Paige demanded as she stood in front of him with her arms crossed.

"Order some grub—good grub, talk guy things, and oh, yeah, celebrate this milestone in the Whitfield family."

"My mother is storming through the store searching for our print ad. Do something!"

"She's yours, not mine. I do like your folks, but, seriously, I've got three brothers to answer to. 'Sellout' is pretty harsh to live down, don't you think?"

"Shampoo. Conditioner. King's new line Dex, the store's mad scientist, whipped up. You are known for football, but also your hair. So it's not a stretch. It's not the *worst*." She put emphasis on the last word.

Jay winced. "About that. I didn't mean *you*, all right?"

The tension drained out of her. She smoothed down

her braid again. "I know. Sorry about that reaction. Didn't see that coming. My folks..." She shook her head. "I expected a grilling, not a welcome with open arms. But you are *the* Jay Whitfield."

He glanced around. "Don't look now, but Mrs. Sumner, followed closely by Mr. Sumner, is storming into the Charmings Beauty Bar."

"Help?" Paige asked, throwing up her hands.

His heart tugged. He didn't like it one bit. Taking pity on her, he held out his hand. She placed her soft palm against his. He sucked in a sharp breath, curling his fingers around her hand. "Come on, let's round up the posse." The weariness settling in his gut colored his words.

A few minutes later, the big glass door whispered closed behind them. The voices, rising to be heard above the blow dryers, screeched to a halt. As a matter of fact, so did the whirling noise of the handheld devices.

It seemed as if every eye in the place were fixed on them. Paige shuddered and retreated a step. If he hadn't clutched her fingers, anchoring her to him, she'd have slipped away.

"Easy now, sweetheart," he nearly purred. *Sweetheart? Why had he called her that?*

"It's them!" Someone near the back of the salon called out.

"Of course. The hair!" A woman twisted in the salon chair and pointed. "I'd know it anywhere."

"Jay." Paige's voice trembled.

Gasps floated through the air.

"Paige, stop it now. We can't go through this again," Alice Sumner cried. "The flashbulbs. The people pressing, pushing, pawing at us. The whispers," she wailed.

"Now, now, honey." Marty Sumner gathered her in his arms. "Paige," he said between clamped teeth, jerking his head to the left.

Following his gaze, Jay spotted the oversized poster.

He swore his gulp matched hers.

Nearly nine feet tall, in brilliant gloss, he stood with Paige in front of him. Her glorious, shiny blonde hair took up most of the shot. But, with his head bent to hers and her looking up at him, his dark hair hung forward. *Dark against light.* She was cradled between his legs, which were encased in the tight black pants.

On the bottom of the ad, so as not to detract from them, it read, King's...A New Beginning In An Age-Old Fairy Tale...

There was no product. Only the King's logo in the corner.

Bold. Powerful. Sexy.

"Is it getting hot in here?" he asked, recalling every incredible moment of that day with Paige touching him, kissing him back.

They groaned in unison.

Was hers a good groan or a bad one?

***

Soft whistles rent the air behind him. *His brothers. Found.*

This time Jay's groan was one of agony.

The brothers didn't hold back.

"Geez, Jay, have some dignity, will you? Jonathan said.

"That wasn't in the contract," Max pointed out needlessly.

"Jay, Paige, how could you do something like that?" Danny asked.

"Help?" Jay whispered to her, hoping she'd lend him a hand here.

"I'll handle yours if you handle mine?" Paige peeked at him from under her lashes.

It did strange things to him. Tingles shot through him. He sucked in a sharp breath. His body buzzed and hummed and shifted to high gear. *Now? Come on. I'm dying here.*

She didn't wait for an answer; she let go of Jay's hand and went to his brothers. Gently, she led them to the poster, pointing to the castle behind them, the horse nearby, to the King's saying on the bottom, and then waving her hand to encompass the whole concept, or so it seemed.

"Jay." Mr. Sumner came up to his side and put a hand on his arm. "You've got to put a stop to it. She's been exploited enough in her life…"

Mrs. Sumner, clinging to her husband, leaned close. "She's just a little girl. How could you?"

He cleared his throat. *Did they really still see her as a kid?* He never asked, but he'd guess she was closer to thirty and not three anymore. "Paige made her own decision about the ad—" He stopped himself from saying ads; they'd freak if they knew she was in more. *Exploited? How so?*

Sighing near his shoulder, Paige nudged him aside. "Good try, Whitfield. Well, not so good. We're handing off families. You take your brothers, and I'll take care of my folks."

***

Paige trudged to the door, held it open for her mom and dad, and refused to focus in on the salon full of curious, gawking stares and especially at Jay.

Not his problem. So stop trying to shield yourself from dealing with yours.

She looped her arm through her father's bent elbow on her left side and her mom's on her right side and steered them across the marble floor of King's. "You've never seen my office, have you? Well, it's more of a work space in the wedding dress department. But, I love it."

"Honey, it's so suggestive." Her mother harped on about the poster. "Everyone knows it's you. Did you even have panties on?"

"Full bodysuit, Mom. Covered from neck to ankle." She didn't dare tell them it was nude and fit her like a glove, so she might as well have been naked in front of Jay. She brushed away the aching in her tummy. Hunger pains. *Hello, it is! For Jay.*

"Sweetie pie." Her father's use of her nickname made her heart tug.

"Daddy. He was a perfect gentlemen." *Well, there was that hot kiss, but they didn't need to know about it or that she practically begged for his lips.*

His deep sigh rushed out. "I always thought he was a good boy."

"He's one of the good ones, Dad. Look how he takes care of his brothers." Jay Whitfield might have been a sports star, but he hadn't forgotten about who he was and what his priorities were. *Family.*

She liked that about him. Liked his sense of duty and loyalty to his brothers. Recalling her visit to his home, she felt the special relationship they shared. They were close.

Gulping hard, Paige envisioned the brothers' reaction to the poster. She hoped they wouldn't hold it against Jay.

It *was* sexy and a tad risqué. While she didn't love every minute of it, Jay was there to lean on and then to cling to.

For the first time since she'd gotten sick in college, she'd been physically close to a guy. *Well, a man.*

He didn't reject her for being different. He didn't treat her like her disease would rub off on him. Granted, he didn't know like the college-age guys she went to school with did. *Nope, can't hide the fact when you're rail-thin and losing your hair.*

Shaking her head, she whisked those painful memories away. Her braid tugged, reminding her how she'd overreacted and went the complete opposite. For all intents and purposes, she'd invisibly flipped her finger off at her illness and she hadn't cut her hair in six and a half years. *Me, sick? Who says? I'm as healthy as a horse. Take that!*

Her parents were talking to themselves and each other at times as Paige positioned them on the escalator to whisk them to the next floor.

"Where did I go wrong?" her mother asked. "Time after time, I warned her. Don't make a scene. Don't draw attention to yourself…"

"My baby. I tried to protect her…" Her father shrugged.

Paige groaned inwardly. *Not this again!*

"You could have said no when that school reporter wanted a story," her mother accused. "Friend?" She snorted. "He'd gotten the scoop and word spread like wildfire."

"He said he was Paige's friend. He wanted to help any way he could."

Stepping off the human conveyor belt, Paige gingerly directed them onward. "Hey, guys, time out, okay? It's over and done. No going back." *How many times had she had to remind them of that fact? While going through the ordeal and now when, on rare occasions like now when discussing it in the open, they skirted around the cold, hard truth? Her illness.*

It always hung there, between them. If not hinted at, or intentionally avoided, it lay there, ripping their existence apart. *Fragile. Vulnerable.*

Her belly clutched. *Was it real hungry pangs or just plain old pain from how much she'd hurt the two people she loved most?*

A dab of perspiration popped out on her forehead. Her legs were wobbly. *Uh oh!*

"Let's get moving here," she said in a chirpy voice. "I've got this—" *Terrible pain slashing through my gut.* She swallowed hard. "Beautiful wedding dress I want you two to see."

"Yours?" Her mother stopped short and turned to her.

"Mom, seriously?" Paige shook her head, the weight of her hair adding to the uncomfortable condition. It weighed a ton and kept all the heat too close to Paige's feverish body right about now.

"You'd tell your mother, wouldn't you?" Her father chimed in.

"Of course." *Why would they doubt her?* "I'm not getting married. Now or anytime soon. I work at King's. I was blessed to have Charlie, the owner, take an interest in my artwork. Fortunately, she saw more than just that and challenged me to try designing clothes, specifically wedding dresses for King's. Next, she asked if I can do a mural for the princess room at King's Café. Now, for the knight room. I'm really lucky."

"And that ad?"

Finally, she entered the wedding dress department, dodging the few customers and even fewer employees, and led her parents into her office workroom. It was small and windowless, but all hers. She went to the completed drawing on her art table. "Take a look. This will be one of the latest designs for the remodeled wedding department at King's." Pride throbbed in her voice. They loved her work and wanted to showcase it even more once the new building was complete. *Now, if only she could design and hide. How was she going to convince the King family when they gave credit where credit was due? Did they really have to use* her *name?*

Her mother's gasp said it all. "I like. Paige, it's beautiful."

Her father nodded. "Nice, honey. You're so talented. But, about that ad—"

Holding up her hand, she went around to her desk shoved against a wall and retrieved the contract and attached check. "This is for you two. I want you to put a down payment on that condo on the golf course."

"What?!" They cried out in unison, glancing from her smiling face to the paperwork.

"How many zeros?" Her father started counting.

"Wowie kazowie!"

"You did it for us?" Her mother's voice trembled with a fresh wave of tears.

"Yeah. You sacrificed so much for me. Now, it's my turn to take care of you." *Yeah, that's what she needed to do, take a page from the book of Jay.* "Dad, you think that unit you loved so much is still available? They can put me on as one of the buyers and they can figure in all our incomes. My future one, too, based one that contract. Mom's job; your two, Dad; mine, plus the ads. It'll be a good chunk of change, right?"

"Oh, honey," her mother exclaimed, throwing her arms around Paige and clutching her tight. "You *are* moving back in with us!"

Paige's heart sank. And her middle heaved.

CHAPTER 9

Her hands shook as she ripped open a protein bar packet she kept in her desk drawer.

Feed the beast.

Taking a bite, she nearly spit it out. Nope, she had to get something to ease the pain in her belly. Now, if only she could take away the hurt in her chest.

It tasted like cardboard right about now. *Ashes in her dry mouth.*

Her mother and father were babbling like excited little children as they hunched over her desk phone, talking to the real estate broker.

Paige chewed the lump and finally swallowed a dozen times to get it down.

No, she was not moving back in with them. *Not now. Not ever.* But how could she break the news to them?

They were so happy, laughing and smiling at each other as they hung up the phone.

"Mom, Dad," she choked out. "That's great it's still

on the market…"

"Our luck is changing, Paige." Her father practically did a jig.

"Ah…there's something you," another difficult swallow, "should know. I can't move in—"

"Yeah, yeah. These things take time. We've got to inform our landlord. You've got to inform yours." He shrugged.

"Ever." The one word dropped into the room like a bomb going off. Their faces fell. Silence roared in the tiny room. *Destruction.*

***

Jay, along with his brothers, stood in the doorway to Paige's office, having overheard the last part of the conversation.

She sat on the edge of her desk, pale and shaking. His heart clutched.

"Do something, Jay," Danny pleaded.

"It's my fault," Jay said, having no idea what he was doing or saying.

All eyes were trained on him.

What the heck was he going to do? He searched for Paige and found her soft, teary eyes directed on his. He swore his heart tumbled. "Paige?"

Why did he think things he shouldn't whenever she was near? Why did he care about her when he shouldn't? He had three brothers to take care of.

"It's part of the ad campaign." He lied. "A modern twist on a fairy tale. Single lady meets single guy. Dating life. Going out. Getting closer." Her frown forced him to rush out the last made-up bit. "You know, the normal progression of a relationship. Engagement. Marriage—"

"Illusion. Smoke. Mirrors," Paige hastened to add. "Playacting, right, Jay? So Mom and Dad, it wouldn't work out all of us living under the same roof."

It was lame.

"That's all you had?" Max asked, shaking his head.

"They'll never buy it," Jonathan put his two cents' worth in to the mix.

"Think of something, Jay," Danny begged.

He recalled something Rico had said about her room being a masterpiece. "Paige's apartment has the all-clear for the photo shoots—"

The woman in question groaned out loud and slapped a hand to her forehead.

"How could you, Paige? Letting people that close. You know better than that. And the germs you could be exposed to." Her mother and father went back and forth.

"Sweetie, you can't. No, not again. It was a disaster the first time."

"First time, Paige?" Jay frowned, wondering what they were talking about. It seemed like they talked in code. One that couldn't be deciphered.

Paige held up her hands and sprang to her feet.

"Enough, okay? I've got work to do. I'll show you out." She skirted around her still arguing parents and squeezed by Jay.

He reached out a hand and tried to stop her. Too late! She slipped past him and cleared his brothers.

"She's bolting again," he murmured under his breath. "Paige, wait up."

Chasing her, he spotted her braid flying out behind her as she rounded the corner to the main wedding dress department showroom. She stopped. But not for him.

The owner, Charlie, reached out to halt her. "Is everything all right, Paige?"

There were several customers nearby, touching the dresses on display or answering questions from an attendant. Now, they stilled and focused on her and Charlie. And him as he made his way to the two ladies.

"It's nothing." Paige tried to brush it off and escape again.

"It's me," he said, coming up behind them.

"Jay?" Charlie glanced from him and back to Paige.

There were a few gasps followed by whispers. Jay turned in time to see another giant-sized poster of them. But this one was different. He recalled setting up for the shoot and joking with Paige. She hid behind him, with her braid draped over his shoulder and along his bare chest. *Hiding again, Paige?*

The slight grin on his face and the look in his eyes jolted him. It was a test shot. But it said more than he'd been willing to admit. There was something there.

More than like. More than desire. Could it be…?

"Holy sassafras and succotash," Peg said, clutching her clipboard, drawing close to his side. "Hey, Jay, you don't mind if I call you Jay, do you? Well, buddy, as my rock-star hubby and I always say, you can't hide that. You got it. Bad."

Love? No, he didn't want it. He had his brothers to parent. Letting his gaze travel from the poster to Paige, he felt the buzz in his veins again. He lingered over her features and gazed into her eyes. She felt it, too. A jolt slashed through him.

As the knowledge of it all was sinking in, Jay heard his brothers' soft whistles and hearty comments.

"Man, bro, why didn't you tell us?"

"Paige and Jay sitting in a tree—" Danny began, but was stopped by a hand to his chest.

"Whoa, now! I'll draw up the pre-nup," Max said.

"You *are* getting married!" Mrs. Sumner exclaimed.

"Not my little girl…" Mr. Sumner glanced at Jay. "Well, okay, if it's to *the* Jay Whitfield I guess it's all right."

"How can you say such a thing? Our baby. You're killing—" She halted, slapping a hand over her mouth.

Paige froze; what little color that was left in her face drained from her. "Mom. No scene, okay?" Her colorless lips barely moved.

There it was again. The awkward silence. The exchange of frightened looks between Mr. and Mrs. Sumner. As if saying something would be a curse if they voiced it.

"But...but the cancer?" Her father whispered in a broken voice.

"Cancer?" He'd heard those words before. His mother's voice, strong and steady, had informed him. *We'll beat this.* But, she hadn't. "You have cancer, Paige?" The bottom of Jay's world just dropped out from under him.

CHAPTER 10

Her feet were like lead. They wouldn't move, wouldn't run away from this horrible moment.

Jay's face, slack and ashen, made her heart twist in agony.

Sucking in a deep, shaky breath, she said, "Not any more, Jay."

It didn't change a thing. Still, he stared. Betrayal was written there in his eyes.

"Hey, guys, we can take this to my office. More private," Charlie said, draping an arm around Paige's shoulders.

Dragging her gaze away from Jay, she said, "You don't seem surprised, Boss."

"Eddie, Dolly's husband, is an ex-cop. He does a very thorough background check on all our prospective employees. We knew about it."

"Hard not to, sweetie. You were all over the papers when it first happened," Peg chimed in. "Holy Toledo, the press ate up your story. Sweet, young college girl fighting for her life. Her devastated parents reaching out for help. The mega search for a bone marrow donor to knock out that hideous bone cancer."

Jay's brothers surrounded him. "You okay, bro?"

"We got you, Jay," Jonathan said.

The four brothers looked at her in a mixture of shock and pity.

She focused on Jay. Tears smarted her eyes. "It was all documented. Unfortunately. It haunts my folks." Glancing at them, she noted how two of the King's employees were helping them sit in nearby chairs. "To this day, they still can't believe I'm well." She shrugged. "Well enough. Stomach issues from the treatments. Small price to pay, right?" Her voice caught.

For years, she'd never spoken of the events. Maybe if she didn't, it wouldn't cause her parents any more pain. It was an unspoken promise to the three of them.

Don't draw attention.

Don't discuss the C word. Or the d-i-e word. Or the death one, too.

Paige didn't know any other way than to pretend, for their sakes, it hadn't happened. But it did. And it sat there between them like a huge concrete block, keeping them stuck in a pseudo world

When it was accidentally mentioned or one of the *bad* words came up, they'd divert the conversation to something safe.

"Chemo sucks," she said in a stronger, louder voice.

"It takes away everything you are, everything you have. Your health—what little you had left. Your dignity. Ever puke your guts out on national TV? Not pretty." She snorted. "Your money. My folks lost every penny they had and then some just to keep me alive and begged to raise funds for the bone marrow transplant. Oh yeah, you ever have to ask a stranger to give up their marrow for your sick kid? They did it. Anywhere. Everywhere."

Hot tears trickled down her face. "You know what. They did it, too. Months of pouring out their hearts and someone stepped forward to be tested. A match. But they were scared. For themselves. Their family. They declined."

"The search went on." Her father's flat voice tore through her.

"And on," her mother added.

"Until an angel arrived. Sweet. Innocent. She gave. I received. She didn't want us to know who she was. Anonymous, except for the doctor letting her gender slip one day. I lived. Thanks to her."

Jay stared, his face white and expressionless now.

Paige swallowed passed the lump in her throat. "I thrived. I rebounded. My hair grew back—"

"And grew and grew." Her mom chuckled softly.

"No way was that cancer going to take the best of our Paige." Her father's voice was filled with pride. "She showed them. All of them who were planning her funer—"He stopped short.

She finished for him. "The press had made contacts. They were staging my last, great goodbye. It was gaudy and grotesque, to put it kindly. Imagine, they even filmed a 'dry' rehearsal. That's how close I was to death's door."

"They blindsided us out of nowhere and showed it to us." Her mother wept. "And filmed our reaction."

"Holy crap, Batman!" Peg dropped down beside Paige's mother and hugged her.

Paige came back to the moment. Aware of the people gathered around, she said, "So that's it. My story in a nutshell." She used Max's phrase from the time she visited the brothers. "Nothing left to tell." She shrugged her shoulders, unable to look away from Jay's now stormy face. *That was that, then. Over. Done. Kaput.*

There were murmurs and most of the onlookers shuffled away a little shell-shocked.

"Nice to see you, Jay, the brothers. I'll see you at the next photo shoot. In what? A week?" She went to her parents. "Mom. Dad. I'll take you home now."

"Peg, can you call Eddie to see if he can take the Sumners home?" Charlie asked, coming up behind Paige and placing a hand on her back. "You're not alone anymore, my friend."

Trust. That's something that had been missing for far too long in her life and her parents' lives. "Thanks, Charlie," she choked out, knowing and feeling she wasn't alone any longer.

"We're your family, too, now. So, if there's

anything you need, don't hesitate to ask."

A few seconds later, Peg ended the cell phone call, saying, "He's on his way. Remember, Boss, Alex is coming to meet with Griff, Shane, and Priscilla on the design for the new addition for the wedding department."

"Thanks, pal," Charlie said. "That's my cue to get moving so I can meet them in the conference room."

"I got this, Boss," Peg offered, helping Mrs. Sumner to her feet.

"No," Jay interrupted. "I'll take it from here, Peg."

Paige stilled, looking over her shoulder at him.

His face had gone from grave to thunderous.

A big alarm went off in her head.

Warning! Danger!

***

Jay Whitfield stood in the center of the new completed knight room in King's Café. He turned slowly, taking in the magnificent mural Paige had created. In a week, most likely working day and night and at breakneck speed, she'd finished it.

In that entire week, she hadn't spoken to him. His chest ached.

He and his brothers had assisted the Sumner family to the awaiting limo with Eddie driving them away. But that was only as far as Paige would let them go. *Shut down.*

Mumbling, I'm sorry didn't cut it. He longed to take her in his arms and tell her how his heart broke for her when she'd confessed. *Cancer. At twenty? A kid really.* But then her hackles went up and the cold, hard truth hit Jay; she'd never planned to share this part of herself with him. *Shut out*.

What he thought was the beginning of them really wasn't anything at all. How could someone keep that from the person they cared about?

Obviously, she didn't care *enough.*

That glaring fact had wounded him. And his brothers. Their concern and questions were the topic of conversation too many times at dinner this last week. Danny had fed them little tidbits of what Paige was doing, keeping different hours, working hard.

Now, catching sight of the not-too-scary dragon, Jay smiled sadly. The detail alone took his breath away. But what she'd gone through and had come back from shook him to his core. He'd been torn between anger at her not telling him and disgust at what had been done to her and her family. But, she'd shown no sign of weakness. God, he admired her.

Shock at the thought of how close she'd come to dying still rattled him. Recalling his mother's ordeal, he could only imagine the days fighting to survive, staying strong for her family, defying the gods and the odds. His mother lost. His brothers had been devastated. The pain etched in their faces and haunting their eyes propelled him to keep them intact, hold the brothers together as one. *And never let that kind of pain happen to them again.*

Still, their concern and worry for Paige echoed in his mind. He couldn't protect them from everything, especially caring for someone like Paige.

He couldn't even protect himself.

The magnificent white horse in the mural bowed his head. Jay regarded the strength and the beauty and thought of Paige. "Amazing," he whispered, both regarding the mural and the woman who'd created it.

"Talking to yourself again, Whitfield?" she asked from the entrance to the room.

He whipped around, seeing her with her hair down and flowing to her knees, standing with her arms crossed. Gazing long and hard, he felt his blood thunder in his ears. Petite, sexy in black leggings and a long white blouse, she was anything but fragile. And by the looks of it, she wasn't turning tail to bolt. *For now.*

Her underlying vulnerability reached out to him. It was the first chance they'd talked alone. What could he say? His heart throbbed in empathy. By the looks of it, she didn't want it.

"Fair maiden," he said, bowing slightly. "Methinks you are a genius."

Her chuckle rushed through him and around him. "I guess that means you like it." She spread her arms to encompass the room.

"Brilliant. However, you left a very big detail out?" She frowned, but he went on. "The maiden for the knight. Or is she invisible, too?" he asked softly.

The smile faded and shadows chased across her beautiful blue eyes. "It's for boys." She shook her head. "No girls allowed, right? So, as a guy with lots of guys in his family, do you think boys will like this room? Not too kiddish?" She cleared her throat. "How are the brothers, anyway? Danny and I have talked. He told me about your mom. But the other two. How are they doing?"

And me? "Getting their classes straight." The large check for the ad was being put to good use.

She walked toward him. He waited, heart drumming. A few steps away, she halted. "Jay." Her soft voice wrapped around him. "I'm sorry. I don't... well, I didn't talk about it to anyone."

He took her in, allowing his gaze to travel over every inch of her. The ache inside him grew.

"Parts all intact," she joked. "No need to check them out."

His grin gave him away. "I happen to like your parts."

"There are some scars." She gulped audibly as she tugged the fabric away from her neck to reveal a few pale lines near the top of her chest. "And lower..."

"You going to show me those, too?" The hopeful tone in his voice wasn't lost on her.

"Funny, Whitfield. On my stomach. Feeding tubes." She shrugged stiffly. "And other things can leave marks."

Looking up swiftly, he watched a shaft of pain chase across her eyes. "And people can leave marks on your heart, too." *She'd left one on his.*

She bit her lip. "How perceptive you are—"

"For a former football player." He tried to make light of it.

"Whitfield." A silent beat pulsed. "No harm. No foul."

"That's more of a baseball term."

"The kiss. All is forgiven."

At the mention of that mind blowing kiss, he dropped his gaze to her lips. He frowned. "Forgiven?"

"In the heat of the moment," she said, waving a hand away. "No need to rehash and all that."

"Really?" He was watching her lips move. *Hypnotizing.* "That's interesting. Why do you get to call the shots?"

"I'm the ref?" she half said, half asked.

"Not in my game, honey." Something pulled inside him. He wanted her. *Big time.*

"You're distracting me," she said softly. "Where was I again?"

"You were about to kiss me right in front of the dragon." He stepped closer and cupped her cheeks in his palms. His defenses crumbled. "Paige. I thought we…thought you could tell me, talk to me. Why?"

Tears shimmered in her eyes as she gazed into his. "Jay. When would have been a good time? When you crashed through the kitchen doors and lemonade spilled on me?"

"I like the wet T-shirt look, by the way. Any time you want to try that again, call me."

She went on as if he hadn't said anything. "When we were sitting by each other at the Kings' big announcement?"

"You kept leaning close. And you ate my quiche," he reminded her.

"At the photo shoot? In that clinch, correction, nearly naked clinch?"

Everything she said made sense. Too much sense. He stilled. "Do you feel anything for me, Paige?" His breath stopped.

"Anything? How about everything?"

He released that breath and another one. "I don't do flings."

She shrugged. "Me either. I have parents… overprotective, frustrating, embarrassing, loving parents."

"Ah, the parents of little discretion. *That* Mr. and Mrs. Sumner." He smiled. "I like them. They love you. We can make it work."

"I…I'm guarded."

He laughed outright at that. "You don't say." His Paige, the one who ran at the drop of a hat, who bottled up all her painful memories of her illness to protect her folks, who was now clutching his sides and holding on for dear life, was now facing the hard stuff.

"It's not easy."

"I've got three brothers to care for." They would always be a priority to him. He wanted her to know what she was getting into. "We live in the same house. We support each other's dreams. We show up, stay for the hard stuff, and cheer when we make it, or give a shoulder to lean on when it doesn't go well. I will always be there for them." *That's how we roll.*

"Sometimes I think they're more worried about you and how alone you are."

"They never complained or said anything." *She knew.* He saw it, too, at times.

"It's there. In their eyes. The way they come to your defense."

"You're not going to bolt, are you?" As much as he wanted her, needed her, he couldn't expose his brothers to losing someone else.

She gulped. "I'll try not to." She winced. "No guarantees."

Something cold and hard dropped into his belly. Jay brushed her soft cheek with a thumb one last time before he took a step back. He disengaged completely. "Not good enough, Paige."

Disappointment crossed her features.

It tore a chunk from his heart. "I can't do that to them. Nothing or forever. No middle ground for me." With that, his hungry gaze took in all of her, and then he was the one who left her standing and walked away.

CHAPTER 11

Numb. N-U-M-B. That was the only word to describe how she felt. *Or didn't feel, was more like it.*

Going through the motions was like trying to pick up your feet as they were sucked into quicksand, dragging her down over and over again.

That's where telling Jay the truth had gotten her. She couldn't give him absolutes. Life wasn't like that. *Not for her.*

Normal? She been drop-kicked so far away from normal her head spun.

Paige plastered on a smile in another meeting. The new addition—well, entire building— for the wedding dress department was coming to fruition. Each step, carefully created and selected by this assembled team, built to an incredible finished design.

In a matter of days, construction would begin. It was an exciting time. Paige sensed it. It was just too bad she didn't feel it.

Rico nudged her. "Your turn, Princess."

All eyes were on her. *Again?* She wanted to shrink. *Yeah, the incredible shrinking woman.* Too bad it couldn't really happen right about now. "What am I supposed to say?" she asked Rico under her breath.

"*The* dress. Girl, where have you been for the last half hour?" He tsked her.

"Yes, of course." She sat up straight and riffled through her sketches.

Charlie seemed to sense her struggle; she stepped in, saying, "Here's the concept for the alcoves. My wedding dress will be at the entrance of this room. Francine's wedding dress will be here, showcasing King's custom wedding dresses."

"And mine in the alternative section," Priscilla chimed in, grinning at her husband, Griff.

"Pixie, it's not alternative." His voice was soft and warm as he talked to his wife. "Well, not in a bad way."

Paige gazed from the usually all-business, no-nonsense man running King's to his smiling, dreamy-eyed wife. God, the man adored his wife. *Go figure!*

"Can I stick a finger down my throat now?" Rico shivered in disgust. "My best friend is all goo-goo eyed. And him, all tough and macho, a big pile of mush. Happens every time, too. God, I need a man. Hey, Jay never came through for me. Ask him for me, will ya?"

"Me? You were supposed to show up at the gym. Did you?" He shook his head. "Didn't think so. And I barely know the man."

He snorted in her ear. "Yeah, like you weren't

licking his face a few weeks ago. Come on, help a buddy out."

"Paige?" Griff asked, turning to her. "Your dress design. How's it coming? It will be the spotlight of the grand opening."

"Ah." She whipped her head back around to face him across the large conference table. "It's in the early stages yet."

"We have a deadline. Charlie?"

"I'll get with you, Paige, after the meeting and you can let me see what you've come up with."

She did that plastic smile thing again on the outside, but, on the inside, Paige groaned. Looking down, she stared at a blank page. *Nothing. Nada.*

"Shamy. Shamy." Rico scolded. "Mr. Football is A-W-O-L and you're down in the dumps. That adds up to mucho trouble."

"Seriously?"

"Just sayin'."

Looking around, Paige discovered all eyes were trained on her still.

Could she just evaporate now? Puff? Be gone?

"One wedding dress. Correction, one fabulous wedding dress, coming right up, folks." *Yeah, right!*

***

"Want to talk about it?" Charlie asked, joining Paige on her ride of shame in the elevator.

“Not really.” Paige prayed for the contraption to hit the first floor soon and the doors to break open.

“Is it Jay?”

Looking at the owner of King’s, her dark eyes filled with empathy, Paige asked, “How did you guess?”

“Oh, I don’t know. A little birdie told me.”

Thankfully, the doors opened, but Charlie lightly touched her arm, directing her through the store and to the café.

Dread filled her as they went through the special tunnel their clients used and out into the bustling café to the knight room.

The finished room bore a large round table in the middle, several smaller round tables, and tall chairs at each one. A plush rug adorned the floor, making their steps soundless. Charlie adjusted the lights and the room was bathed in golden hues from the chandeliers overhead.

“We’re set to open this room in a few days. I’d like you to be here.” Charlie walked to the mural. “Magnificent job, Paige.” She pointed to a few spots near the ceiling.

Looking up, Paige noticed the cameras. Her stomach dropped to her knees.

“These were installed just after you finished the mural. Bruno insisted for security purposes.” Turning to her, Charlie tilted her head and said, “He showed me the tape.”

Clamping her eyes shut, Paige cursed the lovely

night guard. He was a staple here at King's, having begun when Charles King founded and built the store. But, Bruno was ever present, ever knowing. "Can't hide anything around here," she muttered.

"Not likely with my bunch." The smile in her voice softened her words.

"I can't think. Can't concentrate. Can't function." Paige bit her lip.

"As Dolly, Peg, and Rico would say, you've got it bad."

Paige threw up her hands, saying, "It sounds like a disease."

"Love-sick?"

She sucked in a sharp breath, shaking her head in denial. Then she stopped. "I'm afraid, Charlie."

The other lady drew near. "It's natural, Paige. You've been through so much. How can you trust? Who can you be yourself with? I get it. And what if it ever comes back?"

Gulping hard, Paige nodded. *She did know.* "That's just it. I don't want to be another burden or responsibility to Jay—" She cupped a hand over her mouth and stared at Charlie. "I can't believe I said that. I didn't even know I felt it."

Grinning, Charlie said, "Surprised yourself, didn't you?" She touched Paige's long, flowing hair, brushing it away from her face. "Why would you think that of him anyway?"

Paige was surprised by herself for first thinking that

way, but for also allowing someone to touch her long, treasured hair. She'd guarded that and that part of herself for seven years now. It wasn't as bad as she thought it would be. *Well, it certainly wasn't with Jay.* "He takes care of everyone around him. I didn't want to be just another one he felt he had to take care of."

"If that was the *only* thing, then I'd be concerned."

"It's not?" She already had answered that for herself just looking around. He'd treated her like a woman here, touching, holding, kissing…

"What are you going to do about it?" Charlie asked.

"Well…I have some touchups I'd like to do in here, but, is this room available tonight?"

***

Paige dragged a hand across her damp forehead, and then applied the last layer to a crown of flowers. She'd been at it for two hours and hoped she'd gotten it down just right. The fan helped dry it faster and she was careful not to smudge anything.

"He'll be here in forty," Danny said. "Aren't you done yet?"

"Almost. And thanks for helping me out. I knew I could count on you to get things organized."

"Yeah, I'm a regular Peg." He grinned, blowing on his fingers and rubbing them on is shirt.

"Hey, I'm irreplaceable, just ask my hubs. Well, you can when he gets off the road in a few days, that is."

Peg stood tall and surveyed the latest addition to the mural. "Holy moly, me. Mega hot."

"I wasn't going for hot." Paige's concern grew.

"Can't hide chemistry, honey. But it's not indecent or anything." The lady breezed away. "Come on, hotshot or Peg wannabe. We need to get the troops to the kitchen. Paige, finish up in here."

***

Butterflies danced along Paige's nerves and in the pit of her stomach. *Or was that hunger pangs again? Sometimes a girl can't be too sure.*

Making her way into the kitchen, Paige came upon her favorite cook. "Dolly, thanks so much for doing this for me."

"Honey, I wouldn't miss this for the world! I knew the minute you two saw each other, bang, ba-da-boom. Right between the eyes. You just didn't know it yet. Him, neither. But, I swear, I went home that night and told my Eddie. You ask him yourself. I said, Eddie, we're gonna have another King's wedding."

Warmth crept into her cheeks. "I'm not sure about that."

"Listen to me, I know it when I see it. Now, you run along and stop pestering me. I've got some goodies to fix. The gang will be here before you know it, too. Lots of people. Lots of food. Just the way I like it."

"Don't forget the lemonade," Paige called over her

shoulder as she left the kitchen.

"Not when you've reminded me a couple dozen or hundred times," Dolly cried out.

She paced the hall, greeting people as they came. Peg stood at the entrance, checking off the attendees. *Present and accounted for.* The King sisters with their husbands and babies arrived first. More came, a blur of faces and names. Eddie went back and got her parents.

"Mom. Dad." She hugged them tight. "I have some news. Well, news on top of news."

"What's this all about?" Her father looked around at the empty café.

"In the back. The new knight room," she explained. "But first, come with me. I want you two to be there for this."

"Huh?" Her mother's wide eyes couldn't quite focus.

"You'll understand in a minute." Turning, she waved someone forward. "Rico, lead the way."

"It's about time, girl. I've been itching to do this since the day I met you." He fingered her hair. "Oh la la."

"Just go, Rico."

In moments, they were following him through the tunnel to King's Department Store. She nodded to Bruno, who waited for them at the door of the salon. "Thanks, big guy. I owe you more than you'll ever know."

"Well, I do accept food." He smacked his lips. "Any

leftovers, you send them my way."

"Hand delivered by myself," she promised.

"Here? Really, Paige?" Her mother, still owl-eyed, blinked at the brightly lit Charmings Beauty Bar. "The scene of my heartache?"

"They still have that poster up," her father muttered, shaking his head.

"Don't worry. I've completed all the photo shoots. Four in total. Jay…" Her voice caught. She cleared her throat. "He has others to do. More products. His line of sportswear being developed now. A charity thing with King's, too. But, I'm all done." *In more ways than one.*

"Come on. We don't have all day, girl." Rico fussed, drawing her to the back of the salon. Once there, he positioned her. "It's better if you stand." He draped a cape around her neck and dragged out the length of her hair.

"Paige?" Her mother's gasp rent the air.

She leaned forward a little, grabbing a camera. "Here, Daddy, take a picture. Before and after."

"Honey, are you sure?" Tears swam in his eyes.

"I'm donating my hair." Someone could use it more than she could.

"Oh, my baby." Her mother covered her mouth with her hands, weeping openly.

"Definitely. No more hiding. No more running away from the truth." *From life.* "Hit it, Rico!"

He gathered her hair, gingerly putting it in a rubber band near her shoulders. Picking up the nearby scissors, he opened and closed them a few times. “I love this part.”

Thwack! Thwack!

CHAPTER 12

Paige Sumner felt twenty pounds lighter and, if possible, a billion times more nervous than she did an hour ago.

She let her parents and Rico go ahead and now she stalled at the entrance.

Peg's jaw fell, and then she quickly recovered. "Hot dogs and horseradish!" The assistant gave her a thumbs-up and Paige grinned.

"Everyone here?" Her heart raced. "The brothers? Jay?" She stumbled over his name.

"Check. Double check." She tapped her clipboard with her pencil. Leaning close, she said, "He doesn't suspect a thing. Just a little celebration with the King's and friends for the kickoff—no football pun intended—of the knight room."

Giggling, she said, "I like the pun, though." Fingering her shorter hair, Paige filled with wonder at the shoulder-length new style. *Layers? Side swept bangs? Who would have known it would look and feel so good?*

"Go get him." Peg nudged her forward. "Attagirl!"

First, Paige halted near the entrance. Someone brilliant had placed more posters of Jay and her on each side of the entrance to the room. She gulped at the steam rising from the pictures.

"Holy hotness, times two. No denying that," Peg whispered loudly. She nodded her head. "A screen covering your latest handiwork. Danny boy's going to do the reveal for you."

As she grew closer, the murmur of voices from inside increased. Her legs were wooden, her feet clumsy in the new heels Rico had selected for her. The dress, tight and purple, encased her. *Not quite wrapped like a mummy, but close.*

The pep talk jostling in her head the last few minutes petered out the moment she entered.

Run, Paige, run!

She froze.

The chatter died down.

Near the back of the room, Jay sat. The eerie stillness echoed, pulsing in her ears.

He looked to his brother, Danny, and then grinned. Her heart stopped. *God, he was so good with his brothers. He'd make a great dad someday.*

Becoming aware, Jay glanced up and then did another take. "Paige?"

Slowly, she nodded. A sweep of hair moved. She brushed it back.

A few people gasped and then softly clapped.

"J-Jay," she stuttered, taking carefully measured steps toward him. "I'm here. I'm not running anymore."

"No escape route?"

"In these heels? This dress?" She drew within five feet of him.

"Nice," he said with a grin in his voice. "Your hair. Gorgeous." Finally, he stood, looking a little dazed.

"I let it go. It was dragging me down, holding me back." She sucked in a sharp breath. Tall, wide shoulders, white shirt, black pants… "Is there a knight in distress here?"

"I'm not knightly." He stepped away from the table and into the aisle, closer to her.

"Honor. Loyalty. Protecting the ones you love the most. Sounds like a knight to me."

"Paige. You never showed up to the tournament."

That stung. "True enough. I had to drop off some baggage along the way."

The King sisters, their husbands, and friends chuckled.

"She's like you, Jay. Paige was protecting us, too," her father called out.

"We didn't want to admit what had happened," her mother added. "It was easier to deny it all. It hurt too much to remember. It was scary to think how close we'd gotten to losing our baby." Her mother's voice wobbled, but held up.

"Yeah, what they said," Paige choked out, sticking a

thumb over her shoulder in the direction of her mom and dad. Then she dropped her hand and clasped both in front of her.

Jay ran a hand through his hair.

She sensed movement at his table. One by one his brothers rose. "Hey, guys. You know Jay's so proud of all of you. And I know you only want the best for him. I'm that girl. I'm…" She turned back to Jay and gazed into his eyes. "I'm head over heels for Jay. I love him." Swallowing hard, she went on, "I ran every time he was around. You know why? Not because anything he did, but because he made me *feel*. It was the first time in a long time I felt alive. I knew if I could feel again, then I could be hurt again. And so could other people, people I love, when they saw me hurting."

"Paige." He sucked in a sharp breath. "You're the center of attention right now. You sure you want to do this? You sure you want everyone here to know this?"

"Being sick was tough, no two ways about it. But seeing my folks, agonizing over me and what I was going through, tore me up inside. I swore I'd never do it to them again. And I'd never put someone else through it, either. So I bolted. I fled as fast and hard as I could when you were near," she whispered.

"But you came back. Then and now."

She nodded, taking a shaky breath. "I wanted normal. Humdrum. Boring. That's what I told myself. It was much easier to be invisible in my own second chance life. Pictures? Before, yes; during, not because we wanted it. We destroyed all the evidence, as much as we could. After, nothing. As if that part never existed. And there would never be a comparison to before the cancer and after the cancer. Routine. Normal. But…" She shrugged, fighting back tears. "I couldn't be. There were always so many things I wanted to do. Draw. Design. Create. It thrust me into the spotlight, even when I didn't want to be there."

"You're incredible. Talented." He looked around. "You made something from nothing. You brought this to life, Paige."

"You saved your brothers from being split up, being abandoned. Danny mentioned that to me once. You held on to life so fiercely, your hands around its neck, and you shook it and shook it until you showed your brothers how it was done. You're their hero, Jay. Pretty awesome role model." He glanced over his shoulder to find his brothers behind him. Turning back to Paige, he shook his head.

"Do you know when I stopped running, Jay?"

"Now?" It got a grin from her.

"Close. Today. I realized I wanted to live, really live, instead of hide from the world." She gulped hard. "Okay, Danny, it's time."

"That's me, folks." Danny took a bow. He got a chuckle and shot his fans a big, infectious grin.

"What's this all about, Paige?" Jay glanced from her and then to his brother, who easily moved the small divider away from the freshly painted area.

Her heart pounded.

Turning toward it, Jay gasped. “Paige. It’s you.” He gazed back at her, stunned wonder came over his features. “But…you’re the maiden. In the light beside me, the knight. Honey, the press is invited here for the grand opening. There’ll be pictures. Lots of them. Even more questions. Your face. Your name. It will be plastered across TV screens and papers next to mine.”

“I know. I want to do this. For me. For us. No more running. Jay, it hurt worse to not be with you than anything I’d felt when I was with you.” Tears clung to her lashes. She blinked them away to see him holding out his hand.

“Is there a fair damsel in distress?” he asked softly.

“Fair maiden, Whitfield. And, by the way, that’s the name of my new wedding dress line, Fair Maiden.” Reaching out, she grasped his hand and rushed into his arms. He picked her up and crushed her tight. His deep sigh echoed hers.

The room erupted in cheers. His brothers’ whistles and clapping were loudest of all.

Burying his face in her neck, he murmured, “I love you, Paige Sumner. You’ll have to put me and my brothers out of our misery and marry me. We’re a package deal. Can you stay and love us?”

“Just try and stop me, Whitfield.”

“It’s Knight In Shining Armor to you, fair maiden.”

“I’m good with that. But it’s Mrs. Knight In Shining Armor to you then.”

"I want one, too," Rico called out. "Please, someone find me a man!"

Laughter exploded all around Paige and Jay.

"Lemonade, Paigey, coming up, just like you asked for. Jay, honey, I'll save you some for the honeymoon, too," Dolly cried out, making them both chuckle.

"Wet T-shirt contest, coming right up," Paige said softly.

His rumble of laughter reverberated against her, heating every cold spot in her.

Paige pulled back from him and searched his warm, soft gaze. Slowly, she memorized each endearing feature.

"No more hide and seek? No secret ditch and dash?"

"No, Jay. I found what I was looking for."

"And what's that?"

"Me. You. A life worth living and fighting for. A future to cherish. A once in a lifetime kind of love."

THE END

Thank you for reading!

Dear Reader,

I hope you enjoyed reading *Tangled At First Sight.* I just love writing the *Once Upon A Romance Series.*

I've received letters from fans thanking me for writing the *Once Upon A Romance Series* and asking me to write more in the series. I promise more is in the works! As an author, I love feedback. You are the reason why I write about people like Paige and Jay and how they meet and fall in love. So, tell me what you liked, didn't like, even hated. I'd love to hear from you. You can write me at laurie.leclair@aol.com and visit me on the web at www.laurieleclair.com.

Finally, I need to ask a favor. If you're inclined I'd love an honest review of *Tangled At First Sight.* I'd enjoy your feedback.

As you may know, reviews can be tough to come by these days. You, the reader, have the power to make or break a book. If you have the time, please visit my author page at the site you purchased this book from and leave an honest review. You can find all my books there.

Thank you for reading *Tangled At First Sight* and spending time with me.

Thank you,

Laurie LeClair

ABOUT THE AUTHOR

Bestselling author Laurie LeClair writes contemporary romance and women's fiction. Laurie's habit of daydreaming has gotten her into a few scrapes and launched her to take up her dream of writing. Finally, she can put all those stories in her head to rest as she brings them to life on the page. Laurie considers herself a New Texan (New England born and raised and now living in Texas). She lives in Central Texas with her husband, Jim.

You can contact her at:
http://www.laurieleclair.com
https://twitter.com/LeClairbooks
https://facebook.com/laurieleclair.75

Books by Laurie LeClair

Once Upon A Romance Series:

If The Shoe Fits – Book 1

Waking Sleeping Beauty – Book 2

Taming McGruff – Book 3

The Reluctant Beauty – Book 4

Awakened By A Kiss – Book 5

Tangled At First Sight – Book 6

***

The Sweet Spot Series:

The Dating Dilemma – Book 1

***

An Angel Mountain Novel:

The Heart Remembers – Book 1

***

Tempted By A Texan Series:

The Callahans – The Prequel

The Bounty Hunter Series:

Murphy's Law – Book 1

Riley's Rules – Book 2

***

The Heart Romance Series:

Secrets Of The Heart – Book 1

Crimes Of The Heart – Book 2

Lies Of The Heart – Book 3

***

Wanted: Fairy Godmother

***

The Long Journey Home

***

Runaway Wife

***

Sweet Summertime

CPSIA information can be obtained
at www.ICGtesting.com
Printed in the USA
FSOW02n1347221216
28766FS

HEART of the Hunter

MADELINE BAKER

An Ellora's Cave Publication

www.ellorascave.com

Heart of the Hunter

ISBN 9781419964206

Edited by Meghan Conrad.
Cover art by Dar Albert.

Electronic book publication February 2010
Trade paperback publication 2011

HEART OF THE HUNTER

Trademarks Acknowledgement

The author acknowledges the trademarked status and trademark owners of the following wordmarks mentioned in this work of fiction:

Colt: Colt Industries, Inc.

Hudson's Bay: The Governor and Company of Adventurers of England trading into Hudson's Bay AKA Hudson's Bay Company

Jimmy Dean: Sara Lee Foods, LLC

Levi's: Levi Strauss & Co.

Prologue

Indian Territory, 1877

ꟃ

The two men glared at the Indian who stood between their freedom and a king's ransom in gold.

The Indian was tall, his skin the color of dark bronze, his eyes as black as the bowels of hell. His voice was like slow thunder as he ordered them to get out of the cave and leave the gold behind.

Charlie McBride was willing. Life was more precious than gold. Any fool knew that.

Any fool except Denver Wilkie.

As soon as they cleared the cave, Denver drew his .44 and fired at the Indian. Denver was a crack shot and the bullet struck the redskin in the chest, just left of center. Blood oozed from the wound, spreading like crimson tears over the warrior's buckskin shirt.

The Indian fired back. His first bullet struck Denver in the throat, unleashing a fountain of blood.

The second smashed into Charlie McBride's shoulder. He staggered backward, tripped over a rock and landed on his rump, hard. More frightened than he'd ever been in his life, Charlie stared up at the Indian, certain he was about to be given a one-way ticket to hell.

For a moment, the two men stared at each other and Charlie felt as if the warrior were probing deep into his soul, prying into the innermost secrets and desires of his heart.

And then the warrior lowered his rifle. "Take only…what you need," he said at last. "If you take…one nugget more…my spirit will haunt you…for as long as you live."

His mouth as dry as the dust of Arizona, Charlie McBride could only nod.

"My body..." The Indian was swaying on his feet now. "Do not leave it...out here..."

Charlie nodded again. "I'll bury you," he said. "You have my word on it."

"Inside the cave," the warrior said, his voice growing faint. "Swear it..."

"I promise," Charlie said, but the Indian was past hearing.

Slowly, the life faded from the warrior's eyes, the strength left his legs and he fell slowly, gracefully to the ground.

Although he was growing a little light-headed from the blood he'd lost, Charlie McBride kept his promise. He jammed his neckerchief over the wound in his shoulder to stop the bleeding, then wrapped the dead warrior in Denver's faded Hudson's Bay blanket and left the Indian's body on a natural shelf deep in the bowels of the cave, across from the treasure he had died to protect.

Then, his saddlebags filled with a fortune in gold, Charlie McBride rode away from the mountain.

His first stop was the land office, where he bought two hundred acres of land, including the Indian's mountain, even though he knew he'd never set foot in that cave again.

Chapter One

Montana, 1994

ꕥ

She felt it again, a warm breath whispering against the side of her neck and then a chill, as if a cold winter wind had found its way into the cavern.

For a moment, Kelly didn't move, only stood there, her lantern held high, unable to shake the feeling that she was being watched, that unseen eyes were contemplating her with equal parts of curiosity and malice.

But that was ridiculous. There was nothing to be afraid of, she told herself. Nothing at all. If her grandfather was right, no one but members of the family had been in this cave for more than a hundred years.

Taking a deep calming breath, she placed the lantern on the ground and returned to her study of the body that occupied a narrow shelf along the side of the cave wall. The body, wrapped in a faded Hudson's Bay blanket, was located exactly where her grandfather had said it would be.

In her mind's eye, Kelly could see the ancient remains on display in the local historical museum, along with a small white placard that named her as the contributor.

Kelly shook her head. She had never truly believed her grandfather McBride's ramblings about the riches supposedly hidden in a cave in the mountain behind the ranch. She had thought all his talk about a wealth of Indian gold guarded by the ghost of a savage Lakota warrior to be nothing more than the confused yearnings of an old man's mind, a jumbled mix of old legends and fables handed down from one generation of McBrides to the next.

A long sigh escaped Kelly's lips as she stared down at the blanket-wrapped corpse.

She believed her grandfather now.

Answering some call she didn't understand, Kelly drew a corner of the blanket back, then blinked in surprise. She had expected to find no more than an emaciated corpse, a skeleton clothed in tattered shreds of deer hide. Instead, she saw the well-muscled body of a man dressed in a buckskin clout and fringed leggings. His moccasins were unadorned. He'd been tall, long-legged and narrow-hipped. His hair was black and straight and fell well past his broad shoulders. His jaw was strong and square, his cheekbones prominent, his forehead wide. His nose was long and blade-straight.

Kelly stared thoughtfully at the dark stain on his shirt front and then frowned in bewilderment. Why hadn't the body decayed? She had the strangest feeling that the Indian wasn't dead at all, that like Sleeping Beauty he was merely sleeping away the centuries, waiting to be awakened by love's first kiss.

With a shake of her head, she put away such fanciful thoughts and then, impulsively, she touched his cheek with her forefinger. His skin was supple and...warm.

Warm when it should have been hard and cold. When it shouldn't have been skin at all. After all these years, the body should have returned to the dust from which it had been made.

A shiver of unease skated down Kelly's spine and she glanced around the cave, every instinct warning her to run. Abruptly, she jerked her hand away from his cheek. It was then she saw it, a small buckskin bag resting against his chest.

Curious, she opened the small sack and emptied the contents into her hand. For a moment, she could only stare at the large medallion resting in her palm.

Fashioned in the shape of an eagle with its wings spread wide, the amulet was about two inches in diameter. And it appeared to be made of solid gold. Even in the flickering light of the lantern, the fetish seemed to glow with a life all its own. It felt warm as it nestled in the palm of her hand.

Kelly stared at the eagle for a long moment and then, almost of their own volition, her fingers folded over it and her gaze was drawn to the numerous bags of gold dust and nuggets stacked one on top of the other against the far wall. There was enough money there to pay off the mortgage on the ranch, enough to settle her grandfather's hospital bill. Enough to keep her in comfort for the rest of her life.

Her hands were trembling as she pulled the blanket over the face of the dead man. She couldn't put his remains on display. She knew somehow that he wouldn't want that. Tomorrow, she'd bring a shovel and bury the Indian in the furthest corner of the cave where he could rest undisturbed.

Kelly sighed. The body had rested here, undisturbed, for over a hundred years. She wasn't going to bury it so *it* could rest in peace, she was going to bury it for her own peace of mind.

As she stepped away from the narrow shelf, she felt the warm breath against her neck again.

Put it back.

Kelly whirled around, her gaze searching the cavern's dim interior for the source of the deep, masculine voice. But there was no one there.

Suddenly anxious to be gone from this place of death, she slipped the medallion into the pocket of her jeans. Folding her grandfather's map, she stuck it inside her shirt.

For now, she would leave the treasure as she had found it.

For now, she wanted only to go home.

Her boot heels made soft crunching sounds as she hurried toward the entrance of the cavern. The cave was long and narrow, with a high rounded ceiling and a sandy floor.

Extinguishing the lantern, Kelly left it on the ground inside the mouth of the cave. The opening was only a few feet high and barely wide enough for her to fit through. It had taken her over two hours of intense searching to find the cave at all and then it had been by sheer luck.

Kelly squinted against the sunlight as she crawled out of the cave. For some reason, she had expected it to be dark outside.

Her grandfather's old gelding Dusty whickered softly as she stood up. She patted the horse's neck, suddenly glad for the presence of another living creature, and then she swung effortlessly into the saddle and reined the horse toward the Triple M.

Riding away from the cave, Kelly slipped her hand into the pocket of her Levi's, her fingertips moving over the golden eagle.

From behind her, she heard a low rumble, like thunder echoing off the mountains, and then she felt it again, that chill that was colder than the north wind.

Seized with a sudden uncontrollable fear, she drummed her heels into the gelding's sides and raced for home.

Chapter Two

Kelly studied the golden eagle as she ate dinner later that night, intrigued by the intricate carving. It was the most beautiful thing she'd ever seen, tempting her touch again and again. She marveled at the rich feel of the gold beneath her fingertips, at the delicate lines that formed the bird's deep-set eyes and sharp beak. The wings were exquisite, the talons honed to fine sharp points.

Rising from the battered kitchen table, she quickly washed up her few dishes, took a long leisurely soak in a bubble bath, then settled into bed, pillows propped behind her back so she could read.

But she couldn't concentrate on the book. She kept thinking of the body in the cave. How long had it been there? A hundred years, at least, she thought, because the Triple M had been in her family at least that long. Why hadn't the body decayed? She stared at the eagle, propped against the table lamp beside her bed. Why had the body of the Indian felt warm to her touch?

Kelly shook her head. Surely that had been a product of her overactive imagination. But she had not imagined that long, lean body. He must have been quite an impressive man in his day, tall and broad-shouldered. She knew somehow that his eyes had been as black as sin, that his teeth had been straight and white and that when he smiled...

She laughed softly, uneasily. What was the matter with her, fantasizing about a man who'd probably been dead for over a hundred years? First thing tomorrow she would bury the body. It made her uncomfortable just knowing it was there.

She was about to switch off her bedside light when she saw a dark shadow at the window. All the air seemed to leave her body and her heart suddenly seemed too big for her chest as she watched the shadow pause, then move on.

For a moment, she was frozen with fear, then she bounded out of bed, ran into the living room and grabbed the shotgun from the rack over the fireplace, grateful that her grandfather had taught her how to shoot.

Heart pounding, she stood behind the front door, listening, waiting. For the first time, she realized just how alone she was. Her closest neighbor was five miles to the south. She couldn't pick up the phone and dial 911 for help.

Far in the distance, she heard the lonely wail of a coyote and then there was only silence, a silence as deep and dark as the grave.

She stood there for a quarter of an hour, her whole body tense. And then, gradually, the sounds of the night returned. She heard the frogs croaking in the pond behind the house, the song of a cricket, the soft sighing of the wind, and she knew somehow that whatever had been lurking in the shadows had gone.

It took a long time to fall asleep that night, but when sleep finally came, she dreamed of a tall, dark-skinned warrior with hair as black as midnight and eyes as deep and dark as fathomless pools of liquid ebony…

In the morning, her fears of the night before seemed foolish. She'd never been one to be spooked by shadows in the night. She'd lived alone in Los Angeles ever since her father had died five years ago. Lived alone and liked it, but when Grandpa McBride's health started failing, she had tried to convince him to come to L.A. and live with her. But her grandfather had refused to leave the Triple M. Like Kelly, he had cherished his independence. She knew he would have died alone if the hospital in Cedar Flats hadn't called to inform her he was there. She'd taken a two-week leave of absence from her job with Wolfe, Cullman and Chattier and flown to Montana to be with him.

Kelly felt a familiar tug at her heart as she thought of her grandfather. In days past, when she was a little girl, her family had spent their summers at the ranch and Grandpa had charmed her with tales of the Old West, repeating the colorful tales his great-grandfather Charlie McBride had once told him, tales of Indian fights and buffalo hunts and mountain men.

Her grandfather had been on his death bed when he told her about the gold his great-grandfather Charlie had buried in a cave in the mountain behind the Triple M.

"Gold?" Kelly had said with a grin. "If there was any gold up there, don't you think someone would have found it by now?"

"It's there, girl. My great-grandpappy told me so."

"Why didn't he spend it?"

"He was afraid of it, afraid of the ghost who haunts the mountain."

"Ghost!" Kelly had exclaimed.

"I've seen him, Kelly girl," her grandfather had said, his gnarled hand squeezing hers with surprising strength.

"Really?" Kelly had asked, leaning forward. "When? Where?"

"When I was younger and braver. I followed my great-grandpappy's map and found the cave. The gold's in there, girl, a fortune, just like he said."

"And you never touched it?"

"Oh, I took a little dust now and then, when I needed it. But something told me not to try to take more than I needed. Now it's yours, Kelly. Use it wisely."

Those were the last words her Grandpa Frank had said in this world. He was asleep when she went to visit him the next morning. He'd opened his eyes, smiled at her and then, with a sigh, he was gone.

And now the ranch, and the gold, belonged to her.

After a quick breakfast, Kelly went out to the barn and saddled Dusty. She had a grave to dig and it was a long ride to the cave.

Kelly approached the cavern with a growing sense of unease. Chiding herself for her foolishness, she slipped on a pair of heavy work gloves, removed the shovel she'd tied behind the saddle and ducked into the cave.

She paused near the entrance to light the lantern she'd left the day before, felt her heart begin to pound as shadows came to life on the walls. The cavern was roomy inside, high enough for her to stand erect once she was inside.

Nothing to be afraid of, she told herself. The dead can't hurt you.

Her booted feet made hardly a sound on the soft, sandy earth as she went deeper into the cave. She wouldn't have to dig a very deep hole, she decided, just deep enough to cover the body.

Her heart was pounding like a runaway train as she drew near the ledge and then her breath caught in her throat.

The ledge was empty.

The body was gone.

Not believing her eyes, Kelly ran her hands over the surface of the earthen shelf, searching for some sign that a body had actually been there, that she wasn't losing her mind. Nothing.

And then she saw it, the colorful Hudson's Bay blanket, crumpled in a heap beneath the ledge.

For a moment, she felt relief. She hadn't imagined it after all. The body had been there and now it was gone.

Bewildered, she stared at the blanket. Gone, she thought. Gone where?

Lantern in hand, she searched the floor of the cave for some sign that an animal had dragged the remains away, but there was no sign of animal tracks, no footprints other than her own.

She laughed at that. Of course there were no footprints. Ghosts didn't leave footprints.

With a cry, she turned on her heel and ran toward the entrance of the cave, scrambling out of the narrow opening as if Satan himself were snapping at her heels.

She dreamed of the Indian again that night. She was walking in the moonlight when suddenly he was there beside her, his black eyes glowing like dark fires. He gazed at her for a long moment, the awareness growing between them, and then, quite unexpectedly, he brushed his knuckles against her cheek. The touch exploded through her like lightning and while she was trying to recover, she heard a voice echo in her mind. A voice that was husky with warning. His voice. *Put it back.* And then he was gone.

She woke to find the sheets tangled around her legs, her brow damp with perspiration. Unconsciously, she reached for the golden eagle she'd placed beneath her pillow and as her hand closed around its smoothness, she heard the warning again. Only this time it wasn't a dream and she didn't hear the words echoing in her mind.

She heard the words, spoken clearly, from the shadowed corner of her room.

"Put it back."

On the verge of terror, Kelly scrambled across the bed and switched on the light, her eyes wide as they searched the room.

There was no one there.

Chapter Three

ജ

Harry Renford stared at the young woman seated before him with obvious disbelief.

"Pay off the loan?" he said, repeating her words as if he hadn't heard her quite right. "You want to pay off the loan?"

Harry sat back in his chair, his hands folded on the desktop as he studied her face. Kelly McBride was a pretty girl, with long, curly brown hair and large blue eyes. He'd known her grandparents, Frank and Annee, for years. Annee had died almost ten years ago, but Frank had stayed on at the ranch, alone. He'd gotten pretty feeble in his old age, but he'd refused to leave the Triple M, and the ranch, some thirty miles southeast of town, had fallen into a state of disrepair.

Old man McBride had died three weeks ago, leaving behind a mountain of hospital bills and a sizable mortgage. It had been in Harry's mind to buy the Triple M when it went on the market and discover for himself if the rumors of a hidden gold mine were true. It had seemed a safe investment. If there was no gold, and he doubted there was, Harry planned to turn the Triple M into a guest ranch. But then Frank's granddaughter had shown up to claim the old place. He'd made her what he considered a generous offer for the ranch, an offer she had politely, but firmly, refused, thereby upsetting his carefully thought-out scheme.

Harry shifted in his chair. He wasn't a man who liked to see his plans upset, especially by a young city girl who probably didn't know the difference between a dandy brush and a hoof pick.

"Well, that's fine, Miss McBride," he drawled. "Just fine. But where, if you don't mind my asking, did you get the money?"

"I don't believe the source of my funds is a requisite for paying off the loan, Mr. Renford."

"No, no, of course not. Well, it will take me a day or two to get the necessary papers drawn up. Why don't you come back on, say, Friday afternoon?"

"Fine. Until then, Mr. Renford."

Outside, Kelly drew a deep breath and let it out in a long sigh of relief. She was glad to be out of Harry Renford's sight. She didn't like the man, though she didn't know why. It wasn't his looks, she mused. He was quite a handsome man, with a shock of wavy blond hair that was just turning gray at the temples, a charming smile, when he cared to use it, and light gray eyes. It was his eyes, she decided now, they were cold and unblinking, like the eyes of a snake.

Well, as soon as she paid off the mortgage on the ranch, she wouldn't have to deal with him again. Tomorrow she would drive into Coleville and see about selling some of the smaller nuggets. She didn't dare do it here. Cedar Flats was a small town where everybody knew everybody else's business. She didn't want to have to answer any questions about where the gold came from.

Frowning, she started down the sidewalk to where she'd left her car. In a few days, she'd have to decide what to do about the ranch. When she'd first arrived, it had been in her mind to sell it, but once she'd seen the place again, remembered the good times she'd had there, she'd known she couldn't sell the old place. It had, after all, been in her family for over a century. Still, it was horribly run down. The house and the barn were in need of repair, the house needed painting inside and out, the corral fences needed new rails, there was no stock to speak of except for Dusty and a couple of aging chickens.

Nevertheless, she was here and she was here to stay, even though it meant relocating, quitting her secretarial job with Wolfe, Cullman and Chattier, finding other employment…

Kelly laughed softly. She didn't need to work anymore. Having access to those nuggets was like having a trust fund. She was set for life.

She was unlocking the door of her car when a man appeared beside her.

"Miss McBride?"

Kelly hesitated a moment before answering. "Yes?"

"I'd like to talk to you."

He was Indian, she thought, noting his dark skin and high cheekbones, though there was nothing particularly sinister about that. There were lots of Indians in Cedar Flats. Most of them lived out on the reservation.

"Talk?" Kelly said. "About what?"

"The Triple M."

Kelly glanced around, reassured by the presence of other people nearby. "What about it?"

"I'd like to buy it."

Kelly glanced at his faded green shirt, the sleeves of which were rolled up to his elbows, exposing bronze forearms thick with muscle. Frayed blue jeans hugged his legs and his feet were encased in a pair of run-down black boots. She doubted if he could afford to buy a cup of coffee.

"I'm sorry," she said politely, "the ranch isn't for sale."

She opened the door and slid behind the wheel, but before she could close the door, the man took a step forward, placing himself between her and the car door.

"Could we go somewhere and discuss it?" he asked.

Kelly shook her head, thinking that his voice was as deep and rich as dark chocolate fudge.

"Please."

The word seemed torn from his throat and she had the sudden unshakable feeling that this was a man who hadn't done much apologizing in his life.

She looked at him then, really looked at him for the first time, and felt a shiver of apprehension skitter down her spine. He looked remarkably as she had imagined the corpse she'd found in the cave would have looked when he was alive.

Kelly's heart began to pound as she noted the similarities. Like the body in the cave, this man was tall and dark. His thick black hair fell past his shoulders. His legs were long, his shoulders were unbelievably broad beneath the almost threadbare shirt. He seemed made of solid muscle. His eyes were as black as obsidian, just as she'd imagined those of the dead man would have been. His nose was straight as a knife edge and his mouth... Oh my, she had never seen such a sensual mouth on a man in her whole life.

He stared down at her, one black brow arching slightly, as if he knew exactly what she was thinking.

"Are you sure we can't discuss it?" he asked in a voice as seductive as candlelight and champagne. "Maybe grab a cup of coffee in the motel coffee shop?"

"I'm sure," she said, wondering if he was truly suggesting what she was thinking. "Now, if you'll excuse me..."

Kelly stared pointedly at his muscular forearm, which was resting along the top edge of the car door.

His dark eyes flashed with anger as he stepped away from the car.

In an instant, Kelly shut the door and locked it. Shoving the key into the ignition, she gave it a twist, put the gearshift in drive and pulled away from the curb.

But she couldn't resist a look in her rearview mirror. For some reason, she had expected him to have vanished from sight, but he stood in the middle of the narrow two-lane street, staring after her.

Kelly let out a long ragged breath as she turned the corner at the end of the block. Whoever the man was, he intrigued and frightened her as no one ever had.

Lee Roan Horse felt his brows draw together in a frown as he watched the light blue Camaro careen around the corner and disappear from sight.

His first meeting with Miss Kelly McBride hadn't gone quite as planned, he thought wryly. For a moment there, she had looked at him the way most white women did, with a mixture of interest and curiosity, and then, for no reason that he could fathom, she had stared at him as if she were seeing a ghost.

So, he mused, what now?

Hands shoved in the back pockets of his jeans, he crossed the street to where his battered Ford truck was parked and climbed inside, only to sit staring out the windshield, his finger tapping on the steering wheel. She had something he wanted and he had two choices—ask for it, or take it.

He'd tried asking…

* * * * *

Kelly sat up, jerked from a sound sleep by a sudden coldness. She glanced quickly around the room, shivering as a gust of wind blew in through the window across from the bed.

Her mouth went suddenly dry as she stared at the window. She had closed it before she went to bed.

Her heart began to beat triple time as she saw a faint shadow move in the hallway. Instinctively, she reached for the Colt .38 in the drawer of her nightstand. Her hands were shaking as she gripped the gun in both hands. The weapon, small and compact, infused her with a sense of security, though she doubted she had the nerve to actually squeeze the trigger.

A board creaked in the hallway and then she saw a man outlined in the doorway of her room.

Her heart climbed into her throat as she drew back the hammer on the Colt. The noise seemed very loud in the stillness of the room.

"Don't shoot."

Kelly blinked into the darkness. She'd know that voice anywhere.

Transferring the .38 into her right hand, she reached over and switched on the bedside light with her left.

"What are you doing here?"

The Indian shrugged. "I don't guess you'd believe I came to talk?"

Kelly slid a glance at the clock on the nightstand. "At three a.m.?"

"I couldn't sleep."

"So you decided to crawl in my bedroom window and have a look around?"

He frowned. "I came in the front door. You really should lock it, you know."

"The front door?" Kelly glanced at the curtains fluttering in the faint breeze. "Then how did the window...?"

"What?"

"Nothing. You didn't answer my question. What are you doing here?"

"I want to buy the Triple M."

"I told you this afternoon, it isn't for sale."

"This is Lakota land. My land."

"Excuse me, but I believe this is *my* land. I have the deed to prove it." Or she would have, come Friday afternoon.

"I don't care if you have a trunk full of deeds. This is Lakota land, stolen from my people over a hundred years ago."

Kelly grimaced. "And you expect me to give it back to you, just like that?"

"I said I'd buy it."

Kelly let out a sigh of exasperation, wondering how such a remarkably attractive man could be so obtuse. He'd changed clothes, she noticed, and thought he looked even more handsome and more dangerous, dressed all in black.

"And I said it's not for sale. Case closed. Now, get out of here before I call the police and have you arrested for…for…"

"Breaking and entering," he supplied, his voice suddenly as hard as the look in his dark eyes.

"Whatever. Goodbye."

He didn't move, only continued to stare at her from out of eyes as black as the night. The gun wavered in Kelly's hand and for a moment she had the impression that the Indian in the cave was standing in front of her.

Put it back.

Kelly blinked several times. "Did you say something?"

He frowned. "No, why?"

"I thought…I mean… Never mind." She shivered as she felt it again, the same cold chill she'd felt in the cave.

"Are you all right?" the Indian asked. "You look like you're about to faint."

"I'm fine," Kelly said. "I've never…"

The words died on her lips as she stared past the Indian to the wall behind him. She watched in stunned disbelief as his shadow took on the shape of an eagle, its wings spread in flight…

"You've never what?" he asked, frowning.

"Never…fainted," Kelly replied, and then everything went dark.

When she came to, she was lying in her bed. The covers had been pulled up to her chin and there was a cold washcloth over her brow. The Indian—she'd have to ask his name, she thought groggily—was standing beside the bed staring down at her, a frown on his handsome face. He'd taken her gun and shoved it into the waistband of his jeans.

"You okay?" he asked.

Kelly nodded, her gaze fixed on the gun.

He shook his head ruefully. "Would you feel safer if I gave it back to you?"

"Probably, but my hands are shaking so badly I don't think I could hold it. What happened?"

He shrugged. "Beats the hell out of me. One minute we were talking and the next you turned white as the sheet and keeled over."

Kelly's gaze slid past him to the far wall. "It's gone."

"What's gone?" he asked, glancing over his shoulder.

"Nothing."

He grunted. "I put the coffee on. You want some?"

"Yes, please."

Lee Roan Horse shook his head again. She was some piece of work, he thought. First she pulled a gun on him, then she fainted dead away for no apparent reason and now she was as polite as you please.

He left the bedroom, returning a short time later with two mismatched mugs of coffee.

Kelly sat up when he entered the room, her gaze fluttering over the gun still nestled in the waistband of his pants.

"You look like the cream and sugar type," he muttered, handing her one of the cups.

Kelly took the mug, her fingertips brushing against his as she did so. The contact, brief as it was, made her suddenly, acutely aware that she was in the house alone with a man. A very virile, very attractive man who had a gun.

"You're not gonna faint on me again, are you?" he asked.

"No." Quickly, she took a sip of her coffee. Heavy on the milk and light on the sugar, it was exactly the way she liked it.

Lee sat down in the chair beside the bed and looked around. The bedroom was small, containing only a double bed, a mahogany nightstand, a matching chest of drawers and the overstuffed chair he occupied. The walls were blue, bare except for an old gilt-edged oval mirror and a painting of a desert sunset. A colorful rag rug brightened the wood floor.

Stretching his legs out in front of him, Lee regarded Kelly McBride over the rim of his cup. She was a pretty woman, he thought. Not blatantly beautiful, like Melinda, but pretty nonetheless. She had long curly brown hair. Her cheeks were sunburned and there was a light sprinkling of freckles across the bridge of her nose. Her brows were slightly arched above soft blue eyes. Her mouth was wide and generous and he wondered how it would look curved in a smile, how it would taste...

Kelly felt her cheeks grow hot under his intense scrutiny. "Why did you come here?" she asked, disliking the silence between them almost as much as she disliked the way he was looking at her.

"It's my birthright. My ancestors were born on this land. They fought here. They died here."

It was the truth, Lee mused, or at least as much of it as he was willing to tell her.

Kelly stared at him. She didn't believe one word he said. And then she frowned. Did he know about the gold? But that was impossible. No one knew.

Except her. And the ghost.

Lee straightened in the chair and leaned forward. "Why won't you sell? You don't belong here."

"Oh?"

"You're a city girl, Kelly McBride." McBride, he thought. Why did that name sound so familiar? "A city girl," he repeated, frowning. "Anyone can see that."

"Well, I'm a country girl now." Kelly lifted her chin defiantly, trying not to think how right her name sounded on his lips. "Besides, I like it here."

Lee stared into his empty coffee cup. "I have a feeling you aren't going to change your mind," he muttered ruefully.

"Finally we agree on something."

"Yeah." Setting his mug on the bedside table, he stood up. "Well, good night, Miss McBride."

"Good night, Mr.— You never did tell me your name."

"It's Lee," he said as he placed the Colt on the top of the dresser. "Lee Roan Horse."

"Lee Roan Horse." She repeated the name, surprised to find that it conjured images of conical tipis and warriors bedecked with feathers and paint riding across a vast sun-kissed prairie.

Lee turned toward the door, paused, ran a hand through his hair, then turned back to face her again.

"I don't suppose you need any help around here?"

Kelly's brows shot up. "Doing what?"

He shrugged. "Whatever needs doing."

"I'm afraid not."

"I couldn't help noticing the house needs a new roof. And a coat of paint. The barn, too. The corrals could all use some new rails."

Kelly nodded. Everything he said was true, but she couldn't shake the feeling that he didn't really want a job as much as he wanted an excuse to prowl around the ranch. Again, she had the feeling that he knew about the gold.

"The place does need a lot of work," she allowed, "but I'm afraid I can't afford to hire anyone just now."

"That roof on the barn won't hold up much longer."

He couldn't have seen the condition of the roof at night, Kelly thought suspiciously, so how did he know how bad it was, unless he'd been here before, during the day?

"I'd be willing to work cheap. Room and board and whatever you feel you can afford."

It would be a mistake. A big mistake. She didn't trust him, not one bit. But that wasn't what frightened her. It was the attraction she felt for him, the way her heart skipped a beat at the thought of seeing him every day. He was far too attractive for any woman under ninety to ignore and she was afraid he knew it, afraid he knew that just looking at him made her feel good inside.

"No." She shook her head. "No, I can't..."

He took a step toward her, his eyes blazing with ebony fire, his mouth curved in a dazzling smile.

"Sure you can," he drawled softly.

She said yes before she realized she'd spoken the word aloud, afraid if she refused him, the fire that burned in the depths of his eyes would reduce her to ashes.

He had the good grace not to gloat. "You won't be sorry," he promised.

She was already sorry, but he was gone before she could say so.

It was near dawn when Kelly fell into a troubled sleep. She dreamed of her grandfather and in her dreams he was a young man again, strong and vigorous. But then, gradually, his features began to change, his light brown hair darkening to the color of ebony, his freckled face turning to a copper hue, until the man in her dream was no longer her Grandfather Frank, but the Indian who had accosted her in the street.

It's our land, Lee Roan Horse said, his voice ringing out with the strength of his conviction. *Our land!*

And suddenly it wasn't just a single voice clamoring at her, but the combined voices of every Lakota man, woman and child who had ever lived.

Kelly pressed her hands over her ears, but she couldn't shut out the sound of their cries.

Helpless, she stared at the Indian, felt her heart constrict with fear as she saw not one man, but two—one of flesh and blood and one of spirit—two separate beings who stood face-to-face and then blended together until they became one and faded from her sight, leaving her standing alone in the darkness with only the pounding of a distant drum and the faint echoes of ancient voices.

Chapter Four

ꕤ

She woke with the sound of drumming still in her ears.

With a grimace, she buried her head under her pillow, hoping to shut out the noise and go back to sleep, and then she sat up.

Drumming? Cocking her head to the side, Kelly listened a moment and realized it wasn't the sound of a drum at all, but the sound of a hammer.

Muttering under her breath, she slid out of bed, pulled on a short terry cloth robe and peered out the window.

What she saw took her breath away.

Lee Roan Horse was nailing a new fence post into place. It appeared he'd been hard at work long before she became aware of it. His shirt hung over the top rail of the corral, but it was the broad expanse of his back that drew her gaze.

She'd never seen such a magnificent sight in all her life and she couldn't help staring, her feminine eye pleased with the symmetry of broad shoulders that tapered to a firm, narrow waist. His muscles rippled beneath smooth copper-hued skin, skin sheened with a fine layer of perspiration. His hair was long and black and beautiful, surely the envy of every woman who'd ever seen it.

Her gaze drifted down, appreciating the way his faded jeans hugged his long, muscular legs.

She drew back from the window when, unexpectedly, he glanced over his shoulder. Had he seen her watching him? The thought brought a rush of heat to her cheeks. She wasn't in the habit of gawking at handsome men. She'd seen plenty of good-looking guys in Los Angeles. The place was crawling with gorgeous hunks who hoped to be actors or models. She'd even dated a few, but there had been something disconcerting about going out to spend an evening with a man who was prettier than she was.

But Lee Roan Horse...he wasn't pretty. He wasn't even handsome, at least not in the traditional sense of the word. But he had a rugged masculine appeal that she found attractive on some primal, earthy level she didn't care to examine too closely.

Kelly shook his image from her mind and headed for the bathroom. A nice cool shower was just what she needed.

Forty minutes later, she opened the back door and called Lee Roan Horse to breakfast. He entered the kitchen whistling and tucking his shirt into his jeans. He nodded in her direction, then went to the sink to wash his hands. Big hands, Kelly thought. Capable hands that were scarred and callused. She wondered if they could be gentle.

Lee dried his hands on a dish towel, then stood beside the sink, his gaze moving around the kitchen. It was a large, square room. The walls were a pale yellow. Matching curtains fluttered at the open window. A badly scarred walnut table stood in the center of the room.

"Sit down," Kelly said. "Anyplace you like. I'm not used to having company at breakfast."

"Oh?" His look was curious.

"I live alone, remember?"

She filled a plate with hot cakes, eggs and bacon and set it on the table in front of him, along with a cup of coffee, a tall glass of orange juice and a plate of buttered toast.

"Eat it while it's hot," she said, and turned back to the stove to flip the hot cakes on the griddle.

Lee sat down, his nostrils filling with the aroma of bacon and coffee. He couldn't remember the last time a woman had cooked for him, or the last time he'd sat down to a breakfast that consisted of much more than black coffee. But all that would change when he had the gold.

Kelly joined him at the table a few moments later, surprised to find his plate nearly empty. She wasn't used to cooking for a man, but she'd felt certain that six hot cakes, three eggs, four slices of bacon and toast would be enough. Apparently she'd been wrong. If he ate like this at every meal, she'd have to make a trip into town a lot sooner than she planned.

"Would you like some more?" she asked, a smile in her voice. She'd never considered herself much of a cook, but he obviously appreciated her culinary skills. Either that, or it had been a long time between meals.

He shook his head, not meeting her eyes. "No, thanks."

"Are you sure?" As soon as the words were out of her mouth, she knew she'd made a mistake. A muscle worked in his jaw and she had the very real impression that she'd somehow insulted him.

"It's just that…I mean, you must have worked up quite an appetite. I just thought…" Kelly shrugged. "It's just that I made too much and I hate to see it go to waste."

Lee stared at her from across the table, remembering the pitying looks he'd gotten from white women when he was a kid begging in the streets for food, food to feed his invalid grandmother, his little sister, his alcoholic mother.

Kelly frowned. Roan Horse was still hungry. She knew it as surely as she knew the color of her own hair. So she took a deep breath and said, "It's a long time 'til lunch, you know."

"I'm fine, thank you," he said, stiffly polite, and then he stood up and left the room, the rest of his food untouched.

Kelly stared after him, wondering why he was so touchy, wondering what she'd said to offend him.

Outside, Lee ripped the broken rails from the fence, attacking the corral as if it were every man or woman who had ever humiliated him. He'd hated begging for food, for money to buy medicine for his grandmother. He'd hated begging so badly he had turned to stealing instead.

In the old days, stealing from the enemy had been considered a great coup and that was how he had looked at it. He'd been full of hate in his younger days, hate for the whites, hate for the poverty he lived in, for the ugly little house he shared with his family, hate for the father he barely remembered who had run off and left them all behind.

He was breathing hard by the time he'd removed the rails that needed to be replaced. He'd thought it was all behind him, the hatred, the anger, the bitterness he'd grown up with. He'd thought he'd buried it when he buried his mother.

Bracing one hand on a post, he rested his forehead on his arm and closed his eyes. They were all gone now. His grandmother had died peacefully in her sleep. His little sister had died of pneumonia when she was only eight years old. And his mother had finally drunk herself to death.

He swore softly. All his life, he'd wanted a vision. He'd gone alone to the mountains to fast and to pray; he'd offered tobacco to the four winds, to the earth and the sky, but always a vision had been denied him. And then, when he had given up all hope, his vision had come.

Even now, it was clear in his mind. He'd been standing at his mother's grave, dry-eyed and alone, wondering what to do with his life, when the day had turned dark and cold. A heavy gray mist had fallen over the land and then a man had materialized out of the mist. A tall man with long black hair and dark copper-colored skin. A warrior who wore a golden eagle on a thong around his neck.

You are not alone, the warrior had said. *Only believe and all you desire will be yours.*

Who are you? Lee had asked. But the warrior hadn't answered and Lee had wondered if perhaps he had been seeing himself at some future time, but that didn't make sense. How could he foretell his own future?

The warrior had gone on to tell Lee of a cache of Lakota gold hidden in a cave in the mountains to the north.

Find the woman and you will find the treasure, the warrior had said, and then, like shadows running before a storm, he had disappeared.

Well, he had found the woman, Lee mused. His talk of buying the ranch had been just that, talk. He didn't have enough money to fill his gas tank, let alone buy the Triple M, but he'd done what he set out to do. Now all he had to do was find the gold.

A wry grin curved his lips as he recalled a sign he'd seen in an old grocery store in Virginia City.

THE GOLDEN RULE:
HE WHO HAS THE GOLD
MAKES THE RULES

Well, he intended to have the gold, one way or another, he thought grimly. He hadn't spent a year in that damned jail for nothing.

"Lemonade?"

Lee's head jerked up at the sound of her voice. "What?"

He turned around to face her and she offered him a chilled glass of lemonade.

"I thought you might be thirsty," Kelly said with a shrug.

"Yeah, thanks," he replied, and taking the glass, he drained it in two long swallows.

"I guess I should have brought the whole pitcher," Kelly remarked, and then bit down on her lip, afraid she'd offended him again.

But he only grinned at her as he dragged the back of his hand across his mouth.

"You don't have to finish everything today," she said, indicating the corral.

Lee shrugged. "I like to keep busy."

"Oh. Well, I'd better let you get back to work then. I'll call you when lunch is ready."

He nodded, his conscience stabbing at him as he watched her walk away. He hadn't come here to work. He'd come here to steal. He tried to tell himself it wasn't stealing, not really, it was only taking back what was rightfully his. But he hadn't expected to like Kelly McBride. She seemed so open, so honest, not like Melinda...

Muttering an oath, he picked up his shirt and wiped the perspiration from his face and neck.

He'd fix the corral and patch up the roof, even paint the damn house. It was the least he could do for her, he thought, before he went looking for the gold.

Chapter Five

ೞ

Harry Renford leaned forward in his chair, both hands flat on the desktop.

"I cannot believe you actually hired that man," he said, shaking his head.

Kelly frowned, baffled by the banker's obvious annoyance. "He needed a job. I needed some work done." She shrugged. "I don't understand why you're making such a fuss about it. A lot of the ranchers around here hire Indians."

"Don't you know who he is?"

"He said his name was Lee Roan Horse."

"Didn't your grandfather ever mention him?"

"Not that I recall. Why?"

"Your grandfather caught Roan Horse trespassing. He warned him not to come back, but the Indian didn't listen. The next time your grandfather caught him sneaking around, he called the police and had Roan Horse arrested for breaking and entering."

"When was that?" Kelly stared at Renford, not wanting to believe him. And yet, hadn't she known, deep down, that Lee was hiding something? It was the gold, she thought. Lee knew about the gold. That was why he wanted to buy the ranch, why he had been so insistent that she hire him.

"It was quite a while ago, probably four or five years. Roan Horse did a year in the county jail. When he was released, he left town. He's only been back a few months, but he's already been in trouble. Bar fights and the like."

Harry picked up a thin gold pen and rolled it back and forth on the desktop. "Don't trust him, Miss McBride. Lee

Roan Horse is bad clear through. Mean, too. I heard he broke Ronny Brogden's nose in a brawl just last week."

Kelly had a sudden mental image of Lee Roan Horse with his back against a wall, his hands curled into tight fists, his muscles taut as he took a swing at the aforementioned Ronny Brogden. She'd met Ronny years ago on one of her summer visits to Cedar Flats. He'd been a bully and a braggart and she thought it likely that he'd probably only gotten what he deserved, but of course she couldn't tell the banker that

"Please don't trouble yourself about it, Mr. Renford," Kelly said, forcing a smile. "Everything's under control. Now, is the deed ready?"

"Yes, the deed," Renford muttered, not meeting her eyes. "I'm afraid it's missing."

"Missing? How is that possible?"

Renford spread his hands in a gesture of appeal. "I'm not sure. All I know is that it's not in the vault. I'm sure it's simply been misplaced."

"I see."

"I'll call you just as soon as it turns up." Renford smiled. "Signing the deed is just a technicality. Even though your grandfather didn't leave a valid will, there's no question of who the ranch belongs to. Your grandfather had no other kin."

"I understand," Kelly replied. But she didn't, not really, nor could she shake the feeling that there was something Renford wasn't saying, something he wasn't telling her.

"I'll call you," Harry said. Rising, he extended his hand.

It was a curt dismissal.

Kelly was fuming when she reached home. It seemed as if everyone she met was conspiring against her. First she'd had to go into Coleville to exchange a few gold nuggets for cash. A trip that should have taken less than an hour took two because a truck had jackknifed on the road, bringing all traffic to a halt.

From Coleville, she'd driven back to town to settle her grandfather's hospital bill. No easy task. Her grandfather had spent three days in the hospital before he died. They had tried to charge her for six days and then seemed annoyed because she had refused to pay them for the extra three days.

Renford hadn't been able to find the deed and she was having second thoughts about the wisdom of paying off the loan and having nothing other than a receipt to show for it. And now it seemed that Lee Roan Horse had hired on under false pretenses.

Kelly blew out a long sigh. Maybe she should just take the gold out of the cave and sell the ranch to Lee Roan Horse. It would serve him right. And yet, even as she thought about taking the gold, more gold than she would ever need, she felt suddenly cold, as if the chill wind from the cave had blown into the car.

Switching off the ignition, she sat behind the wheel. From where she sat, she could see Lee sawing a new rail for one of the corrals. Of course he wanted to fix up the place, she thought bitterly. He intended to own it.

She let her eyes travel over his broad back. Didn't the man ever wear a shirt? Angry as she was, she couldn't seem to stop watching him. He moved with effortless grace, the muscles in his arms and back bunching and relaxing as he worked.

He'd been in jail for breaking and entering. She grunted softly, remembering the night he'd broken into the house. No wonder he knew what he'd be charged with when she had threatened to call the police. He'd already done time for breaking and entering. She supposed a year in jail could be considered a small price to pay in exchange for a fortune in gold.

Take only what you need. If you take one nugget more, my spirit will haunt you for as long as you live.

That had been the warning given to Charlie McBride when he first found the gold a hundred years ago. Thinking of it now sent a shiver down Kelly's spine. In the bright light of day, it was hard to believe in ghosts and curses, yet she knew she lacked the courage to enter the cave and remove all the gold.

So, what was she to do? Take as much as she needed and run back to L.A.?

She let her gaze sweep over the ranch. In the short time she'd been here, she'd come to love the place—the timeless beauty of the mountains, the quiet nights and peaceful days. She'd thought she'd miss the excitement of the city, but, to her surprise, she'd discovered that she preferred the soft pastoral sounds of tree frogs and crickets to the grinding of brakes and the shrill scream of sirens. She preferred blue skies and green trees to smog and tall, glass-fronted buildings. And she definitely preferred riding Dusty to braving the Los Angeles freeways!

She did miss shopping malls and TV, though, she thought, frowning, and then she smiled. She had money. She could buy one of those big-screen TVs she'd always wanted and a satellite dish to go with it.

With a start, she realized that Lee was standing at the car door.

"You all right in there?" he asked, bending down so he could see her better.

"Fine." She pulled the key from the ignition, grabbed her handbag and opened the car door.

"You look tired," he remarked.

"Yes."

Lee frowned. "Something wrong?"

"No."

With a shrug, he turned away and went back to the corral. If she wanted to tell him what was bothering her, she would. If not...he shrugged. It was none of his business. He'd vowed never to get tangled up with a white woman again, no matter how pretty she was and it was a vow he meant to keep.

Picking up the new rail, he laid it in place, then reached for the hammer, cursing his weakness for smooth pale skin and soft blue eyes.

Melinda Kershaw's image danced across the misty corridors of his mind. Melinda, with her irresistible smile and honeyed words. Melinda, who had teased and tormented the hired help one summer. Lee's knuckles turned white around the hammer. That was a summer he'd never forget.

He'd been seventeen the year he'd gone to work for Melinda's father. Rich and spoiled, secure in her beauty, she had trailed after Lee while he cut the grass and trimmed the trees, flirting shamelessly, fascinated by the fact that he was an Indian and therefore forbidden to her. She had paraded around her family's swimming pool in a hot pink bikini that left almost nothing to the imagination. On more than one occasion, she had begged him to rub suntan lotion on her back and shoulders.

Nights, she had met him on the sly, vowing that she loved him, that it didn't matter that he was an Indian and dirt poor. She had kissed him and caressed him until he was on fire for her and then, when her father had caught her in his arms, she had cried rape. And because Lee was just a dirty redskin, not fit to be in the same room as Frank Kershaw's virginal sixteen-year-old daughter, Melinda's father had believed her every word.

Melinda had spent the rest of the summer in the Bahamas, recovering from her dreadful ordeal.

Lee had spent eighteen months in a correctional institution.

He drove the last nail into place, then hurled the hammer across the corral. Chest heaving, he stared at his hands, remembering the nights he'd spent wishing he could wrap them around Melinda's pretty little neck.

But that was all behind him now. He'd find his ancestor's gold, get the hell out of Cedar Flats and start a new life where nobody would know, or care, who he was.

And he'd never look at another white woman as long as he lived.

Chapter Six

ꟗ

He bent over the hand-drawn map spread on his desk. She wouldn't keep a fortune in gold in the house, he mused, that much was certain. Probably not in the barn, either. She might have buried it somewhere, say in the middle of one of the corrals or in the chicken coop. She might have hidden it in the well, but he didn't think so.

He frowned thoughtfully as his finger made an ever-widening circle around the drawing of the house. Under a rock, perhaps, or in a cave…

His gaze moved to the mountain that rose behind the house. A cave. What better place to hide a king's ransom?

He grunted softly as he lifted his head and stared out the window into the darkness. Roan Horse, a man who had avoided white women like the plague, had gone to work for Kelly McBride. Why?

A slow smile spread over his features. It was all so simple.

Roan Horse knew about the gold.

All he had to do was sit back and wait for the Indian to find it.

Whistling softly, he dialed the phone. "Trask? I need you."

Chapter Seven

ഇ

She woke, knowing immediately that she wasn't alone. Her first thought was that it was Lee. But then she felt that familiar warmth, followed by a breath of cool air that sent a shiver down her spine.

"Who's there?" She sat up, the blanket clutched to her breast. "Lee?" Oh please, she thought, let it be Lee.

Kelly swallowed hard as a corner of the room brightened, felt herself go cold all over when the light coalesced into the form of a man…a tall, dark-skinned man with long black hair. A man who was not a man at all.

"You!" She shook her head, refusing to believe what she was seeing. "No, it can't be."

The Indian stared at her through fathomless black eyes. "You're him, aren't you?" Kelly asked. "The Indian from the cave?"

He nodded and then took a step forward.

Kelly's eyes widened as the Indian closed the distance between them. He looked even more impressive now than he had in the cave. There was no illumination in the room, yet he seemed to be surrounded by an aura of soft blue light. His skin was the color of dark copper, smooth and unblemished save for two faint scars on his chest. There were three white-tipped eagle feathers tied in his hair. A distant part of her mind wondered why he had removed his shirt and why she hadn't noticed the feathers before. His brows were thick and black and straight. Standing so near, he seemed taller, broader. Alive…

He's a ghost. Just a ghost. He can't hurt you.

She repeated the words in her mind as the specter reached the foot of the bed. Arms crossed over his chest, the phantom stared down at her.

Go away from here. He didn't speak, but she heard the words in her mind, as deep and dark as the night.

Kelly shook her head. "No. This is my home."

The Indian continued to stare at her, his expression blank. *This is my home.*

"Who are you?" Kelly demanded, though her voice quivered with trepidation.

The Indian smiled at her, silently applauding her courage. White people were always frightened by his appearance, probably because they had no ties to the world of spirits. They were a peculiar people. They had no bond with Mother Earth, or with their four-footed brothers. They sought no vision to guide them through life. Not that he had known that many white people, he thought, amused. In the last hundred years, only a handful of *washicu* had found their way into the cave.

All had come to steal the gold.

All had left empty-handed.

All except this girl.

"I am Blue Crow of the Lakota."

Kelly blinked at him several times. "So you can talk," she muttered under her breath. "What do you want?"

"I want you to leave here. Like all *washicu,* you take what is not yours."

"This is my house," Kelly retorted indignantly. "It belonged to my grandfather and his father before him and now it belongs to me."

The Indian made a sound of derision low in his throat. "You have taken gold that is not yours."

The eagle, Kelly thought.

"Give it to me."

She hesitated a moment and then reached under her pillow, withdrawing the golden eagle. She couldn't keep her hand from shaking as she offered it to the Indian. His fingertips brushed hers as he took it from her hand. She felt the heat of his touch, the shock of it, sizzle through her like lightning.

Stunned, she stared up at him. Ghosts weren't supposed to have substance. She watched, unblinking, as he opened the small buckskin bag that hung around his neck and slid the eagle inside.

"How…? Why…?" Kelly shook her head. He wasn't real. He couldn't be real.

"You want to know why my body was in the cave."

"Yes."

"I was killed by a *washicu* who wanted the gold. His companion buried me in the cave and I have slept there ever since."

"But how…? Why? I mean, you're not alive and yet…" Her words trailed off as he came around the bed to stand beside her.

"My spirit awakens whenever a *washicu* enters the cave."

"You've been there all this time to guard the gold?"

Blue Crow nodded.

"But why?"

"He mitawa," he said. "It is mine."

"But you don't need it!" Kelly exclaimed.

"Do you?"

Kelly opened her mouth, intending to say yes, of course she needed it. Who wouldn't need a fortune in gold? But the words died in her throat.

"You have taken enough for your needs," Blue Crow said. "You have paid your grandfather's debts, you have enough to live on, you have this house for shelter."

"But it's no good to you. You're..." She couldn't bring herself to say the word.

"Dead," Blue Crow said, supplying the word for her.

"Right. So why do you need a fortune in gold?"

"It is mine," Blue Crow said again. "I will decide who should have it."

"I don't believe any of this," Kelly muttered. "I don't believe you're real. I don't believe I'm sitting here at three o'clock in the morning arguing with something that doesn't exist."

"I am real, Kelly McBride," Blue Crow replied quietly. He held out his hand. "Look at me. Touch me."

She swallowed hard and then, feeling as if she had no control over what she was doing, she gazed deep into his eyes, felt her heart swell with compassion as she sensed the loneliness he had endured for over a century.

Of its own volition, Kelly's hand reached for his, but it was his fingers that closed over hers. For a moment she stared at their locked hands—his was large and scarred, hers was small and very white in comparison to his. But it was the heat of his touch that made her pulse race and her blood sing a new song.

When she tried to take her hand from his, he refused to let go, and for the first time since he'd entered the room, she was truly afraid. Afraid and confused. He couldn't be a ghost. Ghosts were vaporous, without mass or substance.

She blinked up at him, mesmerized by the heat in his gaze, by her sudden awareness that, ghost or no ghost, this was a man with all of a man's desires.

"I will not harm you," Blue Crow assured her, and though that had been his intent when he entered the house, he knew now that this woman was a part of his destiny. He would not harm her and he would destroy anyone who tried. "I will not harm you," he repeated. "It is only that your skin is so soft, so warm and alive, and it has been so long since I have held a woman..."

His fingers tightened on hers and she felt him tremble and then, without warning, he vanished from her sight.

In the morning, Kelly tried to convince herself it had all been a dream. There were no such things as ghosts.

But the eagle was gone.

And when she got up, she discovered a single eagle feather on the floor beside the bed.

Distracted, she dressed and went into the kitchen to prepare breakfast. A short time later, Lee entered the room and took a seat at the table.

Unable to help herself, Kelly stared at him all through breakfast. It was uncanny, his resemblance to Blue Crow.

"Something wrong?" Lee asked when she poured him a second cup of coffee.

"No, why?"

Lee shrugged. "I feel like a bug under a microscope."

With an effort, she drew her gaze from his face. "Sorry."

"You gonna tell me why you've been staring at me?"

"I...it's just...no reason."

"Can't be my good looks," he mused, locking his fingers around his coffee cup. "Did somebody say something to you in town the other day? Maybe warn you to stay away from me?"

She flushed guiltily, remembering Harry Renford's admonition. "No, of course not."

"Maybe you're having second thoughts about my working here?"

"No, it's not that."

"What then? Come on, Miss McBride, tell me what's bothering you."

Kelly shook her head. She couldn't tell him she'd been visited by a ghost. The ghost of Christmas past, she thought, smothering the urge to laugh. Oh Lord, maybe she was losing her mind.

Lee frowned, wondering what was troubling her. She'd gone suddenly pale.

"Somebody told you I'd been arrested, didn't they?"

She started to deny it, then nodded. "Mr. Renford, at the bank, told me you'd been arrested for breaking into my grandfather's house."

A muscle tensed in Lee's jaw.

"He said you did a year in jail." Kelly took a deep breath. "That seems like a rather harsh sentence."

"I was carrying a gun at the time," Lee replied tersely.

"A gun! Why?" She stared at him in horror. "Surely you didn't mean to—"

"Of course not."

"Then why did you need a gun?"

Lee shrugged. He couldn't tell her about the gold and yet...he swore under his breath, wondering if she knew about the treasure rumored to be hidden in the mountains, wondering if that was why she was so determined to stay.

Stalling for time, he lifted the cup to his lips. He wasn't the only one searching for the treasure. He'd seen tracks near the foot of the mountain, tracks that weren't his. Tracks that definitely weren't Kelly's. Somehow, he'd have to warn her she might be in danger without telling her why.

Kelly leaned forward, her elbows propped on the table, her chin resting on her folded hands. "Well?"

"It's dangerous out here after dark, Miss McBride. There are still wild animals prowling around and not all of them are four footed."

Kelly grimaced. Wild animals, indeed, she thought. And then she shivered. Not all of them are four footed, he'd said. Did he know something he wasn't telling her?

Lee stood abruptly. "I'd better get to work," he said, and then paused, his hand on the door, one brow arched in question. "If I'm still working here, that is."

"You are."

His lips flattened into a thin line. And then, as if he'd made a difficult decision, he took a deep breath and blew it out in a long sigh.

"Then you might as well know the rest."

"The rest?" Kelly looked up at him, her fingernails digging into her palms as she waited for him to go on. His expression was bleak, his eyes as hard and black as obsidian. A muscle worked in his jaw.

"When I was seventeen, I was accused of raping a white girl. I did some time for that, too."

He stared down at her, waiting for her reaction.

Kelly's gaze was steady as it met his. "Were you guilty?"

"Only of being young and stupid."

She hesitated only a moment before she said, "I believe you."

Lee studied her for a long moment, wondering if she really believed him. And then he cursed himself for being such a cynical fool. Her face was as open and easy to read as print on a page. If she thought he was lying, it would be revealed in the depths of those amazing blue eyes.

"We're having hamburgers for lunch," Kelly said with a smile. "Don't be late."

With a nod in her direction, he left the house.

Kelly stared after Lee, her mind reeling with unanswered questions. Why had he really come here? What did he know that he wasn't telling her? Was she in danger? Why did he look so much like Blue Crow?

She grunted softly. The answer to that was obvious. They had to be related. If that was so, perhaps it answered her other questions, as well. He'd come to work here because he knew about the gold. And if he knew, perhaps there were others who also knew, or suspected.

If that was true, she would be wise not to trade any more of the nuggets for cash. Cedar Flats was a small town and so was Coleville. Anything out of the ordinary was likely to draw attention and be remembered.

Pushing away from the table, she gathered up the dirty dishes and filled the sink with hot water. The kitchen was on the west side of the house. There was a large window over the sink, affording her a view of the barn and the corrals.

Looking out, she saw Lee carrying a ladder and a can of paint out of the barn. He'd removed his shirt and his skin glistened like fine bronze in the early morning sunlight. His muscles rippled as he placed the ladder against the side of the barn.

The dishes forgotten, she watched as he opened a can of red paint and then, with lithe assurance, made his way to the top of the ladder.

Using a brush pulled from the waistband of his pants, he began to paint the eaves.

She might have stood watching him all day, her hands immersed in a sink of water that was rapidly turning cold, if Harry Renford hadn't called.

After exchanging the usual pleasantries, he informed her that the deed was still missing and that he had sent to the county seat for a copy.

Kelly thanked him for calling, assured him that Lee Roan Horse wasn't causing any trouble at all and hung up.

Resisting the urge to spend the day watching Lee, she quickly finished up the dishes, made her bed and dusted the living room furniture. She hadn't given the house a good cleaning since she arrived and this seemed the perfect time to do it.

It wasn't a very big house. There were two bedrooms in the back of the house, a small but surprisingly modern bathroom, a good-sized living room and a combination kitchen and dining room.

She stripped the sheets and blankets from the bed in the spare bedroom to air the mattress, scoured the bathroom fixtures and mopped the floor.

She was ready for a break when lunchtime came.

The hamburgers were grilling when Lee entered the kitchen. She was relieved to see that he'd donned his shirt. For some reason, the sight of his bare chest aroused feelings she didn't wish to acknowledge or analyze.

Lee hesitated before he sat down, wondering if she'd had a change of heart about his staying on.

"Sit down," she said. "It's almost ready."

Nodding, he pulled out a chair and straddled it. He tried not to stare at her, tried to think of something else, but he couldn't keep his gaze from straying toward her, couldn't help noticing the way she filled out a pair of jeans, couldn't help wondering what it would be like to hold her in his arms.

He swore softly. She was a white woman, he reminded himself sternly, and he'd vowed never to get mixed up with a white woman again. It had been ten years since the incident with Melinda, but he hadn't forgotten what it had cost him the last time he'd let a pretty face override his better judgment and as much as he longed to take Kelly in his arms and discover if she tasted as good as she looked, he had no intention of giving in to that particular temptation.

He ate quickly, thanked her for the meal and left the house, determined to bury his lust under a coat of red paint and a lot of hard work.

By nightfall, Lee was bone weary. Feet dragging, he made his way to the house, convinced he'd managed to subdue his base feelings for a woman he hardly knew, but one look at Kelly's face and he knew he was kidding himself. What was there about this particular woman that drew his gaze again and again? Was it the pull of her soft golden skin, the sky-blue color of her eyes, or the simple fact that she was a challenge he was helpless to resist?

He shook his head imperceptibly. She didn't wear much makeup, only a bit of mascara and a touch of pale pink lipstick, and yet he knew he'd never seen anything as sexy as Kelly McBride clad in a pair of faded jeans and a white turtleneck sweater.

Get hold of yourself, Roan Horse, he chided. You're as randy as a young stud with his first mare.

They ate in silence. The lack of conversation made Kelly uncomfortable and she was glad she'd turned the radio on—until Vince Gill began singing a song called *Nobody Answers When I Call Your Name*. The soft country ballad filled the kitchen, reminding Kelly of how lonely she was. All she'd ever wanted had been a home of her own and a man to share it with, yet she'd never found that one special man. Twice, she'd thought she'd been in love. The first time, she'd discovered that the man she adored was already married. The second time, she had simply lost interest in the relationship. She'd always been told that there was someone for everyone, but she was beginning to doubt it.

The song ended, only to be followed by another song about lost love and broken dreams.

Glancing up, she met Lee's gaze, felt her cheeks grow hot as she saw the barely concealed longing in his eyes. He was lonely, too, she thought.

Her heart seemed to climb into her throat as she watched Lee push away from the table. He rose to his feet with all the sleek, lazy grace of a tiger. He circled the table until he stood beside her chair, one hand outstretched.

Feeling foolish and giddy at the same time, Kelly put her hand in his, let him pull her to her feet, take her in his arms.

Kelly's heart was pounding so loudly she could scarcely hear the music as he waltzed her around the kitchen floor. She marveled at the way she fit into his arms. She had never been a particularly good dancer, yet she followed Lee as if they had danced together for years. She was acutely conscious of his long fingers folded over hers, of the pressure of his hand at her back. He had washed before coming to dinner and she could smell the soap on his skin. Her left hand rested lightly on his shoulder and the flesh beneath her palm was warm and solid.

His leg brushed against hers, sending tremors of excitement through her whole body. His breath was warm against her cheek, his eyes were dark intense, filled with unspoken dreams and secrets she was afraid to learn.

He didn't release her when the music ended. For a long moment they stood there, suspended in time. Kelly stared into his eyes, unable to look away. It was suddenly hard to breathe, impossible to think. She watched his gaze travel to her lips, felt her breath catch in her throat as she waited for him to kiss her. Shivers of anticipation skittered down her spine and her knees went weak as heat spiraled through her.

He took a deep breath, as if gathering his strength, and then he let her go and took a step backward.

"Thanks for dinner," he said, not quite meeting her eyes.

"You're welcome." She glanced around the kitchen, wishing she could find a reason to make him stay. Her gaze settled on the pie she'd made that afternoon. The way to a man's heart, she thought and blurted, "There's apple pie for dessert."

"No." He took another step away from her. "Maybe another time," he added, his voice thick.

"Good night, then."

Her voice moved over him, low and soft, and he knew he had to get out of there before it was too late.

Muttering a hurried good night, he opened the kitchen door and practically ran out of the room.

Chapter Eight

Outside, Lee paused in the shadows and drew in several long breaths. She probably thought he was crazy, running out of the house like that, but he had to get away. Away from the innocent enticement of sweet pink lips and the lure of summer-sky eyes. Away from the intoxicating female scent that clung to her.

He swore under his breath. She'd smelled of lilac soap and minty toothpaste and freshly baked biscuits, of woman and home, of kids and responsibility, and it scared the devil out of him.

He stared at his hand. He could still feel the warmth of her skin against his. His shoulder seemed to burn where her hand had rested. Hell, he was burning all over.

He sucked in another deep breath, blew it out in a long sigh, then made his way to the corral behind the barn. The buckskin whickered softly as he approached. Bending over, he plucked a dandelion from a patch of scraggly grass and offered it to the horse. Then, one booted foot resting on the bottom rail of the corral, he stared into the distance, idly scratching the gelding between the ears.

Gradually, the quiet of the night settled around him, soothing him. He stared up at the stars and from deep within a shadowed corridor of his mind he heard the echo of an ancient Lakota prayer.

He heard the words whisper in his mind and then, feeling awkward and a little foolish, he raised his arms overhead and spoke the words aloud.

"*Wakan Tanka,* whose voice whispers in the wind and the water, whose breath gives life to all the earth, hear my cry. I am small and weak, in need of Your strength and courage and wisdom. If You walk with me, all things are possible…"

After a moment, he lowered his arms and then, very slowly, he glanced over his shoulder.

The house, bathed in moonlight, looked like something out of a fairy tale. Light glowed behind the yellow-checked curtains, warm, inviting. He saw Kelly staring at him through the kitchen window. Lamplight cast soft red highlights in her hair.

His breath caught in his throat as he looked at her. *All things are possible…*

Feeling suddenly naked and vulnerable, he headed for the barn. After putting the horse in a stall, he lit the lamp that hung from one of the rafters. He stood there for a long time, his heart racing as though he'd just run a marathon, his thoughts chaotic.

Kelly. One touch and he wanted two. He held her hand and wanted to smother her with kisses.

Damn! Gold or no gold, he had to get away from here. Away from her.

He dragged a hand through his hair, remembering the beating he'd gotten from Melinda's father. Of course, Frank Kershaw hadn't done it himself. Oh, no. He'd hollered for his two hired bodyguards and they'd beat the crap out of the boy who'd dared lay a hand on his little girl. They'd broken his nose and a couple of ribs before they were done. Lee had wondered how Melinda's old man would explain it all to the police, but no explanations had been necessary. The cops hadn't even blinked. They'd listened to Kershaw's story, readily accepting his word that Lee had raped his daughter without provocation, cuffed Lee's hands behind his back, read him his rights and shoved him into the back of the police car.

Even now he could remember the humiliation of that night. Melinda's tears, her mournful sobs as she accused Lee of dragging her into the bungalow and raping her. He could remember the smiles of anticipation on the faces of the two bodyguards as they backed him into a corner, the sounds of their fists striking his face and body, the smell of his own blood and fear, the stench of their sweat as they worked him over, the look on Kershaw's face as he handed them each a crisp one hundred dollar bill for their trouble.

"It's over. Forget it." Lee muttered the words aloud, knowing he'd never forget it as long as he lived.

"Lee?"

He whirled around at the sound of her voice.

Kelly paused, her hand on the door. "I'm sorry, I didn't mean to bother you, but..." She shrugged, a faint smile flitting over her face. "I went for a walk and I seem to have locked myself out of the house and I was wondering if you could..."

Her voice trailed off and she felt a rush of color flood her cheeks.

His eyes narrowed ominously. "And you knew I'd be able to pick the lock, since I'd done it before."

Kelly bit down on her lip. Of course, that was just what she'd thought, only it sounded awful when he said it aloud.

"I... Never mind. I'll..."

"Forget it," he said brusquely. Hands clenched into tight fists, he swept past her.

"I'm sorry," she mumbled, but he didn't seem to hear her.

Needing time to compose herself, she spent a couple of minutes glancing around the barn. She hadn't been inside since Lee moved in. The floor had been swept clean. An assortment of tack hung from pegs on the far wall; there were several bales of hay and straw piled in a corner, along with a half-dozen bags of sweet feed. Her grandfather's saddle, cleaned and oiled, sat atop a wooden sawhorse. An old cardboard box held an assortment of curry combs and brushes

She walked down the aisle that separated the stalls. Dusty whickered softly and she paused to rub the gelding's nose.

Glancing at the stall across the way, she saw that Lee had made a bed of sorts in the stall; the adjoining stall served as his closet. She saw a few shirts draped over the partition, an extra pair of boots, a couple pairs of blue jeans, a well-worn black hat. But what held her eye was the war bonnet hanging from a nail. Made of black-tipped eagle feathers that trailed to the ground, it was a thing of rare beauty, tempting her touch.

Giving Dusty a final pat, she crossed the floor and entered the stall, letting her fingertips glide over one of the feathers. And into her mind came an image of Blue Crow astride a black and white paint pony. He was dressed in a clout and moccasins, his face streaked with war paint, a feathered lance in his right hand. And a war bonnet on his head, a war bonnet that looked exactly like the one beneath her hand.

A shiver curled up Kelly's spine. Snatching her hand away, she left the barn and made her way to the house, anxious to ask Lee about the war bonnet.

Lee was waiting for her. The front door stood ajar. A stream of lamplight illuminated the porch.

"Thank you," Kelly said.

A corner of Lee's mouth curled up in a wry grin. "No problem."

Lifting her head and squaring her shoulders, Kelly met his unblinking gaze. "I'm sorry if I offended you earlier."

"Forget it."

"I didn't mean anything, honestly. I…sometimes I say things without thinking. I really am sorry."

"Why should you be sorry? You didn't do anything wrong."

"But—"

"Listen, Kelly, I'm not a very nice guy. It's no secret that I've done time and lots of it. Everybody in town knows it."

He paused and then went on, deciding he might as well tell her everything and be done with it. "I got busted for stealing, for vandalism, for burglary." He shrugged. "You name it, I probably did it."

"Why are you telling me this?"

"Because you've got a right to know who's sleeping in your barn."

"It doesn't matter."

"Doesn't it?"

"It's all in the past. Isn't it?"

He couldn't meet her eyes. He couldn't lie to her, he couldn't make promises to those innocent blue eyes, promises he had no intention of keeping.

"Isn't it?" Kelly gazed at him intently, suddenly aware that she was shivering and that it had nothing to do with the weather.

"I don't know, but if I were you, I'd keep my doors and windows locked."

Kelly glanced pointedly at the open front door and then at the piece of wire in his hand. "Would it do me any good?"

"Kelly—"

"I'm trusting you, Lee Roan Horse. I hope you won't let me down. Goodnight."

Only after she'd closed the door did she realize she'd forgotten to ask him about the war bonnet.

Lee stared at the closed front door, listening to her footsteps fade as she made her way toward her bedroom in the back of the house.

I'm trusting you…

Lee grunted softly. No one had ever trusted him before. He'd never realized what a burden it could be. He had to get out of here, he thought again, before it was too late.

But even as the thought crossed his mind, he knew he wouldn't go and he wondered which temptation was more enticing, the age-old lure of soft feminine curves and sweet pink lips or the equally ancient lust for gold.

It was a question that kept him awake far into the night.

Chapter Nine

Kelly stared out the kitchen window, her mouth agape. Where had that horse come from? She was about to go outside to find Lee when she saw him walking toward the corral, a bridle in one hand. Mercy, he didn't mean to ride the beast! It was the biggest, blackest, wildest-looking horse she'd ever seen. The animal darted toward the far side of the corral when it saw Lee approaching. Nostrils flared, ears laid flat, the horse watched the man.

Whistling softly, Lee ducked into the corral. For a long while, he simply stood there, the bridle swinging from his hand. And then, moving without haste, he crossed the corral, his free hand outstretched.

Kelly held her breath, certain Lee was about to be killed before her very eyes, but as soon as he got near the horse, the black bolted to the other side of the corral.

For the next half hour, she watched Lee stalk the horse, never able to get close enough to slip the bridle over its head.

Wild-eyed and wary, the black pranced around the corral, tossing its head, blowing loudly, until it had worked itself into a sweat.

Finally, muttering what Kelly assumed was an oath, Lee left the corral.

She was stirring eggs in a pan when he entered the kitchen.

"Morning," she said brightly.

"Morning."

"Where'd the horse come from?"

"I took it in payment for some work I did." A wry grin tugged at his lips. "I think I got taken."

"He's not broken to ride?"

"He's barely broken to a halter. I had to lead him here from the Montgomery place."

"That's five miles from here."

"I know." He accepted the cup of coffee she handed him and sipped it appreciatively.

"What kind of horse is it?"

"He's a mustang and as wild as they come."

"Can I ask you something?"

"You can ask."

"Where'd you get the war bonnet in the barn?"

"From my grandfather."

"Do you...do you know who it belonged to?"

"My grandfather's grandfather, I think. Why?"

"No reason. It looks old. I was just curious."

* * * * *

It took four days before the stallion would accept the bridle without a fight and another two days before the horse would stand still while Lee tightened the cinch. Even then, swinging into the saddle was like straddling a block of dynamite. And it wasn't because Lee didn't know what he was doing. He was a good rider, the best Kelly had ever seen, but the horse bucked like it was powered with TNT. Time and again, Lee went sailing through the air, only to regain his feet and try again.

After a while it was almost painful to watch and Kelly wondered which stubborn creature would win—the man or the stallion.

It was late one night about two weeks later when something roused Kelly from sleep.

Rising, she went to the window and peered out-side. A bright silver moon illuminated the yard. At first she didn't see anything and then a bit of movement caught her eye. Leaning forward, she glanced to the left toward the corrals.

"Oh." The word whispered past her lips and then she grabbed her robe and left the house.

Moving silently through the shadows, she made her way to the corral, stopping out of sight behind a tall pine, her gaze focused on the man and the horse silhouetted in the moonlight.

She watched Lee walk toward the horse, speaking softly in a language Kelly did not understand, but assumed was Lakota. Slowly he closed the distance between himself and the black, a constant stream of words wrapping magically around the horse.

The stallion stood in the center of the corral, ears twitching, eyes watching the man's every move, until the man stood at its head and very slowly reached out to stroke its neck.

Kelly eased forward, listening to the soft words that seemed to have woven a fairy spell around the wild stallion.

She pressed a hand to her heart as Lee placed his hands on either side of the horse's head and blew softly into the animals nostrils.

And then, to her utter surprise, Lee vaulted onto the stallion's bare back. She held her breath, expecting to see the horse start to buck. Instead, the black craned its head around to look at the man on its back. Lee gave a gentle squeeze with his thighs and the horse began to walk around the corral as if it had been doing it every day of its life.

Speechless, Kelly left her hiding place and went to stand near the corral gate. Man and horse circled the corral, moving together as if they were one creature.

When they reached the gate, Lee spoke softly to the horse and the stallion came to a smooth halt. Lee slid off the horse, gave the animal a pat on the neck and left the corral.

It was only then that Kelly realized it wasn't Lee at all. It was Blue Crow.

"How did you do that?" she asked. "Lee's been trying to break that stallion for days."

"Lee Roan Horse is a good man, but he has wandered far from the true path. He has forgotten how to be one with his four-footed brothers."

"Oh. The war bonnet Lee has in the barn, it belonged to you, didn't it?"

"*Han*. How did you know?"

"I saw you wearing it."

"You saw me?"

"Yes. I don't know how to explain it, but I touched it the other day and I saw you riding a paint horse."

Blue Crow nodded. "At the Greasy Grass."

"You were at the Little Big Horn?"

"*Han*. It was a day to be remembered, *tekihila*. The Blue Coats fought bravely, but *Wakan Tanka* was on our side that day. It was a great victory for my people. I would have liked to share it with you."

Kelly took a step backward, suddenly aware that she was standing outside, clad in a nightgown and robe, alone with a ghost. A very sensual ghost.

A small smile flickered over Blue Crow's face. "You feel it, too."

"Feel what?"

"The magic between us."

"No," Kelly said, shaking her head for emphasis. "I don't feel anything."

"Do not lie to me, *tekihila*."

"What did you call me?"

Blue Crow made a vague gesture of dismissal. "It is not important." *My love,* he thought to himself. How easily he had come to think of her as his. Day and night, he watched her, pleased because she had a good heart, a good soul.

"I'd better go inside," Kelly said. She wrapped her arms around her middle as a cool breeze stirred the air.

Blue Crow took a step forward. Before Kelly could object, he enfolded her in his arms and drew her close, his embrace gentle, nurturing.

"You shouldn't... I shouldn't..." All thought of protest fled her mind as his warmth infused her. She stared into his eyes, eyes as soft and dark as black velvet, as deep as a midnight sea. Eyes that glowed with a fierce desire, a barely suppressed hunger that created a wild fluttering in Kelly's stomach and made her heart beat faster.

"Tekihila."

The sound of his voice enveloped her like a silken web. Mesmerized by his nearness, by the strength of his arms, she could only stand there, her gaze trapped in his, waiting, hoping that he would lower his head and kiss her.

As if he'd read her mind, he did just that.

And there was magic between them, she thought, dazed. His lips were warm and firm, yielding and demanding. Desire seared through her, brighter than the tail of a comet, hotter than a thousand suns.

"Tekihila," he murmured. *"Skuya, skuya."*

"Skuya?"

"Sweet," he said. "So sweet."

"Tekihila?" It took an effort to form words when he was standing so close to her, the heat of his deep black eyes glowing like twin coals, warming her in places that had long been cold.

"My own love."

His love. It never occurred to her to argue. Standing on tiptoe, she touched her lips to his. This couldn't be happening, she mused. He wasn't real. Maybe he was only a figment of her imagination. But there was nothing imaginary about his mouth on hers, or the way her blood hummed in her veins. There was nothing imaginary about the rapid beat of her pulse, or the hard male thighs pressed against hers.

She was breathless, mindless when he took his mouth from hers.

Effortlessly he swung her into his arms and carried her into the house, moving confidently through the dark hall until he came to her bedroom. Removing her robe, he put her to bed, drew the covers up to her chin.

She stared up at him, wanting him as she'd never wanted anything in her life, but instead of crawling into bed beside her, he kissed her lightly on the forehead.

"Rest well, *tekihila,*" he murmured, and then he was gone, leaving her alone, and lonely, in the dark.

Chapter Ten

ꭍ

She was still slightly dazed in the morning. Standing at the stove, she touched her lips again and again, remembering the touch and the taste of his mouth on hers, the sound of his voice calling her *tekihila*. My own love.

She might have stood there daydreaming until the bacon caught fire if Lee hadn't entered the kitchen, letting the door slam shut behind him.

"What the devil!" he exclaimed. "You trying to burn the house down!"

"What? Oh!"

Startled out of her reverie, Kelly jerked the frying pan off the fire and turned off the gas.

"From the smoke filling the room, I'd say breakfast is ready," Lee drawled. Pulling out a chair, he sat down, his brow furrowed in thought.

Kelly didn't bother to answer. Instead, she spooned some bacon and eggs on a plate and plopped it down in front of him. Filling a plate for herself, she took a seat across from Lee.

"Something wrong?" he asked.

"No."

He studied her face a moment, then sighed. "Okay, okay, I'm sorry about that crack about the smoke," Lee muttered.

"What?"

"Where are you this morning?" Lee waved his fork in the air. "First you practically set the bacon on fire and now you look as if you're a million miles from here."

"I'm fine. I just have a lot on my mind."

"Anything I can help you with?"

"No."

He frowned and then shrugged. "Funny thing," he remarked. "I threw a saddle on the black before I came up here. For the first time, he didn't fight me, so I climbed aboard."

"And?"

"Nothing happened. He just stood there like we were old friends." Lee shook his head. "It was the damnedest thing."

And that wasn't all of it, Lee thought, bemused. The black had whickered at him like he was glad to see him.

"Maybe he just got tired of fighting," Kelly suggested.

"Yeah, maybe, but..."

"But?"

"An outlaw like that doesn't just give up overnight."

"It hasn't been overnight," Kelly pointed out. "You've been trying to break him for the last two weeks."

"Yeah," Lee muttered in agreement, but he didn't sound convinced.

"More coffee?"

"Thanks." Lee watched Kelly cross the room, admiring the way she filled out her Levi's, the feminine sway of her hips. For a moment, he wondered if she'd been riding the black, but quickly dismissed the idea. The horse would have chewed her up and spit her out.

Kelly refilled Lee's cup and then her own before she sat down at the table again.

"So," Lee said, his hands folded around the mug, "now that we've got two horses, what do you say we take the day off and go for a ride?"

"A ride? Where?"

He shrugged. "Up in the foothills, maybe. Pretty country up there. Lots to see."

You don't know the half of it, Kelly thought.

"What do you say?" He lifted the cup to his lips and took a drink, watching her over the rim.

"It's gonna be hot again today. I'd rather ride along the creek bed, maybe take a dip."

A flicker of disappointment shadowed his eyes and then was gone. "Sounds good." Rising, he drained his cup. "I'll saddle the horses."

"And I'll pack a lunch. Ham sandwiches okay?"

"Fine."

Kelly stared after Lee as he picked up his hat and left the room, shaken by the feeling that he knew about the gold.

She'd have to be careful, she thought, and then wondered if maybe she should just fire him and be done with it. She considered it for a moment and then decided that if he was really looking for the gold, she'd be better off to let him stay where she could keep an eye on him.

An hour later, they were riding side by side along the narrow creek that flowed down the south side of the mountain and meandered, snakelike, across the southern portion of the Triple M.

Kelly had ample opportunity to observe Lee, since he had his hands full keeping the stallion under control. The horse might be saddle-broke, but he was still green. And young. He shied when a rabbit skittered across their path, bucked when a jay flew out of a tree, wings flapping loudly.

Kelly shook her head when the stallion bucked again, this time because he'd seen his shadow. Leaning forward, she patted Dusty on the neck, grateful she was mounted on a reliable old gelding instead of a high-spirited young stallion.

Lee was grinning when, a few miles later, he drew rein in the shade of a cottonwood tree.

"He's a great horse," he exclaimed.

Leaning forward, he stroked the black's neck affectionately, thinking that maybe he hadn't made such a bad bargain after all.

Dismounting, he turned to help Kelly from the saddle. It shouldn't have meant anything when his hands circled her waist. He was, after all, only helping her dismount, but she felt the heat of his hands penetrate her shirt, searing the skin beneath.

He felt it, too. She saw it in the brief flare of surprise in his eyes, heard it in the catch in his breath.

A muscle worked in his cheek, as if he were keeping himself in tight control, and then he swung her out of the saddle. Her hands rested on his shoulders, feeling the play of powerful muscles beneath her fingertips as he lifted her from Dusty's back.

As soon as her feet touched the ground, he released her and took a step backward.

Kelly stared up at him. They weren't touching anymore, but she was acutely aware of the male scent of him, of the remembered touch of rippling muscles beneath the thin cotton of his shirt. His eyes were black. Dark. Hypnotic. Somehow warning her away even as they burned with unspoken desire.

She was plagued by a fierce urge to caress his cheek and see if she could wipe the bitterness from his face; instead, she slipped her hands into her pockets. But, try as she might, she couldn't draw her gaze from his. It was like being caught in a whirlpool, being sucked deeper and deeper in black water until she was helplessly caught.

"Kelly..." Her name whispered past his lips, a prayer and a groan combined.

She blinked at him, unable to speak for the fierce pounding of her heart.

He shook his head, his face twisted with pain. "I don't want to hurt you."

"I don't understand."

"I'm no good, Kelly. Tell me to go, now, before it's too late for both of us."

"It's already too late."

She spoke without thinking and knew that no truer words had ever been spoken. Right or wrong, she was drawn to this man in ways she could not fathom or explain.

Lee shook his head in denial. He didn't want to care for her. He couldn't care for her. She was a white woman, his enemy. He had come here to steal from her, to take what was rightfully his, not to become infatuated with sky-blue eyes and pretty pink lips.

He swore under his breath as he read the wanting in those same blue eyes. How could he steal from this woman? She was so innocent, so trusting. And yet that gold was his. His grandfather's grandfather had been killed on the mountain that rose behind Kelly's house, killed by a pair of greedy white men...

Lee frowned as a distant memory niggled at the corner of his mind. McBride...

"You don't happen to have an ancestor named Charlie McBride, do you?" he asked.

Kelly nodded, wondering at his sudden change of topic. "I saw his name on a genealogy sheet once. He was born back in 1854 or 1855, as I recall. Why?"

Lee shook his head. Charlie McBride had been one of the white men responsible for the death of his grandfather's grandfather, Blue Crow.

He felt a rush of adrenaline. He was on the right track. The gold was here, in the mountains, as his great-grandfather had told him so many years ago.

"Lee, what's wrong?"

"Nothing."

He tried to ignore the hurt, the confusion, in her eyes. In the old days, she would have been his enemy. He would have thrown her across his horse and carried her off into the mountains. He would have made her his woman, willing or not. He would have buried himself in her pale flesh and exorcised the demons that haunted him.

He felt his blood heat at the mere thought of possessing her. For a moment, he was tempted to forget everything...the silent festering wound that Melinda's betrayal had left in his soul, his determination to have the gold, to forget everything but the woman standing before him.

He glanced at the black stallion. It would be so easy to grab Kelly, throw her on his horse and run like the devil. But where would they go? In the old days, they could have lived off the land. He could have taken her far away, hidden her, kept her until he tired of her. But not now. Sooner or later they'd find him and he'd be back in jail, or dead.

A twinge of unease made Kelly take a step backward. A moment ago she had thought Lee was going to kiss her. Now he looked as if he were contemplating what it would be like to slit her throat, or worse. Unwanted came the memory that he had been accused of rape.

"Maybe we should go home," she suggested.

"No. Come on, let's take a walk."

She hesitated a moment, then nodded in agreement. "Okay."

Side by side, they walked along the winding creek. Willows and cottonwoods grew in scattered clumps. Wildflowers swayed in the breeze. Birds flitted from branch to branch, or dusted themselves in the sandy soil along the creek bank.

Once, Kelly's hand brushed Lee's. It was as if a spark of electricity arced between them. When it happened again, she came to an abrupt halt.

Lee...

He didn't say anything, only drew her into his arms and kissed her. His lips were firm and warm, asking but not demanding, entreating, hopeful. Of their own accord, her arms twined around his neck and she pressed against him, hoping to ease the ache that was spreading through her, an ache made stronger by the probing fire of his tongue.

The strength seemed to be draining from her legs. She was aware of Lee's arms around her, slowly pulling her down until they were kneeling on the grass.

"Kelly…" He groaned softly. "Kelly, tell me to stop."

"I can't."

She leaned toward him, her breasts pressing against his chest as her lips sought his again.

His hands slid down her back, drawing her hips to his. Kelly's breath caught in her throat as she felt the evidence of his desire. Her head fell back, giving Lee access to her neck, and she shuddered with pleasure as she felt his mouth glide over the sensitive skin of her neck, behind her ear, at the pulse point in the hollow of her neck. She was tingling with delight, burning with need, as her restless hands explored his arms, his shoulders, his back. She pressed her hand to his chest and felt the rapid beating of his heart.

She'd never felt like this before. It was frightening, exhilarating.

He fell back on the grass and drew her down on top of him, his mouth covering hers. She felt the rumble of a groan in his chest and wondered if he was experiencing the same exquisite pain she was.

She wanted him, wanted him in a way she'd never wanted any other man. Wanted him in the most elemental, primal way that a woman could want a man. But, more than that, she wanted to hold him, to comfort him, to make a home for him…

She drew back so she could see his face, not knowing that her thoughts were as transparent as a pane of new glass.

With an oath, Lee sat up and then stood up, carrying Kelly with him. Gently, but deliberately, he put her feet on the ground, removed her arms from his neck.

"We'd better head back, Miss McBride," he said, his voice as hard and cold as winter ice, "before one of us gets into trouble."

Without waiting for her reply, he turned on his heel and started walking back to where they had left the horses. How easily she broke through his resolve! How quickly she made him forget Melinda and all that happened afterward.

He shook his head ruefully. Some men had a weakness for firewater. He seemed to have an incurable weakness for women who were sure to cause him nothing but trouble.

Swinging into the saddle, he renewed his determination to find the gold and get the hell out of Cedar Flats.

Chapter Eleven

ℰ𝒪

The man seated behind the desk drummed his fingers impatiently. "Well, Trask, what have you learned?"

"Nothing, boss. Roan Horse spends all his time working around the ranch, patching up the roof and fixin' the corrals. When he's not fixin' the place up, he's working with a black devil horse. If he's searching for the gold, he's doing it at night when we can't see him."

"And the woman?"

Trask's companion shook his head. "She rarely leaves the house. They went on a picnic." He shrugged. "Maybe all that talk about Indian gold is just that, talk."

"When I want your opinion, Bradford, I'll ask for it. In the meantime, I'm paying you two for information."

"Yessir."

"Next time I see you, you'd better have news. I'm getting damned tired of all this waiting around."

"Maybe we can stir something up," Trask mused.

"Do that. Now, go on, get out of here. And don't let anyone see you leave."

Chapter Twelve

ꙮ

Kelly stood at the kitchen window watching Lee put the last coat of paint on the barn. Two days had passed since their ill-fated ride. Two tension-filled days. Lee had avoided her except at mealtimes and then he had been sullen and withdrawn.

She'd been tempted to take her meals in her bedroom, but had refused to let him chase her out of her own kitchen. If he didn't like her company, he could take his meals in the barn!

Dragging her gaze from his sweat-sheened back and quietly cursing the fact that he rarely wore a shirt when he worked, she studied the barn. He'd done a good job, she couldn't fault him there. The freshly painted white trim made a vivid contrast to the dark brick-red paint. As soon as he finished the doors, the barn would be done and he'd start on the house.

Kelly wrapped her arms around her waist. She should let him go, she thought. He had warned her that there were wild animals prowling around and that they weren't all four-footed. She wondered suddenly if he'd been warning her against himself.

She had no doubt that Lee Roan Horse could be a dangerous man. If she wasn't careful, he was going to steal her heart.

At five, he opened the back door and informed her that he was going into town.

Startled, Kelly had no time to do more than nod before he was gone.

The rest of the day seemed like a week. She hadn't realized how accustomed she'd become to Lee's company, how often she'd looked out the window to see what he was doing, until he wasn't around.

At loose ends, she wandered through the house, seeing things she hadn't really paid attention to before, like the old photograph of her grandparents in the spare bedroom.

Sitting on the edge of the bed, she studied the couple in the picture. Her grandfather was sitting in a straight-backed chair, his expression solemn, a black bowler hat balanced on his knee, but it was her grandmother's image that drew Kelly's eye. Annee McBride stood slightly behind her husband, one hand on his shoulder.

Kelly stared at the photo, wondering why people in old photographs never smiled. Had life in the old days been that hard, or was it simply "not done"? What had it been like, living back then, when women were considered nothing more than property, like a man's horse, when they couldn't vote or wear pants or do any number of things that women did today?

Kelly stared out the window as darkness fell over the land. Would she have meekly obeyed the rules of the day, or would she have dared to speak out for what she believed in? Would she have defended a woman's right to own property, to vote, to smoke and drink in public?

Probably not, Kelly mused. She'd never been much of a fighter. And she wouldn't have wanted to live back then, either.

With a sigh, she fell back on the bed and closed her eyes.

A hand on her arm. A breath of warm air against her neck. The scent of sage and smoke.

Only half awake, Kelly opened her eyes and blinked into the darkness.

"Tekihila."

"Blue Crow."

She felt the mattress sag as he sat down beside her.

"Soft," he muttered. "How do you sleep on such a thing?"

Kelly shook her head. "What should I sleep on?"

"Mother Earth is the best bed."

She made a soft sound in her throat, neither agreeing nor disagreeing, mesmerized by the slash of his profile in the room's dim light, by the hypnotic touch of his fingertips slowly gliding up and down the inside of her forearm.

"Walk with me, *tekihila?"*

At her nod, he took her hand in his and helped her to her feet.

Outside, he turned north, walking toward the distant mountain.

"Where are we going?" Kelly asked.

"Does it matter, *skuya?"*

"No."

He smiled at her, his teeth gleaming whitely in the darkness.

"In the old days, we would have been enemies." He lifted his hand and let it slide through the thick fall of her hair. "Your scalp would have made a fine trophy."

Kelly shivered. "Did you…did you…do that?"

"Han!" he said, his voice ringing with pride. "I am a warrior." His hand slid down to her neck, resting lightly on her nape. "But I never took the scalp of a woman, *tekihila."*

"I'm glad."

"I would not have wanted your hair, *skuya,"* he murmured, his voice washing over her like liquid sunshine.

"No?"

"No. I would have stolen you had I seen you then," he said fervently. "Had you been married, I would have killed your man and made you mine."

Kelly stared into his deep black eyes, not knowing if she should be flattered or afraid.

"I would take you now, *tekihila,* if I could."

"Would you?" It was an effort to speak past the thickness in her throat.

"*Han*. I would carry you high into the *Paha Sapa,* where all life was born. And there, in the shadow of the sacred mountains, I would give you laughter in the light of the day, and at night, in our lodge, I would give you sons."

No man had ever promised her anything as beautiful. Unable to speak, she took his hand in hers and cupped it to her cheek. His palm was hard and callused and warm.

For a time they stood there in the darkness, not speaking. Slowly his hand slid from her neck and he wrapped his arm around her shoulder, drawing her against him.

Wordlessly she moved into his embrace, placing her head against his chest. She could hear his heart beating, strong and sure, and she wondered how that could be. He was a ghost, a spirit, yet he was the most solid thing in her life.

As though drawn by an invisible hand, she looked up, her eyelids fluttering down as his head lowered toward hers. His kiss was gentle, yet she felt as though she had been branded as his for all time.

Her lips felt bereft when he drew away. Gently he cradled her head to his chest again, his arms holding her close, making her feel as if nothing could ever hurt her again.

"Where is Roan Horse?" Blue Crow asked after a while.

"I don't know. He said he was going into town."

"Do you believe him?"

"Why shouldn't I?"

"He is a troubled young man, haunted by his past, afraid of his future."

"Afraid? Of what?"

"Who can say what another man fears? His life has not been easy. He does not trust others, or himself."

"Do you think he means to hurt me?"

"There are many kinds of hurt, *skuya.*" His hand caressed her cheek. "Holding you brings me more pain than you will ever know."

"Does it? Why?"

"Because I have waited for you my whole life and now that I have found you, I know you can never be mine."

Kelly gazed into his fathomless black eyes. There were no words to describe the emotion that his soft-spoken words aroused within her heart, no words to describe the tenderness that swelled in her soul.

She could only look at him, hoping he could read her feelings in her eyes, in the touch of her hand as she pressed it over his heart.

"You never married, did you?" she asked.

"No. I was waiting, searching, for you."

"And I was waiting for you," Kelly murmured, realizing only as she spoke the words that it was true.

She would never have been happy with the men she'd dated. She knew that now, knew it as surely as she knew the sun would rise in the morning, or that winter would follow the fall.

She loved Blue Crow.

"No, *skuya,*" he said, his voice as deep and dark as the night that surrounded them. "You must not love me."

"It's too late," she said, her voice breaking. "Too late."

She buried her face against his chest, her eyes burning with unshed tears.

"Do not weep, *tekihila,*" he murmured as he stroked her hair. "Your tears are like a knife in my heart."

"Kiss me," she begged, and threading her fingers through his long black hair, she drew his head down toward hers, losing herself in his touch, in his nearness.

She felt the instant response of his manhood as their lips met and she pressed herself against him, tears coursing down her cheeks because she'd fallen in love with the one man she couldn't have, a man who wasn't a man at all, but a ghost.

"Kelly! Kelly, are you out there?" Lee's voice ripped through the darkness. "Kelly?"

"Answer him," Blue Crow whispered.

"I'm over here." She clung to Blue Crow's hand when he started to pull away. "Don't go," she said, but he was already gone.

A moment later she saw Lee striding toward her.

"What the hell are you doing out here alone in the middle of the night?" he demanded, his voice laced with anger.

"I felt like taking a walk."

"You little idiot. Didn't I warn you it was dangerous to go prowling around alone out here?"

"It's no concern of yours what I do!" Kelly retorted.

Lee frowned at her. "Have you been crying?"

"No." She wiped her eyes with the backs of her hands. "Of course not."

"Have it your way. Come on, I'll walk you back to the house."

"I don't need a chaperon."

"Fine," he muttered crossly, "*You* can walk *me* back to the house. Does that soothe your feminine vanity?"

"I don't know what you mean!"

"You're probably one of those feminists, right?" He muttered an oath. "All that women's lib crap, it makes me sick."

"That's because you're not a woman."

"Damn right."

"Why are you so angry?"

"Why are you so stubborn?"

"I'm not."

"The devil you're not."

Kelly came to an abrupt halt, her hands fisted on her hips as she glared at him. "I hate you."

"Good. I hate you, too," he growled, and then, because he could no more resist the lure of her pouting pink lips than he could refuse to take his next breath, he yanked her into his arms and kissed her. Hard.

Kelly struggled against him, her fists pounding impotently on his back and shoulders.

"Quit that, you little hellcat!"

"Let me go!"

Ignoring her futile protests, Lee backed her against a tree, his hips grinding against hers, letting her feel the strength of his need. His lips slid to her neck, her ear.

"Skuya," he murmured, his tongue delving into her ear.

"Don't call me that!" Kelly exclaimed.

"What?" He drew back a little.

"Skuya. Don't call me that."

"Why not?" he asked, and then frowned. "You know what it means?"

"Yes…no…just don't call me that."

Lee studied her face closely. In the moonlight, her skin was like porcelain touched with star dust. Her tear-dampened eyes were luminous, her hair fell loose around her shoulders, a perfect frame for her beauty. A single tear hovered on the tip of her lashes.

His anger evaporated like smoke. "What is it, Kelly?" he asked quietly. "What were you doing out here alone? Why were you crying?"

She shook her head, refusing to meet his eyes.

With a muffled curse, he drew her into his arms and held her close.

"It's all right, Kelly," he murmured. "You don't have to tell me." He rocked her gently, his hands making lazy circles on her back. "It's all right, sweetheart, everything's gonna be all right."

And swinging her into his arms, he carried her home and tucked her into bed as if she were no more than a child.

"Lee? I...would you mind staying with me awhile?"

"No, I don't mind." And sitting on the bed beside her, he held her hand until she fell asleep.

The hand holding hers was strong yet gentle, telling her she was safe, telling her she was loved. She glanced up at the man walking beside her, the warmth of his smile washing over her like sunshine, heating her flesh with only a look, sending shivers of sensation running through her.

When they reached the river, he drew her into his arms, his lips covering hers in a kiss that made her blood flow like warm honey and drained all the strength from her limbs so that she swayed against him.

*"*Tekihila.*" His breath teased her neck.*

"Kiss me," she murmured.

"Gladly, skuya.*"*

Little soft sounds of pleasure rose in Kelly's throat as his mouth covered hers. His tongue was a flame of fire, threatening to engulf her until only cinders remained. She felt the need of his need and knew she longed for nothing more than to ease his ache and her own.

Slowly they sank to the ground, surrendering to the soul-deep need between them.

She had never known a man.

He had not held a woman in more than a hundred years.

Their coming together was like an inferno, two fiery stars that collided in the night, coming together in fury and exploding in a thousand bursts of flame until only ashes remained...

"Blue Crow?"

Kelly sat up, awakened by the cold and a sense of being alone. Glancing around, she saw that she was in her own bed, still dressed as she had been the night before.

Confused, she stared around the familiar room, her heart growing heavy with disappointment when she realized it had only been a dream.

She heard footsteps in the hallway, felt her heart give a little leap of anticipation as the door to her room swung open. The smile of welcome died on her lips.

It was Lee.

"I'm glad to see you, too," he muttered. "Here, I brought you a cup of coffee."

"Thank you." She took the blue flowered mug from his hand.

"You feeling any better today?"

"Better than what?"

Lee took a deep breath, striving for patience. She made him angrier quicker than any woman he'd ever known.

"Better than last night," he said brusquely. "You want to tell me why you were crying?"

Kelly stared into the cup to avoid his eyes. "I wasn't."

"Dammit, Kelly…"

"Let it go, Lee."

"Fine. I'm gonna start on the roof today. If you need to go into town, this might be a good time. I'll be making quite a racket tearing off the old roof."

Kelly nodded. She did need to go to town. All week she'd been expecting Harry Renford to call about the deed. This might be a good time to find out just what was going on

Putting the mug on the bedside table, she swung her legs over the edge of the bed. "I'll fix breakfast."

Lee nodded, wondering what was bothering her, wondering why she'd been crying last night.

"I'll go feed the stock," he muttered. On the way to the barn, he gave himself a stern reminder of what he was doing at the Triple M, a reason that had nothing to do with Kelly McBride.

Two hours later, Kelly was sitting in Renford's office, her hands clasped together in an effort to control her rising temper.

"How long does it take to get a copy of a deed?" she demanded. "It's been weeks!"

"I know, I know," Renford agreed with exaggerated patience. "But they're having some trouble in the records department at the county seat. Some nonsense about transferring the records to computers. You understand?"

"No, I don't. I have a good mind to drive up there and see what's going on for myself."

"Now, Kelly, I've told you before, there's no need to worry. The Triple M is yours, free and clear." The smile that curved his lips didn't reach his narrowed eyes. "Free and clear, except for the balloon payment on the mortgage."

"What balloon payment? I thought I'd paid the mortgage in full. I have a receipt."

"Yes, well, I'm afraid I made a little mistake when I calculated the amount due. There was a rather stiff payoff penalty I neglected to allow for."

"How much?"

Renford made a vague gesture with his hand. "I believe it comes to just under six thousand dollars."

"I see."

Kelly looked out the window. Six thousand dollars wasn't a vast amount of money. She had a hundred times that much in gold, but she had very little cash in the bank. Well, she thought resolutely, there was no help for it. She'd just have to take a few of the larger nuggets and cash them in.

"How soon is the payment due?"

"It's…ah, past due now."

"Past due! Why didn't you let me know?"

"You're not the bank's only client, Kelly. I'm afraid I was unaware of the problem until my secretary brought it to my attention. The foreclosure papers have already been drawn."

"When's the money due?"

"Closing time tomorrow. Shall I expect you?"

"Damn right!"

Quivering with anger, Kelly stood up and slammed out of Renford's office. She had the feeling that the man was up to something, but what? He had nothing to gain from foreclosing on the ranch.

And what about Lee? She couldn't shake the feeling that he knew about the gold, that the only reason he had come to the ranch was to look for the treasure. And when he found it, he would leave without a backward glance.

Heavy-hearted, she slid behind the wheel of her car and headed for home.

Chapter Thirteen

"You look worried, *tekihila,*" Blue Crow remarked. "Is something wrong?"

"I'm having trouble with the bank."

"What kind of trouble?"

"I owe them some money for the ranch. If I don't have it by tomorrow, the bank will foreclose."

"Foreclose? What does that mean?"

"It means I won't own the land anymore. It will belong to the bank and they'll sell it to someone else."

Blue Crow traced the curve of her cheek with his fingertip. "Then you have no problem. The gold is there. Take what you need. Take it all, if you must."

"Not very long ago you told me quite emphatically that the gold was yours."

"I remember. And I also said I would decide who should have it."

"But you've spent an eternity guarding it. Somehow it doesn't seem right for me to take it."

"The gold is yours, *tekihila,*" he murmured. "I want you to have it. You may do with it as you wish."

Kelly smiled at him, relief mingling with gratitude as she murmured her heartfelt thanks.

As always, Blue Crow had come to her in the dark of the night and now they were sitting in the living room on the Navajo rug in front of the fireplace. Shadows danced over Blue Crow's bronzed chest and broad shoulders, sliding over his bare torso like a lover's caress.

The vast expanse of heavily muscled male flesh drew Kelly's hand. He shivered at her touch, a sensual shiver that bespoke his pleasure at her touch.

"Why don't I ever see you during the day?" she wondered aloud.

Blue Crow shrugged. "I guard the cave."

"What's it been like for you all these years?"

"I don't understand."

"You've been...you've been dead for over a hundred years. Have you been in the cave all that time?"

Blue Crow nodded.

"Do you ever get hungry?" Her gaze skimmed his bare chest. "Or cold?"

He smiled, his dark eyes bright with amusement. "No, *tekihila,* I don't get hungry or cold. Only lonely."

She covered his hand with hers. How had he stood it, staying in that cave, alone, for over a hundred years?

Blue Crow laced his fingers through hers. "Most of the time, I sleep," he said, answering her unspoken question. "And when I sleep, I dream, *tekihila.*"

"Do you? Of what?"

His beautiful black eyes caressed her. "I dream of you, *skuya.* You have been my companion, the light in my darkness, my only weapon against the loneliness of a hundred years."

The man had the soul of a poet, Kelly thought.

"How could you have been dreaming of me all that time? I mean," she grinned at him, "I'm only twenty-two."

"I cannot explain it to you. I only know that when I saw you, I knew you were the woman I had seen in my vision quest."

"You saw me in a vision?"

"*Han.* When I went to seek a medicine dream, I saw a woman with hair as brown and curly as a buffalo's and eyes as blue as the sky above. All my life, I searched for you. And now, too late, you are here."

His hand cupped her cheek. "You are in danger, *tekihila.* I have seen a man scouting the mountain. He has a bad heart."

"A man?"

"A *wasichu.* He has dark hair and yellow eyes, like a coyote."

Her relief that he wasn't describing Lee was almost painful.

"You should leave this place, *skuya.* You are not safe here."

"But this is my home. I don't want to leave." Tears burned her eyes. "Will you go with me?" she asked, her voice thick.

"I cannot." He brushed his knuckles against her cheek. "I cannot leave this place."

"Then I'm not going, either."

"You must."

"No, I won't leave you."

"You are a young woman, *tekihila.* You deserve a man of flesh and blood, one who can share your life, give you children."

"I won't leave you," Kelly said.

"Ah, *tekihila,*" he murmured, drawing her into his arms. "What a warrior's wife you would have made."

"I wish I had known you before," Kelly said, the tremor in her voice speaking of the pleasure his touch gave her. "Tell me, how did you come by the gold?"

"It was in the time of Long Hair," Blue Crow said. "The government had promised the *Paha Sapa* would belong to the Lakota for as long as the grass was green and the water was blue, but then Long Hair invaded the sacred hills and found the yellow iron that the white men crave as they crave firewater."

Kelly nodded. She'd never been a history buff, but she'd seen enough movies to know about Custer and the Black Hills and the Little Big Horn.

"The government tried to buy the *Paha Sapa,"* Blue Crow went on, "but *Tatanka Iyotaka,* the one your people call Sitting Bull, said no. He was a man of vision and cunning and he knew that if the white man could not buy the hills, he would steal them. Another of our chiefs who was wise in the ways of the whites decided we should gather as much gold as we could find. He, too, believed the whites would steal the hills, but he thought if we could gather enough gold, we might be able to buy them back.

"We picked up gold whenever we found it and hid it in the cave, along with whatever gold was taken in raids. But then Custer was killed at the Greasy Grass and the Army began to hunt our people. Those who were caught were sent to the reservation.

"I refused to surrender. I came here to guard the gold, hoping that one day I might be able to buy freedom for my people." He shook his head ruefully. "I never had the chance."

"And you've guarded it all these years. Has no one ever found the cave?"

"Some have come looking for the gold. None have lived to tell the tale."

Kelly bit down on her lower lip as she digested that bit of news.

"The yellow iron is mine," Blue Crow said. "I gave my life for it. Now I give it to you. Take it and leave this place. Find the happiness you deserve."

"You might as well stop trying to send me away," Kelly said, "because I'm not leaving."

"You are a stubborn woman, *skuya."*

"That's what Lee says."

Blue Crow grunted softly. "Roan Horse is blood of my blood, but he has strayed from the true path."

"That explains it, then," Kelly mused.

"Explains what?"

"Why you look so much alike. When I saw you riding the stallion, I thought it was Lee."

"He would have made a fine warrior in the old days. The blood of fighting chiefs runs hot in his veins."

"He has hot blood, that's for sure," Kelly muttered, remembering the two times when they had kissed. She had felt his hunger, the desire that arced between them whenever they were together. Kelly frowned in confusion. She loved Blue Crow, not Lee, yet she felt the same desire for both men. It was most disconcerting.

"Has he touched you?" Blue Crow asked.

"No."

"You would be good for him, *tekihila.*"

Kelly stared at Blue Crow, too astonished to speak. Good for Lee!

"He needs a woman in his life, someone to believe in him, to reawaken the softness that he has buried beneath his anger and bitterness."

"You're talking about the girl that hurt him, aren't you? How do you know about her?"

Blue Crow shook his head. "I don't know how to explain it. When I am asleep in the cave, visions of my relatives sometimes come to me. Roan Horse was shamed and dishonored by the father of the white girl. I felt his frustration when he was locked in the white man's iron house. I felt his anger, his need for vengeance. It festers deep within him."

Blue Crow put his arm around Kelly and drew her close. "Think about it, *tekihila.* Perhaps Roan Horse would be good for you, as well."

"Are you trying to get rid of me?" Kelly asked. She tried to keep her voice light, but failed miserably.

"No, *tekihila,* never think that. I love you more than life, but it is a love that can never be." He smiled at her, his expression melancholy. "The thought of you in another man's arms is like a knife in my soul, but I cannot have you, *skuya,* and since I cannot have you, it would give me great joy to know that you are still a part of me, a part of my family."

Kelly shook her head. "I don't trust Lee."

"Why is that?"

"I think he knows about the gold. I think he came here to steal it from me."

Blue Crow grunted softly. "I fear you may be right," he remarked thoughtfully, "but clouds do not always mean rain and rivers do not always run true."

"What do you mean?"

But he wasn't listening to her. He was staring at the front door through narrowed eyes. Kelly followed his gaze, wondering at his sudden wariness. When she turned to face him again, he was gone.

"I hate it when you do that," she muttered, and a moment later she heard a knock at the door.

"Kelly? You in there?" The knocking came again, louder and more insistent. "Kelly!"

It was Lee. Scrambling to her feet, she opened the door. "What's wrong?"

"Nothing now. I heard someone moving around behind the barn, but whoever it was was gone when I got there." He held out a small can of gasoline and an oily rag. "I found this."

Kelly frowned. "So?"

"So I think someone was planning to torch the barn."

"Why would anyone do that?"

"I don't know. You got any enemies around here?"

"No...well, not that I know of, anyway." She chewed the inside of her lip a moment. "What about you?" she asked. "*Have you* got any enemies around here?"

"What do you mean?"

"You're the one who sleeps in the barn." Kelly took a step backward, one hand holding the door open. "Come on in. I'll fix some coffee."

Leaving the can and the rag on the porch, Lee followed Kelly in and closed the door, then turned the key in the lock before making his way to the kitchen. He noticed she had to turn the lights on as she went. Apparently she'd been sitting in the dark.

He straddled a chair while Kelly brewed a pot of coffee. He'd assumed whoever had been prowling around was trying to drive Kelly away to get at the gold, but what if she was right, what if they'd been after him? But that was ridiculous. He didn't have any enemies around here, or friends, either, for that matter. His death wouldn't mean a thing to anybody. He didn't own anything other than a beat-up truck, a wild stallion, an old saddle and a moth-eaten war bonnet, certainly nothing worth killing for.

Lee shook his head. It had to be because of the gold. That was the only reason that made sense.

He lifted his gaze to Kelly. She was standing near the stove, her arms crossed over her breasts as she waited for the coffee to boil. Her hair, unbound, fell in a mass of unruly curls down her back and over her shoulders, a perfect frame for her tanned skin and sky-blue eyes.

He felt the first stirrings of desire as he let his gaze move over her, lingering on the swell of her breast, her narrow waist, her long shapely legs.

He cleared his throat, shifting uncomfortably on the hard wooden chair.

"What are you doing up so late?" he asked, hoping to take his mind off the enticing image of Kelly writhing beneath him.

"Nothing."

She took two mugs from the shelf over the sink and filled them with coffee. Lee took his black, but she added a generous amount of milk and sugar to her own before carrying the cups to the table. She set one down in front of Lee, then sat in the chair across from him.

"So," Lee said after taking a sip of his coffee, "you got any ideas about who might have been prowling around at this time of night, or why?"

"No." Her gaze met his, unblinking, unflinching and slightly accusing. "Do you?"

He felt a sharp stab of guilt as he shook his head. "No."

Was he imagining things, or did she look disappointed?

"Maybe it was just some kids," Kelly suggested. "You know, a prank, or an initiation of some kind."

"Maybe. Do you sit alone in the dark often?"

"What if I do?"

Lee shrugged. "Hey, calm down. I didn't mean to ruffle your feathers."

"Sorry. I've got a lot on my mind, that's all. And that reminds me, I've got to go into Coleville tomorrow. I'll be gone most of the day."

"Want some company?"

"No," Kelly said quickly. Too quickly, but she couldn't have him with her when she cashed in the gold. "I mean, well, you are working for me and I'd like to have the roof done as soon as possible. They're predicting a wet winter this year."

"Yes, ma'am, I'll get on it first thing in the morning."

"I didn't mean it that way, Lee."

"Didn't you?"

He laughed softly, bitterly, his dark eyes blazing with such anger she was surprised she hadn't been incinerated on the spot.

"Lee…" She held out her hand, palm up, in an ancient gesture of peace.

"Hey, I understand. I'm just the hired help, not somebody you'd want to be seen with in town."

"I told you I didn't mean it that way."

"Forget it," he said brusquely, and rising to his feet, he stormed out of the kitchen.

She heard the front door slam behind him and then only a long, lonely silence.

Chapter Fourteen

ஐ

He didn't come to breakfast the next morning and when she went out on the back porch to call him, she saw that his battered old truck was gone.

Frowning, she went to the barn, certain she'd find his few belongings gone, too. She tried to tell herself it would be better if he was gone, that he was a complication she didn't need in her life, but even as she tried to convince herself of that fact, she was breathing a sigh of relief that he hadn't taken his things with him.

She gave Dusty a scoop of oats, then went back to the house and ate breakfast. Forty minutes later, she was riding toward the mountain.

Her heart was beating double time when she reached the cave. Dismounting, she hurried inside, wondering if she would see Blue Crow.

Lifting the lantern high, she stared at the shelf cut into the side of the cavern. The blanket was there, but he wasn't.

She was trying to fight her disappointment when she felt a warm breath whispering against the nape of her neck.

"Tekihila."

She whirled around, her heart fluttering with happiness even before she saw him standing in the shadows.

"Blue Crow!" She put the lantern on the ground, then went gratefully into his arms, resting her head on his shoulder. "I'm so glad to see you."

"My heart soars at your nearness." He drew her closer, delighting in her nearness, in her vitality, in the bright spark of life that glowed like a flame within her.

Lightly, he stroked her hair, thinking of all the years he had dreamed of her, waited for her. "Have you come for the gold?"

Kelly nodded, though it was hard to think of such earthly things as gold and foreclosures when Blue Crow was near, when his hands were moving in her hair, when his body was pressed intimately against her own.

"Be careful, *skuya,"* he said, his arms tightening protectively around her. "I sense danger riding toward you."

"Danger? From whom?"

"The man with the yellow eyes. Be wary of strangers, *tekihila.* Trust no one."

"Not even Lee?"

"Not even Lee."

Kelly shivered, frightened by the warning in Blue Crow's voice, the concern in his eyes. "Lee left the ranch."

"I know." Blue Crow held her tight, wishing that he could go beyond the boundaries of the ranch, that he could be constantly at her side. "I will ask *Wakan Tanka* to watch over you."

"Thank you." She hugged him quickly, fiercely. "I have to go."

"Tekihila." There was a world of wanting in his voice as he cupped her face in his palms and slowly covered her mouth with his.

It was a kiss unlike any Kelly had ever known, filled with soul-deep yearnings and heartfelt dreams that could never come true. It was a kiss that spoke of caring and concern, of a love that could never be consummated.

Kelly's eyelids fluttered open and she gazed into the depths of his eyes, seeing hopelessness and the loneliness of eternity in their depths.

"Blue Crow." She could hardly speak past the lump in her throat.

"Go, *tekihila.*" Reluctantly he let her go and took a step backward. "Hurry. The sun is already high in the sky."

He was right, it was time to go, and yet leaving him there, alone in the darkness of the cave, was the hardest thing she'd ever done.

When she returned to the ranch, she saw that Lee's truck was still gone. Hurrying into the house, she quickly changed her clothes, brushed her hair, applied fresh lipstick.

Moments later she was on the road, heading east toward Coleville. She switched on the radio, only half listening as Jimmy Dean extolled the value of his pure pork sausage.

She felt a sudden heartache as Vince Gill's voice drifted over the speaker singing the same song that had been playing that night in her kitchen when Lee had almost kissed her.

Lee. Where had he gone? She hadn't meant to hurt him, but she had. No wonder he had such a low opinion of white women, she thought ruefully. Either they were accusing him of rape, or making him feel that he wasn't good enough to be seen in their company.

Well, she couldn't worry about that now. She'd apologize when she got home.

She finished her business in Coleville quickly, adroitly sidestepping the questions that came her way about where the gold had come from and how she happened to have it.

Slipping the money into her purse, she left the store and walked down the street toward her car. With each step she took, she had the feeling she was being followed. She was probably just being paranoid, she thought, seeing muggers behind every face because she had six thousand dollars in her handbag.

Reaching her car, she slipped behind the wheel, locked the door, looked over her shoulder, then pulled away from the curb.

She breathed a little easier once she'd left Coleville behind, certain she'd been imagining things.

"Good day, Miss McBride," Harry Renford said, shaking her hand. "Sit down, won't you?"

"Yes, thank you," Kelly said, unable to shake the feeling that he was surprised to see her.

"So, what can I do for you?"

"I came to settle the final payment on the ranch," Kelly said.

"Oh yes, of course. That was six thousand dollars, I believe."

"Yes, I have it right here."

"I see." He took a deep breath. "Well, then, that settles that."

"I beg your pardon?"

"Nothing. I have your receipt right here."

"And the deed?"

"Yes, it's here, as well."

Kelly stared at him, wondering at his wan expression, at the way he tugged at his collar, as if it were suddenly too tight.

"Is something wrong?"

"No, no, nothing at all."

Kelly handed him the wad of bills, watched while he counted it, twice, then wrapped the bills with a thick rubber band and deposited it in his desk drawer.

"If you'll just sign here," Renford said, "and here. That's fine."

He handed her a handwritten receipt for the six thousand dollars and the deed to the Triple M.

"I'm sure you'll find everything in order, Miss McBride, and if we can ever be of service again, please let me know."

Kelly stuffed the deed and the receipt in her purse, then stood up. "Thank you for everything."

Renford nodded. "Good-bye, Miss McBride."

His tone and the look in his eyes sent a shiver down her spine. Without a backward glance, she hurried out of his office and out of the bank.

Outside, she took a deep breath, welcoming the fresh air and the cool breeze on her face.

She was walking toward her car when she felt it again, that eerie sense of being followed, of being in danger.

Crossing the street, she stopped abruptly and whirled around, but there was no one there. Or was there? Was she imagining things again, or had she seen Lee Roan Horse duck around the corner? Or was it just that she wanted to see him?

She didn't breathe easily until she was sitting inside her car with the doors locked. For a moment, she clutched the steering wheel and then, releasing a deep sigh, she turned the key in the ignition and started for home.

It was almost dark when she pulled into the yard. The first thing she saw was Lee's truck parked near the barn. She was surprised at the relief she felt just knowing he was there, relief not only because he was back, but because it meant he couldn't have been following her in town.

He emerged from the barn as she stepped out of the car.

Kelly felt the pull between them vibrate like an electric wire. What was there about this man that attracted her so? It was more than his rugged good looks. Perhaps it was the air of vulnerability that he tried so hard to hide, perhaps it was the knowledge that he so badly needed someone to love, someone to love him. Whatever it was, it hummed between them, vital and alive and irresistible.

She watched him cross the yard toward her, felt her insides turn shivery as every step brought him closer.

"I'm sorry. Lee," she said. "I didn't mean to hurt you."

"It's all right."

"No, it's not. It's just that I needed to be alone today. I handled it badly and I'm sorry."

"Forget it."

The hunger between them was almost palpable, as was the distrust that kept them apart. Invisible, unmentioned, it rose between them, shimmering like heat waves on the desert.

A muscle throbbed in Lee's cheek. "What did you do in town?"

"I went to the bank."

"Oh?"

"Yes. I needed to pick up the deed to the ranch."

He grunted softly, clearly not believing her.

"I thought I saw you there." The words were out before she could stop them.

He grunted again, neither affirming nor denying her suspicions.

"Have you eaten?" Kelly asked.

"No."

"Me either. I've got some steaks in the fridge."

"Sounds good."

"Dinner in half an hour then?"

"Fine," he replied, but he didn't move and neither did she.

An awkward silence stretched between them.

"I wasn't in town today, Kelly. I drove out to the reservation."

"Really? Why? Do you have family out there?"

"No." He dragged a hand through his hair. "I don't know why I went out there."

He still didn't know. He'd driven around for hours before winding up at the cemetery. The graves of his family were untended, grown over with weeds. He'd spent an hour on his knees, clearing away the debris, trying not to remember how his little sister had followed him around, always wanting to be where he was, to do what he was doing. Why hadn't he spent more time with her when he'd had the chance?

Kneeling in the dirt, he'd begged for her forgiveness. For his mother, he felt nothing at all. Not love, not hate, not bitterness. She had courted death and it had found her.

He looked up, realizing Kelly was speaking to him

"I've never been to the reservation," she was saying. "I'd like to see it."

"No," he said flatly, "you wouldn't."

"Oh."

Silence settled around them again. Kelly stared down at her hands. She should go to the house, take a shower, fix dinner, but she couldn't seem to move. She slid a glance at Lee. He was standing so close, she could feel his heat, smell the perspiration and the scent of aftershave that clung to his skin. His hands were balled into tight fists, his eyes as dark as a winter night, his expression tormented.

"Kelly."

All he said was her name, but she heard more, so much more. He wanted her, wanted her in the most elemental way. He offered no promises, no words of love, nothing but a cry for help, a plea to be held while he battled the demons that were tormenting him.

She had never thought of herself as particularly maternal or nurturing—she'd never fussed over babies or felt any driving need to take on the hurts of the world. Being an only child, she tended to be selfish and self-centered. But now, gazing up into the haunted depths of Lee's eyes, she was overcome with the need to hold this man, to comfort him, to ease his loneliness.

Wordlessly she reached for his hand and led him to the house, down the narrow hall to her bedroom.

She didn't turn on any lights, didn't want him to see the indecision in her eyes.

"Kelly, maybe this isn't a good idea."

"Probably not."

"Then why...?"

"Don't talk."

She put her arms around his neck and pressed her lips to his.

It was all the invitation he needed.

With a strangled cry, he crushed her in his arms, his lips grinding against hers. She tasted blood in her mouth, felt his hands roaming restlessly over her back. And then he swung her into his arms and carried her to bed.

Somehow their clothing disappeared and they were lying in each other's arms, his hard-muscled body surrounding hers, the curves of her body filling the hollows of his.

It was everything she had ever dreamed of and more. All the fire and excitement that she'd only read about, all the wonder and magic she'd hoped for, she found in Lee's arms. His kiss gentled, his hands caressed her, aroused her, until all her doubts and fears were gone and she was aching for something she had never known.

She gasped with pain and pleasure when she felt the first sweet invasion by his body, but even as she was reaching for him, wanting to hold him closer, he was gone.

She opened her eyes to find Lee standing beside the bed staring down at her, a look of stunned disbelief on his face.

"Why didn't you tell me?"

"Tell you what?"

"That you've never done this before."

Kelly shrugged, confused by his anger. "It doesn't matter. What difference does it make?"

"It matters to me."

A vile oath escaped his lips as he pulled on his jeans, remembering other slim legs that had wrapped around his waist, other blue eyes cloudy with passion, other pink lips, lips that had spoken only lies.

He closed his eyes, his hands shoved deep into the pockets of his jeans. He felt the bile rise in his throat as he recalled the horror of being accused of rape, of being locked up, of having his every minute watched and regimented. Even in jail, rapists were considered the scum of the earth.

"Lee? What is it? What's wrong?"

He yanked his shirt over his head, grabbed his boots and headed for the door.

"Lee!"

"Leave me alone, Kelly. Please, just leave me alone."

She sat up, drawing the sheet over her breasts. "Won't you tell me what's wrong? I didn't mean to…to offend you."

He groaned low in his throat. "Kelly, it isn't you." He took a deep breath. He could feel her gaze on his back, feel her hurt and confusion. He wanted nothing more than to crawl back into bed and take her in his arms, but he couldn't.

Kelly McBride had been a virgin when he took her in his arms. She was still a virgin, at least technically, and he didn't intend to be the one to change that. He'd already ruined one girl. He didn't intend to make the same mistake twice. It had taken every ounce of self-control he possessed to let Kelly go, to back away when he felt the resistance of her maidenhead.

"Lee…"

"Good-night, Kelly."

"Wait! You aren't leaving, are you?"

He closed his eyes. Leave, he thought, that was just what he should do. But he'd come here for the gold and he wasn't leaving without it. But that wasn't the only reason he had to stay. Someone else was prowling around out there, searching for the treasure, someone who might not be averse to killing

Kelly to get what he wanted. Until he found the gold, or knew that it was gone, he'd stay and keep an eye on Kelly.

"No," he said hoarsely, "I'm not leaving."

And then, before she could ask any more of him, before his self-control shattered, he bolted from the room and shut the door behind him.

In the hallway, he braced one hand against the wall and pressed his forehead to the cool plaster. He was shaking all over, trembling from his need to protect Kelly and the startling, frightening realization that he was falling in love with Kelly McBride.

Chapter Fifteen

ꕥ

Kelly stood beside the front-room window, watching Lee wax her car. She had never known a man to work so hard. Lee was like a man driven by demons. He rose with the sun and didn't go to bed until long after dark. He had put a new roof on the house, repaired all the corral fences and the hole in the barn roof. Every day, he curried the horses, mucked the stalls. He tore down the old chicken coop and built a new one, then went into Cedar Flats and bought a dozen hens and a rooster.

Her grandfather had once kept a garden beside the house. Lee turned the soil under, fertilized it, raked it and planted a variety of vegetables.

Tomorrow he was going to start painting the house. She'd already picked out the paint, a dark blue-gray for the walls and white for the trim.

She'd mentioned once, in passing, that she'd like a brick border along the walkway that led to the house. The next day, he'd come home with a truckload of bricks and she now had a nice winding red brick path leading to the porch.

With a sigh, Kelly left the window and went into the kitchen to fix lunch. The tension between them was almost unbearable. Lee no longer took his meals in the house but ate in the barn. He was careful to keep his distance from her, never getting close enough to touch, never saying or doing anything that could be considered personal.

She still didn't understand what had happened to cause the breach between them. It didn't make sense for him to be upset that she hadn't known a dozen men before him, yet she'd never seen such anger in a man's eyes, such a look of betrayal.

And then, like dawn bursting on the horizon, she knew and wondered why it hadn't occurred to her before. He was remembering that other girl, the one who had accused him of rape.

Of course, that had to be it. Kelly grimaced. He was afraid that because one white girl had accused him of rape, it might happen again.

She experienced a moment of blinding anger that he would think her capable of such a reprehensible thing and then, as quickly as it had risen, her anger was gone, deflated by an overwhelming sadness for all he'd been through.

She made Lee a couple of thick ham and cheese sandwiches, added some potato chips and pickles to the plate, got a cold beer out of the fridge and then, taking a deep breath, she carried it outside.

He knew she was there even before he turned around. He could sense her presence, smell the faint scent of lilac soap that clung to her skin, the sweet womanly fragrance that was hers and hers alone.

"You've been working hard," Kelly said. "I thought you might be ready for a break."

"Thanks."

He tossed the rag on the hood of the car, wiped his hands on his Levi's.

"Looks good."

He lifted the sandwich from the plate, took the beer from her hands. His fingers brushed hers. That was all, just the merest touch of her fingers against his, but his body reacted instantly, warming, hardening with need.

He could mask the hunger in his eyes, but there was no way to hide the very visible evidence of his desire.

"Lee…"

"Let it go, Kelly."

"We need to talk."

"No, we don't."

"Yes, we do. I can't go on like this."

He took a long swallow of beer, wiped his mouth with the back of his wrist. "Do you want me go?"

"No, I want things to be the way they were before. I miss you. I don't like eating alone. I don't like having to watch every word I say."

"Do you think it's any easier for me?"

"No." Her gaze strayed to the telltale bulge in his jeans. "I know it isn't. I have needs, too, Lee."

"Then find someone else to satisfy them."

"I don't want anyone else."

He shook his head. *No more white women.* He drained the beer can, crushed it in his hand. *No more white women.* Kelly might think it didn't make any difference and in a lot of places, it didn't. But here in Cedar Flats, decent white women didn't sleep with Indian men. It just wasn't done. And even if it had been, she deserved far better than he could give her.

He stared at the untouched sandwich in his hand. He was a man with a police record. If it weren't for Kelly, he'd be a man without a job. He'd almost stolen her virginity. And how did he intend to repay her? By stealing the gold.

"Here." He thrust the sandwich into her hands. "You eat it."

"You must be hungry," Kelly protested. "You haven't eaten since breakfast."

Lee shook his head, knowing he'd never be able to swallow past the lump of self-disgust that was threatening to choke him.

"Talk to me," Kelly urged. "Please. Let me help."

"You want to help? Then leave me alone, Kelly, just leave me the hell alone."

He watched the effect his words had on her, each one slicing into her like a knife until she stood bleeding before him, valiantly fighting the urge to cry.

"Kelly, I'm sorry."

He wanted to take her in his arms and beg her forgiveness, but he was afraid to touch her, afraid that it would be his undoing.

Kelly squared her shoulders and raised her chin. Pride drove the tears from her eyes. She looked at him for a long moment and then, very deliberately, she dropped the sandwich in the dirt at his feet, pivoted on her heel and walked back to the house. Conscious of his gaze, she didn't run and she didn't look back.

Lee watched her walk out of sight, knowing he had to get the hell away from the Triple M before it was too late. He had put off searching for the gold, telling himself that he owed it to Kelly to fix the place up as best he could before he robbed her. He'd convinced himself she didn't need the gold. She had a decent name, a good piece of land, a career to go back to. She'd be all right and if worse came to worst, she could sell the Triple M for a good chunk of change. Anyway, she'd get married eventually and her husband would look after her.

Lee shook his head ruefully. He knew now he'd only been kidding himself. He'd been stalling because he didn't want to leave her, because he liked it here. It was the first real home he'd ever had. He'd left a part of himself on this land. His sweat and his labor were making a difference. The ranch didn't look neglected anymore. For the first time in his life, he felt a sense of pride in something he'd accomplished with his own two hands.

And as long as he was being honest with himself, he might as well admit that he'd kill any other man who dared lay a hand on her.

With an oath, he grabbed the rag and began removing the wax from the hood, hoping that the work would drive Kelly from his mind.

But it was no use. Kelly's image danced before his eyes, her curly brown hair the perfect halo for an angel's face, her lips as pink as a new rose, her eyes as blue as a midsummer sky.

He stared at his reflection in the hood of the Camaro, wondering if it was too late to start over. For too long he'd lived under the shadow of Melinda's accusation. It had followed him like a bad habit, turning up to haunt him again and again. Filled with anger and frustration, he had left home, determined never to return. But no matter how far he ran, he couldn't outrun who and what he was.

As far back as he could remember, people had been pasting labels on him. His teachers had called him a bad boy, incorrigible, wild. Time and again they'd warned him that he would come to a bad end. As he grew older, people called him a dirty Injun, a no-account redskin, and he'd proved every one of them right. Instead of trying to make something of himself when he got out of jail after he'd been arrested for breaking and entering, he'd left the state and headed west, the chip on his shoulder as big as the Grand Canyon. He had no family left, no one to give a damn if he lived or died, and he hadn't much cared, either.

He'd spent six years wandering from state to state, working at odd jobs just long enough to earn enough money to move on. He'd wasted his time and his money drinking, fighting and gambling, never letting anyone get close to him until, finally, he'd gotten so disgusted with himself that he'd gone back home, back to the reservation, drinking himself into a stupor every night in an effort to forget how miserable he was. He'd spent six months feeling sorry for himself and then, from out of the blue, he had remembered something old Frank McBride had said while they were waiting for the police to arrive.

"It ain't for you, boy. You'll never get your hands on that treasure, not you, nor none of your kin."

Treasure. That one word had sobered Lee up. He had spent the next three weeks asking questions, gradually putting together bits and pieces of stories he had heard as a child, stories the old ones had told around the campfire, tales of an ancient warrior named Blue Crow who had died protecting a fortune in gold.

Lee glanced at the mountain that loomed behind the house. Somewhere in that mountain there was a cave and in that cave was a fortune in gold. But to take what he wanted meant stealing from Kelly. When he had thought of her as the enemy, the thought of taking the gold hadn't bothered him at all. It was the Lakota way, to steal from the enemy.

But Kelly wasn't the enemy anymore.

And he didn't know how he could steal from her and live with himself afterward.

Chapter Sixteen

Lee stood in the doorway of the barn, his gaze on the house, the cigarette in his hand forgotten. Now and then he could see Kelly framed in the window as she moved around the kitchen fixing dinner.

He missed eating his meals with her, missed her nearness, the conversations they had shared. After his father left home, his family had rarely sat down to meals together. His grandmother had taken to her bed, heartbroken that her only son had shamed the family. His mother was usually barhopping at dinner time, or too drunk to eat. There had been only his little sister Tanya to keep him company and more often than not he had ignored her, too caught up in his own bitterness to think that she might be as lonely and unhappy as he was. He regretted the callous way he'd treated his sister more than he regretted anything else he'd done in his life. She'd adored him and he'd repaid her love with indifference.

A light went on in the kitchen, shining like a beacon of welcome in the gathering dusk. He saw Kelly at the sink, felt the brush of her gaze over his face.

More than anything, he wanted to go up to the house, walk into the kitchen, fold his arms around her and bury his face in her sweet-smelling hair. He wanted to tell her he was sorry for hurting her, beg for her forgiveness and start over. But the lure of the gold, of the new life it promised, held him anchored to the ground.

He dropped the cigarette butt into the dirt and stubbed it out with his boot heel.

A few minutes later the back door opened and he saw Kelly walking toward him, a cloth-covered plate in her hands.

Kelly's heartbeat accelerated when she saw Lee silhouetted in the doorway. The black T-shirt he wore clung to his torso like a second skin, outlining his muscular chest and biceps. His jeans were so old and faded they were almost white.

"Fried chicken tonight," Kelly said, her voice deliberately cool. "Hope you like it."

"I'm sure it's fine," Lee murmured. He took the plate from her hands, but his mind wasn't on food and when she turned to go, he caught her by the wrist. "Kelly…"

She kept her back to him, refusing to meet his eyes. "What?"

"I said I was sorry. I didn't mean to hurt you."

His voice poured over her, deep and dark and rich, as enticing as a chocolate sundae on a hot summer day. She wanted to forgive him, to trust him, but he'd hurt her once, hurt her more deeply than she had believed possible. She didn't want to be hurt again.

Resolutely she squared her shoulders. "My dinner's getting cold."

"Fine."

He dropped her arm as if it were something loathsome. He'd tried to apologize and she wasn't having any and maybe it was just as well. If she didn't hate him now, she would soon, so maybe it was just as well.

But he couldn't ignore the grinding ache in his gut as he watched her walk back to the house.

Cussing under his breath, he tossed the chicken into the bushes for the coyotes.

It was time to remember why he'd come here and what he hoped to gain, time to remember that Kelly McBride was just another white woman, the enemy. In the old days, her people had taken everything from his people—their land, their pride, their way of life.

Now it was time to get even.

Sitting on the sofa in the front room, Kelly stared into the darkness while her dinner grew cold. She'd reached a decision about Lee and it had killed her appetite. She stared at the food congealing on the plate. Tomorrow she would tell him she didn't need his help anymore.

A single tear rolled down her cheek. She started to wipe it away when a large, callused hand closed over hers.

"Why do you weep, *tekihila?*"

"Oh, Blue Crow," she murmured, and fell sobbing into his arms.

He held her for a long time, rocking her as he would have rocked a child, whispering her name as he stroked her hair, her back. His lips grazed her cheek, tasting the salt of her tears.

Gradually her sobs subsided. When she would have pulled away, his arms tightened around her. "Stay, *tekihila.*"

And because it felt so good to be in his arms, so right, she relaxed against him, her head pillowed on his broad shoulder.

No words were needed. She knew somehow that Blue Crow was aware of what had happened between herself and Lee, that he knew and understood.

"Do you love Roan Horse?" Blue Crow asked after a long while.

"I don't know. I thought..."

"Tell me."

"Maybe I was trying to love him because he's so much like you. I guess I thought if I couldn't have you..." Kelly raised her head from his shoulder and gazed into his eyes. "Why can't I have you?"

A sad smile lifted one corner of Blue Crow's mouth. "I would think the answer to that would be obvious, *tekihila.*"

"But…what difference does it make if you're…if you're a ghost? I can see you, touch you, hold you. You're more real to me than anyone I've ever known."

"*Tekihila…*"

"You said you'd waited for me your whole life, that you saw me in a vision."

"Perhaps I misinterpreted the vision. Perhaps you were not meant to be mine. Perhaps I was only to keep you safe for someone else."

"Who?" Kelly asked suspiciously.

"Who do you think? He needs help, *tekihila.* He has lost his faith in himself and others. Maybe you were meant to give it back to him."

Kelly shook her head. "It's the gold. He came here for the gold. That's all that's important to him."

"He may think so now."

"I've decided to send him away."

"You must do what you think is best."

"But you think I'm wrong?"

"I think you cannot change what was meant to be, *tekihila.* You may fight it, you may run from it, but in the end you cannot change it."

"So it doesn't matter if Lee stays or goes, is that what you're trying to say? That whatever is meant to happen will happen?"

"*Han.*"

She was suddenly too tired, too discouraged, to argue. Resting her head on his shoulder again, she closed her eyes, grateful for his arms around her, for his nearness.

She remembered the night that Lee had broken into her house. Just before she fainted, she had seen Lee's shadow on the wall, seen his shadow take on the shape of an eagle…

She should tell Blue Crow, she thought. Maybe he would know what *it* meant, but she tumbled over the abyss into sleep before she could form the words.

Blue Crow held her all through the night. In her sleep, she felt his nearness; when she hovered near consciousness, she was aware of his arms holding her close.

Once—she didn't know if she was awake or asleep—she let her hands wander over his broad chest, exploring the texture of his skin, the scars on his chest. She felt his lips on hers, felt her body sing a new song as his love enfolded her.

Dawn came too soon. When she woke, she was in bed alone, her cheeks damp with tears.

Staring out the window, she saw that it was raining. Lightning split the skies. Thunder rolled across the land, booming like the echo of distant drums.

Kelly turned onto her stomach and punched her pillow. On days like this, she liked nothing better than to curl up in front of the fireplace with a good book and a cup of hot chocolate. But that would have to wait. Rain or not, she had to go into Cedar Flats.

She groaned softly. She should have gone yesterday, but she'd put it off and now she was out of virtually everything.

She could send Lee, she thought, and then grimaced. *No,* she was going to fire him today. If it was fated for them to be together, then Fate could find a way to bring him back, but she wanted him gone, the sooner the better.

She'd tell him she wanted him to leave and then she'd drive into town so she wouldn't have to watch him go.

Her decision made, she jumped out of bed, took a quick shower, then pulled on a heavy sweatshirt, jeans, sweat socks and a pair of old boots.

Tying a scarf over her head, she paused with her hand on the door. She'd never fired anyone before. How, exactly, did one go about it? She puzzled over it for a moment, then shrugged. She was the boss here. She didn't have to explain her decision. She'd tell him to pack his gear and then she'd go to Cedar Flats and pray Lee would be gone when she got home.

Resolutely, she opened the door and stepped out into the yard. She was picking her way through the mud toward the barn when a sharp report cut through the storm.

Kelly felt her heart skip a beat. She'd never heard thunder like that in her life.

She had almost reached the barn when another report rang out.

Only then did she realize it wasn't thunder, but gunfire.

Kelly's gaze followed the sound of the gunshot, wondering who would be out hunting on a day like this.

With a shrug, she started walking toward the barn again when Lee barreled into her, driving her down to the ground only seconds before another gunshot rang out.

Her breath whooshed out of her body as his weight landed on top of her. She felt Lee jerk as if he'd touched a live wire and then he was firing wildly at a clump of mesquite near the barn.

There was a yelp and a moment later, the sound of a truck roaring to life.

Lee scrambled to his feet, intent on following the truck.

Kelly screamed "No!" as a tan pickup emerged from the woods behind the barn, screamed "No!" again as she saw someone poke a rifle barrel out the window. It was aimed directly at Lee.

Suddenly, everything seemed to be happening in slow motion.

Flame spurted from the barrel of the rifle.

Lee staggered backward.

Kelly saw the blood then, a bright crimson stain blossoming near his left shoulder. Another splash of red was spreading down his right thigh.

And then the truck roared out of sight, leaving behind an appalling silence broken only by the gentle whisper of the rain.

Kelly stared at Lee. He was lying on his back on the ground, one arm flung out from his body. He didn't seem to be breathing.

"Lee..." Her legs seemed to be made of wood as she walked toward him. "*Lee?*"

His eyelids fluttered open. "Kelly?"

She murmured a quiet prayer of thanksgiving as she slid her arm under his shoulders. "Can you stand up?"

"I think so." He shoved the gun into the waistband of his pants, then put his arm around her waist.

"We need to get you to a doctor," Kelly said.

She pushed the terror of the last few moments into the back of her mind. She'd cry and fall to pieces later, but now she had to take care of Lee.

"No doctor." He hissed the words through clenched teeth.

"No? What do you mean, no? You're bleeding."

"No doctors, Kelly. Gunshot wounds have to be reported."

"Lee, those men tried to kill you!"

"Could we argue later?" he asked, grimacing as pain lanced through his side and down his thigh. "I don't think I can stand up much longer."

Exasperated, Kelly helped Lee into the house and down the hallway into the spare bedroom. She threw back the covers, then stood fidgeting while he pulled the gun from his waistband and placed it on the table beside the bed, then slowly sat down on the edge of the mattress.

"Can you...? Should I...?" She took a deep breath. "You need to get out of those wet clothes," she said, not meeting his eyes. "Do you need help?"

"I'm afraid so."

With a curt nod, she knelt on the floor and pulled off his boots and socks. He obligingly unfastened his fly, stood up while she tugged on his jeans, exposing dark blue briefs and a pair of long, muscular legs.

Lee sank down on the edge of the bed while she unbuttoned his shirt and eased it off his shoulders. He didn't wear an undershirt.

She gathered up his blood-stained clothes while he crawled under the sheet.

"I'll be right back," she said, and hurried out of the room. She tossed his clothes in the hamper in her room, then went into the kitchen where she filled the teapot with water and put it on the stove. While she waited for the water to heat, she went into the bathroom to towel dry her hair and change out of her wet clothes, then she rummaged around in the medicine cabinet to see what kind of first aid supplies she could find.

Ten minutes later, fortified with a cup of strong black coffee, she went back into the bedroom. She drew the sheet away from Lee's injured thigh and shoulder, sucking in a deep breath when she saw the two bullet wounds. For all the bloody *Lethal Weapon* and *Rambo* movies she'd seen, she wasn't prepared for the real thing. Both wounds were red and ugly and dripping blood. Lee's face was pale and sheened with perspiration.

Kelly's hands were trembling as she placed squares of cloth over the wounds to stop the bleeding.

"Lee, I don't know what to do. Please let me take you to a doctor."

"No, Kelly. Just pour some iodine over it and bandage me up. I'll be okay."

When she started to argue, he jackknifed into a sitting position and grabbed her by the arm.

"Dammit, Kelly, just do as I say. I'll explain later." He took a deep breath, fighting against the blackness that was hovering all around him. "Please, *skuya*."

"All right."

"If I pass out, don't worry. Just do what I said. Did you lock the front door?"

"No."

"Do it now, before you do anything else. Check the back door, too, and the windows."

He was scaring her, he could see it in her face, gone suddenly pale, in the way her eyes widened.

"Trust me, Kelly, just this once. Do as I say. And don't go outside. I'll explain everything later."

Driven by a rising, all-encompassing fear, Kelly ran into the front room and locked the door. She checked all the windows, drew the curtains, then did the same in all the other rooms before returning to the back bedroom.

Lee's eyes were closed. His face was drawn and pale. The makeshift bandages on his shoulder and thigh looked very white against the dark bronze of his skin.

"You got any whiskey, *skuya?*"

"Yes."

"Think you could bring me some?"

"Sure." She didn't drink, but her grandfather had liked a snort every now and then.

She found a bottle in the cupboard in the kitchen, poured a good-sized amount in a glass and added some water. She started back toward the bedroom, paused and retrieved the bottle.

Lee's eyes were still closed when she returned to the guest room. If possible, he looked even paler than before.

"Lee?"

He opened his eyes and she placed the bottle on the table, then slid one hand under his head while he took a drink.

"I think you could use a little fortifying yourself," Lee remarked. "Your hands are shaking."

"I'm scared."

"I know. Drink a little of the whiskey, Kelly, it'll calm your nerves."

She lowered his head to the pillow, then stared skeptically at the small amount of whiskey left in the glass. She'd never tasted anything stronger than wine, but she was game to try anything that would still the shaking in her hands. The whiskey was strong and burned a path all the way down her throat to her stomach. Amazingly, it did make her feel better.

"Thatta girl," Lee murmured.

For Kelly, the next forty minutes were the most nerve-wracking she'd ever spent. She swallowed the bile that rose in her throat as she washed the ugly wounds in his shoulder and thigh, trying not to notice the blood on her hands or the way the water in the bowl turned from clear to scarlet.

When that was done, she poured iodine over the bullet wounds, front and back, acutely aware of the pain she was causing Lee. He endured her amateurish doctoring in stony silence, his hands clenched into tight fists, while perspiration dripped from his face and neck, soaking the pillowcase. She breathed a sigh of relief as she taped the last bandage into place.

When she was finished, she stared at the bowl of blood-stained water on the bedside table. Never in her life had she treated anything more serious than a paper cut.

"You okay, Kelly? You look a little pale."

"I'll be all right."

"You sure?"

She wanted to say yes. Instead, she shook her head, then bolted for the bathroom where she was violently ill.

Grabbing a towel from the side of the tub, Kelly wiped her mouth and face, then stood up. She rinsed her mouth, brushed the hair from her forehead and went back into the bedroom.

Lee regarded her through eyes that were faintly amused. "I think you're in worse shape than I am.

"I doubt it. Can I get you anything?"

"Some more whiskey?"

"Is that a good idea?"

"At this point I don't much care."

She poured some whiskey into the glass. When she would have added water, he shook his head.

"I'll take it straight," he said, and drained the glass in two quick swallows.

"Lee, what's going on?"

"Later, Kelly," he murmured.

"You promised..."

"I know, but I'm...so...tired." His eyelids fluttered down. "The gun," he said, his voice growing faint. "Keep it close..."

Kelly stared at him. The whiskey and the pain and the loss of blood had caught up with him, she thought and wished that she, too, could lose herself in oblivion, but she was too frazzled even to think of sleep.

She took the gun from the bedside table, its weight somehow reassuring as she walked through the house, rechecking the doors and windows.

She was surprised to see that it was still raining, a slow, steady drizzle.

Returning to the guest room, she sat down in the faded overstuffed chair in the corner, the gun in her lap. Drawing her legs up beneath her, she stared at Lee, watching the shallow rise and fall of his chest. He'd been shot. He could have been killed. Why? Who was after him and what did they want?

She knew the answer, knew it as surely as she knew the rain would stop and the sun would shine.

They hadn't been after Lee at all.

They were after her.

They were after the gold.

Chapter Seventeen

"So, what have you learned?"

The two men standing in front of the desk exchanged glances. "Nothing."

"Nothing?" Renford leaned forward, his gaze intent on the face of the man with the odd-colored yellow eyes. "You assured me you'd be able to locate the gold within a week."

"I miscalculated."

"I'm not paying for miscalculations, Trask, I'm paying for information."

"Yeah, well..." Trask slid a glance at his partner.

The shorter man shrugged. "We...uh...changed our tactics a little."

"A little!" Trask exclaimed. "Bradford took a shot at the girl."

"You idiot! She's the only one who knows where to find the gold."

"He didn't hit the girl," Trask said brusquely.

Harry Renford squirmed in his chair. It had been a mistake, hiring these two thugs. Both were wanted men. He'd thought the promise of easy money would keep them in line but now he wasn't so sure.

He resisted the urge to wipe the perspiration beading on his brow. He was in too deep and they knew too much for him to turn back now. Secretly, he was afraid of Trask, afraid of the greed that burned in the man's cold yellow eyes.

"I don't want any more shooting," Harry said. "Is that clear? I only want to know if the gold exists, nothing else!"

"Sure, boss, don't worry." Trask fixed his partner with a hard stare. "This time we'll do it my way."

Chapter Eighteen

☙

Kelly sat with Lee until he fell asleep and then, after checking all the doors and windows one more time, she went to bed, only to toss and turn restlessly. Twice, nightmares woke her.

The third time she woke up, she found Blue Crow sitting on the foot of her bed.

"Go back to sleep, *tekihila,*" he whispered. "I will keep watch."

"You know what happened?"

"*Han.* It was the man I warned you about, the one with the yellow eyes."

"I'm scared, Blue Crow."

"I know." He rose from the bed and padded quietly to her side. "I will keep you safe, *tekihila,* so long as I am able."

"Hold me?"

He murmured a soft sound of assent as he sank down on the bed beside her and drew her into his arms. The long blue sleeping gown she wore felt like dandelion fluff against his bare chest.

They fit together perfectly, Kelly thought as she snuggled against Blue Crow, like a hand in a glove, or two halves of the same whole.

She ran her fingertips over his broad back, amazed anew at the pleasure she found in touching him. He seemed so real, so alive, it was hard to remember that he was a ghost, a phantom who came to her in the dark of the night.

"*Tekihila...*"

His voice was low and husky, filled with the yearning of a hundred years. His hand played in her hair, caressed her nape, slid down her back, and everywhere he touched, she felt little frissons of sensual delight.

She gazed up into his eyes, eyes dark with passion, as Lee's had been dark the night she had almost lost her virginity. It was eerie, the resemblance between the two men. Sometimes she thought Lee and Blue Crow shared the same soul.

Blue Crow's gaze met hers. "You are thinking of Roan Horse," he remarked.

Kelly nodded. "You're so much alike, sometimes I forget you're not him."

"You have learned to care for him?"

"Yes."

Blue Crow nodded. It was what he wanted, what he hoped for, yet he couldn't suppress the sharp stab of jealousy that coursed through him when he thought of Kelly in another man's arms.

"Has he made you his woman?"

Kelly felt the heat flood her cheeks in bright red waves. Mute, she stared into Blue Crow's eyes, wondering what to say. Though they had been intimate, she wasn't sure if Lee considered her to be his woman. As far as that went, she didn't know if she wanted to be Lee's woman—she didn't even know if she trusted him.

"Do you love him?"

"I don't know."

"Does he love you?"

"I don't think so."

"Think again, *tekihila. I* have seen into his heart. He holds only good feelings for you, though he tries to fight them." Blue Crow smiled pensively. "He is afraid of you."

"Afraid? Of me?"

"*Han.*"

"Why?"

"You are white, *skuya.* Roan Horse has no good memories of anyone who is white."

Blue Crow's finger traced the line of her jaw, the curve of her cheek. "You did not answer my question, *tekihila.* Has he made you his wornan?"

"Not exactly."

Blue Crow stared at her, one black brow arched in confusion. "I do not understand."

"He...we...that is, we started to..." Kelly shook her head. "He did and he didn't."

"Are you still a maiden?"

"Yes, but a very experienced one."

Blue Crow frowned. "You talk in riddles."

"We started to make love, but when he discovered I'd never been with a man that way before, he got angry and left."

"Ah, now I understand." Blue Crow smiled with pride. "He did not wish to defile you. Truly, he has the heart of a warrior."

"I guess so," Kelly said, and then yawned.

"Sleep, *tekihila.* I will stay with you until *anpetu wi* chases *hanhepi wi* from the sky."

"Lie with me."

With a sigh, he slid under the covers beside her, then drew her into his arms. It was torture of the sweetest kind, lying next to her, holding her close. The faint flowery scent of her perfume rose in his nostrils. Her hand rested against his chest and he could feel the warm swell of her breast against his side.

"Good night, Blue Crow."

"Rest well, *tekihila.*"

"You, too," she replied sleepily.

Blue Crow grunted softly. He would not rest this night, not with Kelly nestled against him, the heat and curves of her body playing havoc with his senses.

Holding her close, he stared into the darkness and prayed his self-control would last until dawn.

It was still raining when Kelly woke the following morning. She pulled on a pair of comfortable jeans and an oversize sweatshirt, stepped into a pair of furry bedroom slippers, then headed for the kitchen. There was just enough instant coffee left to make two cups.

While she waited for the water to heat, she called Brewer's Market and learned, to her dismay, that they didn't deliver except in rare cases of emergency.

Kelly hesitated and then assured Tom Brewer that this was, indeed, an emergency and she was too ill to drive into town.

Brewer was sympathetic as he took her order, assuring her that his son would be out sometime before noon with her order.

Thanking him effusively, Kelly hung up the phone, made two cups of coffee and carried them into the guest bedroom.

Lee was still asleep. After setting the mugs on the antique oak dresser, she laid her hand on Lee's brow. His skin was hotter than it should have been, she thought.

She watched him for a couple of minutes while she debated which he needed more: rest, or something to bring down his fever.

Frowning, she went into the bathroom and rummaged through the medicine cabinet for a bottle of aspirin. She filled a glass with water, then returned to the bedroom.

Lee was tossing restlessly, his hands clutching the covers, his knuckles white with the strain.

"Cowards! Turn me loose!"

Kelly bit down on her lip as she watched Lee's body go rigid. His lips drew back in a grimace and then he began to swear, his voice harsh, raspy with pain.

She couldn't bear to watch. Bending over him, she placed her hand on his uninjured shoulder and shook it gently

"Lee. Lee, wake up."

A vile oath hissed between his teeth and he sat up, thrashing wildly.

Kelly gasped as his fist slammed into her face just below her left eye. She reeled back, momentarily stunned, her hand automatically cupping her bruised cheek.

Lee fell back on the pillows, a low moan rumbling in his throat. "Don't hit me again," he whispered. "For the love of God, don't hit me again."

Cautiously, Kelly approached the bed again. "Lee, wake up."

A muscle worked in his jaw. "Damn you!" he roared. "If my hands were free, I'd beat the shit out of all of you!"

Where was he, who was he hiding from? Taking her courage in hand, she shook his shoulder again. "Lee, wake up. It's Kelly."

"Kelly?"

He opened his eyes, eyes that were dark and wild. For a moment he looked disoriented and then his gaze focused on her face.

"Kelly?"

"I brought you a cup of coffee."

"Coffee?"

"Lee, are you all right?"

He stared past her, his gaze sweeping over the room. Gradually he released his death grip on the covers.

"Let me help you sit up." She reached behind him, plumping the pillows, then helped him to a sitting position. "That better?"

"Yeah, thanks."

"Here." She handed him one of the mugs.

He drank it quickly, welcoming the warmth, the bitterness.

"Would you like some more?" Kelly asked, and when he nodded, she handed him her cup. "Go on, take it," she said when he started to refuse. "That's all there is until the Brewer kid shows up with the groceries I ordered. Go on, drink it. You need it more than I do."

For once, he didn't argue.

"Can I ask you something?"

"You can ask," he replied guardedly.

"What were you dreaming about?"

He stared up at her through eyes gone suddenly cold. "Why?"

"I...you were talking in your sleep and I wondered... Never mind, it doesn't matter."

"I'll tell you, if you'll tell me something?"

"What?"

"What happened to your eye?"

Kelly lifted a hand to her bruised cheek. "My eye?"

"It's turning black and blue."

"Is it?"

"What happened, Kelly?"

"Nothing."

"Did I do it?"

She turned her head to avoid his probing gaze.

"Did I?"

Kelly nodded. "You were having a nightmare and when I tried to wake you, you struck out. It was an accident."

"I'm sorry."

"It's all right. It doesn't hurt." She grinned at him. "Much." She folded her arms over her breasts and looked at him expectantly. "Now it's your turn."

"I'd rather not talk about it."

"That's not fair, Lee."

He stared into the empty coffee cup clutched in his hands. "I got sick while I was in juvenile hall. Ran a high fever for a couple of days. Sometimes when I get sick, it brings back memories I'd just as soon forget."

"Did someone beat you while you were there?"

His hands tightened around the mug until she thought it would shatter.

"Yeah."

"Who?"

A muscle worked in his jaw as the memories came flooding back, memories of constantly being teased and harassed because he was an Indian, memories of being cornered in the shower, of four white guys holding him down on the cold tile floor while a fifth beat him.

"Lee?"

He couldn't tell her. He couldn't tell her how bad it had been, how alone he had been. His sister had been too young to visit him. And his mother—she'd come once in eighteen months, so drunk she could hardly stand up. He'd never forget the humiliation he had felt when she walked into the rec room, her long black hair stringy and unwashed, her steps uneven. He'd never forget the way she had cried and carried on about seeing "her boy" locked up because of what some *wasichu* girl had accused him of. That was the night the five white boys had ganged up on him, threatening to castrate him if he ever looked at another white girl.

"Don't ask me, Kelly."

"All right."

Teeth clenched, he put the mug on the night-stand, then swung his legs over the side of the bed.

"What are you doing?" Kelly asked, alarmed.

"I need to…dammit, I need to use the bathroom."

"I'll help you."

"No."

"Lee, you've been shot, remember? You've got a fever. Now stop being foolish and let me help you."

"I can do it."

"Let me get you a bedpan."

"No!"

Shaking her head, Kelly gathered up the mugs and stomped out of the bedroom. Men! Stupid macho jerks, all of them!

Standing up was a mistake. His legs felt like rubber and a wave of dizziness sent the room spinning out of focus. He knew he would have fallen if Kelly hadn't chosen that moment to return.

With a cry, she ran forward and wrapped her arm around his waist.

"Now will you let me help you?" she asked dryly

Lee nodded. Draping one arm over her shoulders, he let her help him down the hall to the bathroom, thinking there was nothing like sickness to rob a man of his pride.

Kelly kept her head lowered as she helped Lee down the hallway. For all her bluster, she was as embarrassed as he was. Embarrassed and acutely aware of the fact that he was wearing nothing but a pair of skimpy briefs. Why hadn't she thought to wrap a blanket around him, if not to keep him warm, then to cover up all that bronze flesh? She tried not to remember the night they had almost made love, tried not to think of how warm and solid and intoxicating his touch had been.

Don't think about it, she chided herself. You were going to fire him, remember? If he hadn't gotten shot he'd be gone by now…

She glanced up, her cheeks flaming with the memory of that night, when he opened the door.

Wordlessly, she slipped her arm around his waist. trying not to notice the way his skin felt beneath her hand.

When he was settled back into bed, she poured him a glass of water, handed him a couple of aspirin and fled the room.

She spent the next hour scrubbing the kitchen floor and scouring the old tin sink and when that was done, she washed the stove inside and out.

She was about to start on the bathroom when there was a knock at the front door.

"Who's there?" she called.

"It's me, Jeff Brewer."

Kelly let out the breath she'd been holding, then opened the door. "Come on in, Jeff. I'm sorry you had to come in this weather."

"That's okay. Where do you want this?"

"In the kitchen on the table, please.

"There's another box and a bag in the truck."

"I was out of just about everything."

"My pa said you were sick."

"I'm feeling better, but I didn't want to go out in the rain."

"Yeah. I don't blame you." He put the box on the table, then went out to get the rest of her order.

Feeling safe with Jeff there, she ran out to the barn to feed and water the horses, then hurried back to the house.

Jeff was waiting for her on the front porch. "Anything else I can do for you, Miss McBride?" he asked politely.

"No, thanks, Jeff," Kelly said. "Tell your dad I really appreciate this."

"Sure 'nough. Take care of yourself, Miss McBride."

"Thank you, Jeff. Goodbye. And drive carefully."

He waved at her as he climbed behind the wheel of a bright green truck with the name BREWER'S FAMILY MARKET outlined in white letters on the side.

Kelly closed and locked the door, then went into the kitchen and began putting the groceries away. She'd emptied one box and was starting on another when she realized she was no longer alone. Glancing over her shoulder, she saw Lee standing in the doorway, a blanket draped around shoulders.

"You should be in bed," Kelly said.

"I got…lonely."

"You'd better sit down before you fall down. You look as pale as a ghost," she said, and then grinned. The only ghost she knew wasn't pale at all.

"Something funny?" Lee asked as he sank down on one of the kitchen chairs.

"No. Are you hungry? We have food again."

He shook his head. "Got any coffee in there?"

"Sure. But you need to eat. Some oatmeal, maybe?"

"Oatmeal!" He grimaced as though he were in pain.

"It's good for you." She sighed in exasperation. "How about some scrambled eggs and toast? And some orange juice?"

"Anything," he said, "just quit nagging me."

Kelly watched him out of the corner of her eye while she brewed a pot of coffee and scrambled a half-dozen eggs. He looked as though he were in pain, but she thought the hurt went far deeper than the two gunshot wounds.

With a weary sigh, he crossed his arms on the table and rested his head on his forearms. He looked terribly vulnerable.

The urge to comfort him rose up within her until it was all she could do not to reach out and stroke his head, to tell him that everything would be all right, that he wasn't alone any longer.

But she didn't. Fear of being rebuffed kept her from reaching out—the memory of his voice telling her to just leave him the hell alone made her turn away.

He was asleep by the time the eggs were cooked and this time she let him sleep, deciding he needed rest more than anything else.

She stared at the eggs and then, with a shrug, tossed them into the garbage.

Leaving the kitchen, she went into the guest room and changed the sheets on the bed. She filled the pitcher at his bedside with fresh water, then went into her own room and made up the bed.

When she went back into the kitchen, Lee was awake.

"How do you feel?" she asked.

"Like hell."

She grunted softly as she placed her hand on his brow. "You're burning up. Come on, you need to get back into bed."

He didn't argue and that worried her more than anything else.

Chapter Nineteen

ജ

His fever worsened during the night. Nothing she gave him seemed to help. Time and again she paced to the window and stared out into the darkness, wishing the rain would stop, wishing she hadn't promised not to call the doctor. If Lee wasn't better by morning, she'd call the hospital, promise or no promise.

She made him drink as much water as he could hold, applied more antiseptic to his wounds, noting that the one in his shoulder looked raw and red. She taped a fresh bandage in place, knowing she was wasting her time. Lee needed more help than she was capable of giving.

In despair, she went to the window and gazed out into the darkness. "Please, God, help me..."

"Tekihila?"

"Blue Crow!" She ran to his arms. "I've never been so glad to see anybody in my life."

"What is wrong?"

"Lee's got a fever and I can't bring it down. I think the wound in his shoulder is infected." She shook her head. "I don't know what to do."

"It will be all right, *skuya,"* Blue Crow murmured.

And she believed him. Standing in his embrace, his arms warm and strong around her, she believed him.

Blue Crow smiled down at her and then, because she was so close, because her eyes were as blue as the wildflowers that grew along the Little Big Horn, because her skin was smooth and soft, because she glowed with life, he bent his head and kissed her.

It was only a gentle kiss, meant to reassure her, but it quickly built to something much more intense. He groaned as her arms went around his neck, felt his heart begin to pound like a Lakota war drum as she pressed her body to his. Her heat went through him like chain lightning, making him feel strong and vitally alive.

Holding her, knowing she could never be his, filled him with a soul-deep sadness, a hurt that went deeper than pain.

"*Tekihila.*" Holding her close, he rested his chin on the top of her head, wishing that he had known her when he was alive, when he could have claimed her for his own. Why? he thought, his heart twisting with anguish, why had he found her now when she could never be his?

"Blue Crow?"

He drew back a little so he could look down into her eyes. "What is it, *tekihila?*"

"I don't know. You seem so sad."

"I am not sad, *skuya.*"

"You wouldn't lie to me, would you?"

"No," he replied quietly. "I would not lie to you. I am not sad, *tekihila.* Only filled with regret that we did not meet a hundred years ago. I would have courted you as ardently as ever a warrior courted a maiden. I would have gone to one of the Buffalo Dreamers to obtain a love song and then I would have played my flute outside your lodge. When the time was right, I would have taken horses to your father, as many as he required. And if he had refused to let you be my wife, I would have kidnapped you and taken you far away."

"Would you?"

"*Han.*"

"And then what?"

"I would have made a home for you and given you sons, *tekihila,* many sons."

"And daughters?" Kelly asked tremulously.

"Maybe one," Blue Crow allowed with a smile. "If she was as beautiful as you."

"I wish I had lived back then," Kelly said. "But wishing won't make it so."

"No."

"But you're here with me now." Her arms tightened around him and she buried her face against his chest. "Never leave me, Blue Crow," she murmured. "Promise me."

"I don't know if I can make a promise like that, *tekihila.* If *Wakan Tanka* calls me, I must go."

"No!"

He held her close, rocking her against him. "Let us not speak of parting," he said. And then, because it was painful to hold her close and not possess her, he drew away. "Come, let us look in on Roan Horse."

Lee! She'd forgotten all about him.

She followed Blue Crow into the guest room, stood on the opposite side of the bed while Blue Crow examined Lee's wounds, his face lined with concern.

"He'll be all right, won't he?" she asked.

"The wound in his shoulder is not healing."

"I wanted to take him to a doctor, but he wouldn't let me. Maybe…"

"There is no need for a *wasichu* medicine man," Blue Crow said.

"You mean it's too late, that nothing can be done?"

"No." Blue Crow drew the covers over Lee, then went to Kelly and took her in his arms. "There are plants nearby that will draw the poison from the wound. I will gather some."

He smiled down at her. "Do not worry, *tekihila,* all will be well." He pressed his lips to her brow. "I will be back soon."

"Hurry."

Blue Crow returned an hour later. Kelly watched as he built a small fire in an old tin bucket, then dropped a handful of sage and sweet grass onto the flames. Soon a plume of sweet-smelling smoke rose from the bucket.

Plucking an eagle feather from his hair, Blue Crow drew it over the bucket, drawing the smoke toward Lee. When that was done, he ground some leaves that Kelly thought looked like comfrey and marigold into a thick paste, then spread it over the wound in Lee's shoulder and all the while he chanted softly.

The words, sung in a minor key, filled Kelly's mind with images of running buffalo, of tipis scattered over a grassy plain, of sun and wind and the sound of rushing water.

"I brought some herbs which you must brew," Blue Crow remarked, turning away from the bed. "When he wakes up, you must make him drink as much of it as he can hold."

"Okay."

"Okay?"

Kelly smiled. "I mean I will."

"Han." Deftly he wrapped Lee's shoulder in a length of soft cloth. "He will recover, *tekihila.* He is young and strong." Blue Crow's gaze moved slowly over Kelly's face. "And he has much to live for."

The heat in his eyes burned through her, as warm and welcome as sunshine. The faint hint of jealousy in his voice filled her feminine heart with joy.

"Blue Crow…"

"You will be good for him, *skuya.* With you at his side, he will become the man he should be."

"What are you saying?"

"He cares for you," Blue Crow replied. His hands curled into tight fists. "You care for him. What else is there to say?"

Kelly shook her head. "No, it's not like that."

"Tekihila, did you not tell me that he made love to you?"

"Yes."

"You would not have let him do so if you did not care for him."

"That's true, but it's you I love, Blue Crow. Only you."

Her words were the sweetest pain he had ever known. But, as much as he loved her, desired her, yearned for her, she could never be his.

"Your love is wasted on me," he said, his voice harsh.

"No!"

The sight of her tears tore at his heart. Regret sliced through him, sharp as a Lakota skinning knife.

"*Tekihila,* forgive me," he implored. Tenderly he drew his thumbs across her cheeks to wipe away her tears and then he drew her into his arms. "Do not weep, *wastelakapi.* I cannot bear your tears."

"My love is not wasted," she said, her voice muffled against his chest.

"I know. I was wrong to say such a thing."

Kelly sniffed. "What was that word you said?"

"*Wastelakapi?*"

She nodded. "Yes. What does it mean?"

"Beloved."

"Am I? Your beloved?"

Blue Crow placed his forefinger under her chin and tilted her head up. "Do you not know that you are? There has been no other woman for me, *tekihila.*"

"You've never been in love?"

"No."

"But you've…you know?"

"I am a warrior," he replied, as if that explained everything.

"Of course," Kelly said, but inwardly she was seething with jealousy. She told herself she was being foolish. Any woman he might have had was long dead, but it didn't matter. He'd had other women.

Blue Crow looked past Kelly to the window. Outside, the rain had stopped. In the east, the sky was growing light. His arms tightened around Kelly's waist.

"I must go. Do not forget about the tea. Make it strong."

Kelly nodded. When he started to pull away, she held him close, pressing herself against him, drawing his warmth, his strength, into herself.

"Tekihila..."

"I know. It's just that I miss you so much when you're gone."

"No more than I miss you." He lowered his head to hers and kissed her then, savoring the sweet taste of her lips. She was light and life, banishing the darkness from his existence, and he loved her beyond words. One last kiss and then he was gone. Gone before his resolve disappeared, weakened by the tears that shimmered in her eyes and the silent invitation of moist pink lips.

Kelly stared after him for a moment, then sank into the chair beside the bed. Taking up the cloth from the bedside table, she dipped it in the bowl of water, wrung it out and began to sponge Lee's fevered face, neck and chest.

He stirred restlessly on the bed, muttering incoherently in a language she didn't understand. His hands worried the covers, clenching and unclenching. Once he cried out, as if in pain.

Dropping the cloth into the bowl, Kelly took one of Lee's hands in hers.

"Rest, Lee," she murmured soothingly. "You're safe here. No one will hurt you."

At the sound of her voice, his eyelids fluttered open. "Kelly?" His gaze darted around the room. "Where am I?"

"At the Triple M."

"The Triple M?"

She nodded. "Just rest, Lee, everything will be all right."

"I thought I saw an Indian."

"An Indian?"

He stared up at her. "I know it sounds crazy, but...never mind."

"Tell me."

"Not now. I'm cold, so cold."

Rising, she went into the linen closet and pulled out another blanket. After covering Lee, she went into the kitchen, filled the teapot with water and put it on the stove to heat.

She thought about Blue Crow while she waited for the water to boil. She was in love with a ghost, but a ghost unlike anything she had ever imagined. Ghosts were supposed to be invisible, weren't they? Able to walk through walls, to make things go bump in the night. But there was nothing spectral about Blue Crow. He was flesh and blood, as warm and real as any man she had ever seen. How was it possible?

The whistle of the teakettle scattered her thoughts. She dumped the herbs into the pot, let them steep until the water was dark green, then filled a mug with the bitter-looking brew.

Lee was staring out the window when she returned to his room.

"Here," she said, "I've brought you something to drink."

"What is it?"

"Herb tea. It'll do you good."

She piled the pillows behind his head so he could sit up, held the cup while he drank even though he insisted he didn't need her help.

He grimaced as he took a drink. "Tastes awful," he muttered.

"Drink it anyway."

"Where'd you get this stuff?"

"Just drink it, Lee."

He drained the cup and then made a face, as if he were in pain.

"What's wrong?"

"I don't think that hot tea was such a good idea. I need to… you know."

"I'll get the bedpan," Kelly said. "I don't think you should get up."

"I don't want a bedpan."

"Lee Roan Horse, you are the worst patient I've ever had."

"I'm probably the only one you've ever had."

"That's beside the point."

She left the room in a huff, returning a moment later with an old slop jar she had found in her grandfather's closet. It was an antique. She had painted blue flowers on it and filled it with a bouquet of dried flowers, which she now removed. "Do you, uh, need help?"

"No." Lee ground the word out through clenched teeth. Damn, but it was humiliating being waited on by a woman, especially a woman he wanted as much as he wanted Kelly McBride.

With a curt nod, Kelly left the room, grateful that he'd refused her help.

She gave him ten minutes, hoping it would be enough. When she returned to his room, the pan was on the floor. She emptied it, washed her hands, then went back to Lee's bedside.

"Can I get you anything else?"

"Would you lie down with me?"

"Why?"

"I'm still cold."

She hesitated a moment, then crawled under the covers and took him in her arms. She could feel him shivering against her, feel the length of a long bare leg pressing against hers. His arm was heavy across her waist, his breath warm against her neck.

Her emotions ran riot as she remembered lying naked in his arms, on the brink of discovery. She looked down at him, at the long black hair that fell over his shoulders and tickled her cheek.

She tried to think of something other than bare bronze skin, or the fact that they were pressed intimately together, that she had lost her innocence, if not her virginity, to this man.

She held him a long time, her fingertips gliding over his arm. Gradually his shivering ceased, his breathing grew even and she knew that he was asleep.

She'd get up in a minute, she told herself. Just another minute. But he snuggled against her, his head resting on her breast, his arm holding her close. The minutes turned to hours, but she didn't get out of bed.

Lee woke to darkness, instantly aware that he was holding a woman in his arms, that their legs were entwined, that her head was pillowed on his shoulder.

Kelly! What was she doing in his bed?

He frowned. He'd been sick with a fever and she'd cared for him. He'd had one of his old nightmares, reliving the days he'd spent in that damned correctional facility. Funny, he always dreamed about getting the crap kicked out of him, but never about getting even. And he had gotten even. In spades. He'd found the five guys who'd beat him up. Found them alone, one by one. They'd never touched him again.

His frown deepened. Had he imagined it, or had he seen an Indian beside his bed? An Indian who wore a golden eagle on a leather thong around his neck. The same Indian he'd seen in his vision.

Lee shook his head. He must have been dreaming.

He looked down at Kelly, felt his heart turn over in his chest. She was so lovely. So young. So innocent. He felt his body harden as he remembered how she had felt in his arms, how close he had come to stealing something from her that was more precious than the gold he coveted.

She made a soft sleepy sound as she turned onto her side, her breasts pressing against his chest, igniting a fire in his body hotter than any fever.

He tore his gaze from her face and stared out the window. Someone had tried to kill Kelly. The reason seemed obvious. Someone besides himself knew about the gold and wanted it badly enough to kill for it. But who?

It had all happened so fast, he hadn't gotten a good look at the truck, or the two men inside. He remembered the rifle, though. He'd looked down the barrel and knew he was looking into the face of death, but his only thought had been to save Kelly.

He moved his injured shoulder tentatively. It was as stiff and sore as the very devil. His thigh, too. But his fever seemed to be gone. And he was hungry. Always a good sign.

He glanced down at Kelly to find her staring back at him, her cheeks rosy with embarrassment.

An awkward silence stretched between them.

Kelly wished she could think of something to say, but she was all too aware of Lee's bare legs entangled with her own, of the solid wall of his chest against her breasts, of the very tangible evidence that he was feeling much better.

Lee broke the silence with a muttered, "Good morning."

"Morning," Kelly replied. She lifted a hand to his brow, pleased that his skin was cool to the touch.

There seemed to be no graceful or tactful way to extricate herself from his arms, so she simply rolled away from him and got up.

"I'll go fix breakfast," she said over her shoulder and hurried out of the room.

She washed quickly, changed into a pair of dark blue sweats and a loose-fitting white sweater, socks and her boots. After looking out the window, she opened the door and ran to the barn. The horses whinnied at her, obviously upset because she had neglected to feed them the night before. She tossed them each two flakes of hay, made sure they had water, threw a couple of handfuls of chicken feed to the hens, then ran back to the house.

In the kitchen, she made a pot of strong black coffee, fried up some bacon and eggs and poured two glasses of orange juice.

She'd spent the night in Lee's arms. Worse, she'd been glad to be there when she woke up.

She could hear him moving around in the bedroom. A moment later she saw him walk unsteadily down the hallway toward the bathroom, a blanket draped over his shoulders. Stubborn man. Why did he insist on doing everything the hard way?

She was placing his breakfast on a tray when he entered the kitchen.

"I'd rather eat in here," he said, sinking down on one of the chairs.

"You should be in bed."

"I've been in bed for two days."

"You ought to be in a hospital."

"Are you always such a nag in the morning?"

"Are you always this stubborn?"

"I'm not stubborn. I'm hungry."

"You are?" She smiled, pleased. Surely that meant he was getting better.

She handed him his breakfast, put her own plate on the table and sat down across from him.

He was indeed hungry. He wolfed down everything on his plate before she'd made a dent in her own meal.

"There's more," she said, and before he could argue, she got up and refilled his plate. "More coffee?"

Lee nodded. "Thanks."

After breakfast, she insisted on checking on his wounds. Lee frowned when she took the bandage from his shoulder.

"Did you do this?" he asked, gesturing at the poultice on his shoulder.

"I..." Her gaze slid away from his. "Of course."

Lee looked at her suspiciously. "This is an old Indian remedy."

"Is it?"

Lee stared down at the table for a moment, trying to remember what he'd seen, what he'd heard, but it was all so hazy.

Muttering an oath, he fixed his gaze on Kelly's face again. "He was here, wasn't he?"

"Who?"

"I don't know his name. Until now, I thought I'd dreamed it all, the chanting, the smoke, everything. But it was real, wasn't it."

Lee leaned across the table, his gaze holding hers. "Who is he, Kelly? What was he doing here?"

Chapter Twenty

ꕤ

Kelly put her hands on her hips and stuck out her chin. "I don't know what you're talking about."

"Dammit, Kelly, no city girl would know how to mix a poultice like this. There was an Indian here and I want to know who he is."

"His name's Blue Crow."

"Blue Crow!" It couldn't be, Lee thought. It had to be someone else. Either that, or he was going slowly insane. "What does he look like?"

"He looks like you."

"Like me?" Lee dragged a hand through his hair. He had seen the resemblance between himself and the Indian during his vision, but he had thought it was part of his medicine dream, that he was seeing himself a few years down the road. "Does he wear a gold eagle on a thong around his neck?"

Kelly nodded, wondering at Lee's agitation.

Lee sat back in his chair. It couldn't be, but it was. Blue Crow had been the warrior in his vision, the man Charlie McBride had killed over a hundred years ago.

Kelly leaned forward, worried by Lee's sudden pallor. "Are you all right?"

Lee shook his head. He was going out of his mind that was the only answer that made sense.

"Come on," Kelly said, rising to her feet. "I think you'd better go back to bed."

"Yeah," he muttered bleakly, "I think you're right."

Kelly helped Lee back to bed and when he insisted he wanted to be alone, she went back to the kitchen and washed the dishes.

The rain had finally stopped, leaving the world looking bright and clean.

Lee slept most of the day.

Left to herself, Kelly wandered through the house. She found her grandfather's photo album on a shelf in the hall closet and spent an hour looking at old pictures, remembering the balmy summer days at the ranch when her grandfather had taught her to rope and ride. They'd gone fishing together, too, though Kelly had never gotten over her queasiness at baiting a hook or gutting a trout.

She wished now that she had spent more time with her grandfather during the last few years, but instead of taking the time, she'd made excuses, she was busy at work, she was taking an accounting class, she couldn't afford the plane fare. Sorry excuses, she thought, and even the knowledge that she'd called often and sent cards on his birthdays and holidays didn't ease her conscience.

"I did love you, Grandpa," she murmured. "I hope you know that."

Lee woke up long enough to eat dinner and use the bathroom and then he went back to bed, quickly falling asleep.

Kelly dashed out to feed the horses before it got dark, then ran back to the house and locked the door.

Once she was safe inside, she felt foolish for sprinting across the yard as if she were being pursued by demons, but she couldn't shake off the memory of those gunshots, or ignore the fact that those men had meant to kill her. Most frightening of all was the possibility that they might come back.

Unable to shake off her fears, she turned on all the lights in the house, then built a roaring fire in the fireplace.

Changing into her nightgown and robe, she curled up in the corner of the couch with her favorite author's latest romance, but as good as the book was, Kelly couldn't concentrate on the printed page. Every night sound, every creak, every shadow made her jump.

Maybe, if Lee felt better tomorrow, she'd leave him long enough to go into town and buy a big dog and a couple of geese, she thought. She'd keep the dog inside, for company and protection, and let the geese patrol the yard. Their noisy honking would alert her to prowlers and maybe the dog would make intruders think twice about trying to get into the house.

Her eyelids were getting heavy when she felt his presence and then he was there beside her, gathering her into his arms, comforting her with his touch.

With a sigh, she rested her head against his shoulder and closed her eyes. She was safe now. Nothing and no one could hurt her while he was here.

Time lost all meaning as he held her. Her fragrance engulfed him, her nearness made him feel alive. He lifted a callused finger to her cheek, drawing lazy circles over her smooth skin, marveling at how lovely she was. He outlined the shape of her nose, her brows, the fullness of her lower lip. Fire shot through him when she took his finger into her mouth and caressed it with her tongue.

"*Tekihila...*" He murmured her name, then groaned softly as she wriggled against him.

Her eyelids fluttered open and she looked up at him, her beautiful blue eyes glinting with mischief. Her lips pressed butterfly kisses to his palm.

"*Tekihila,* I am not made of stone."

"Is something wrong?" she asked with mock innocence.

He stared at her, mute, afraid to move for fear he would come into contact with some tantalizing part of her anatomy that would shatter his hard-won self-control.

"Blue Crow?" She ran her hand through his hair, slid her fingers over his nape. And smiled when she felt him shiver.

"*Tekihila...* Kelly, you must stop."

"Why?"

"You are a maiden..."

"A maiden who wants you."

He groaned again, as if he were in pain, and Kelly drew back, frowning. Maybe he *couldn't* make love to her. He was a ghost, after all.

"Why aren't you invisible?" she asked, her passion momentarily swallowed up by curiosity.

"I do not know."

"Lee saw you last night."

Blue Crow grunted softly.

"Can anyone see you?"

"*Ban.*"

Kelly shook her head. "I just don't understand. You're not like any ghost I've ever heard about. I mean, you've been, you know, gone, for over a hundred years. Why didn't your body...?"

Kelly shook her head, unable to go on. The whole subject was just too gruesome.

Blue Crow shrugged. "I cannot explain it, *skuya.* Perhaps I walk between life and death because of you. Perhaps I was meant to guard the gold until you came to claim it." He gazed deep into her eyes, his soul touching hers. "Perhaps *Wakan Tanka* knew I would not be happy in the land of spirits until I had seen the woman of my vision, until I had held her in my arms."

He cupped her face in his hands and kissed her lightly. "The reason matters not. It only matters that you are here, that I can see you and hold you."

His words, soft-spoken and fervent, touched Kelly's heart. He was right. It didn't matter why he had been allowed to linger on the earth. She was only glad that he was here, able to hold her in his arms. He was a part of her, more necessary than her next breath.

And she wanted him, wanted him desperately, but she didn't say so again. Instead, she relaxed in his arms, content to be held.

"Ah, *tekihila,*" Blue Crow murmured. "I wish..."

"What?" Kelly whispered. "What do you wish?"

"You do not know?"

"I can guess. It's what I want, too."

"I know, *wastelakapi,* I know, but it is not to be. Not now."

The words *not ever* hung in the air, but neither wanted to acknowledge them.

"You should leave this place, *tekihila.*"

"Still trying to get rid of me?" she asked.

"I fear for your safety."

"I'm not leaving you. I told you that before."

"Ah, *tekihila,* you have the heart of a warrior."

"No, I don't. I'm scared to death, but I'm more afraid of losing you."

Blue Crow sighed heavily. If he couldn't convince her to leave, he would just have to watch over her more carefully, at least until Roan Horse was feeling stronger.

Lee woke with the dawn, feeling better than he had in days. He flexed his shoulder, pleased that the sharp pains had dulled to a mild ache.

He grimaced as he swung his legs over the side of the bed. His leg was still sore, but he could stand on it. Crossing the floor, he gazed out the window. In the east, the sun was rising, painting the sky with vivid hues of vermilion and ocher.

Pressing his head against the cool glass, he closed his eyes. When he'd been very young, he'd spent a summer with his grandparents. Even now he could remember how his grandfather had left the house at dawn each morning. Standing outside, his face lifted to the rising sun, he had prayed to *Wakan Tanka,* his voice rising in a song to the dawn. Sweeter than the trill of a meadowlark, his grandfather's words had climbed skyward.

"Hear me, Father of us all, maker of heaven and earth and all living things. Grant me the wisdom to listen to the wind, to remember that I am one with all Thy creatures—the two-footed, the four-footed and those that ride on the wind. *Mitakuye oyasin.* We are all related."

"Mitakuye oyasin," Lee murmured. "We are all related."

Opening his eyes, he gazed at the sunrise once again. Yesterday he had been certain it had all been a dream born of fever and loss of blood. Today he knew deep within himself that, incomprehensible as it seemed, impossible as it was to explain, it had indeed been Blue Crow who had treated his wounds.

Lee shook his head. Blue Crow hadn't looked like a ghost, nor felt like one. Weren't ghosts supposed to be made of spirit? But the hands that had treated Lee's wounds had been warm, callused. As tangible as his own.

A sound at the door drew his attention and he turned to see Kelly standing there. Belatedly, he realized he was wearing nothing but briefs.

Kelly flushed as Lee met her gaze and then he shrugged, a glint of amusement dancing in the depths of his devil-dark eyes.

"No need to be embarrassed, Kelly," he said. "You've seen it all before."

But he'd been sick then, lying in bed with a fever. She'd been able to ignore the fact that he was too handsome by half, that he stirred feelings within her she didn't want to acknowledge.

She tried to drag her gaze away, but she couldn't stop looking at him. The bandages on his shoulder and thigh were very white against his skin. Smooth, dark bronze skin that she yearned to touch.

She blinked and looked away. What was the matter with her? She loved Blue Crow, not Lee. But they were so much alike. Had the two men been the same age, she wondered if she'd be able to tell them apart.

"Kelly?"

With a start, she realized Lee was standing in front of her, apparently unconcerned with the fact that he was nearly naked.

"I want to thank you," he said.

He was close, so close. His heat, his maleness, seemed to encompass her. "Thank me?"

"For taking care of me. I owe you my life."

Kelly shook her head, wishing he'd get back into bed under the covers. "I didn't do anything. It was Blue Crow."

Lee grunted softly. "Blue Crow. Where is he now?"

"He's…" She caught herself in time. "I don't know."

"He isn't here?"

"No. He only comes at night."

"At night? Why?"

Kelly shrugged. "I don't know."

Lee's gaze held hers and she had the distinct impression that he knew she was lying, that he knew about the gold.

She saw him shift his weight from one leg to the other. "Is your leg hurting?" she asked, hoping to steer the subject away from Blue Crow. "Maybe you should sit down?"

"Yeah." He limped across the room and sat down on the edge of the bed.

"I'll fix breakfast," Kelly said.

"Maybe you could bring me something to wear?

With a curt nod, Kelly left the room.

Lee stared out the window, his thoughts drifting like sparks in the wind. Blue Crow was here. And the Lakota gold was here, too, somewhere on the ranch. He wanted Kelly, wanted her in the most primal way. Wanted her as he wanted the gold, as he wanted the freedom it represented, as he wanted this land. An unwanted image of Melinda flashed across his mind. Melinda, with her sweet lying smile and her empty promises of love. He'd measured every woman he'd known since then by Melinda's treachery, refusing to trust any of them.

His hands curled into tight fists. He didn't trust Kelly McBride, either. She was a rotten liar. But he couldn't ignore the way his body hardened whenever she was near, couldn't deny that he wanted her. Just as she wanted him.

He swore under his breath. Hell would freeze over before he let himself get involved with another white woman, he thought grimly, and then he swore again. Whether he liked it or not, whether he wanted to admit it or not, he was already involved with Kelly McBride. He wanted her gold. And no matter how he tried to deny it, he wanted Kelly in his bed.

Filled with self-contempt, he called himself ten kinds of a fool, but the fact remained. He wanted her in his bed, in his arms, wanted her as he'd wanted no other woman he'd ever known.

Kelly stood in the doorway, watching the emotions that played across Lee's face as he stared out the window. He looked vulnerable sitting there, vulnerable and alone. She had a sudden urge to sit beside him, to draw him into her arms and cradle his head against her breast, to stroke his brow and tell him that everything would be all right, that he wasn't alone.

And then he glanced up, his eyes as hard and dark as obsidian, his jaw tense with anger and the urge to comfort him was swallowed up in the urge to run away before it was too late.

"How long have you been standing there?" Lee asked, his voice harsh.

"Not long. I…here." Kelly thrust an armful of clothes at him. "Breakfast is ready when you are," she said, and hurried out of the room.

In the kitchen, she braced her hands against the sink and took a deep breath. His eyes, she thought, she had never seen eyes filled with such desire, or such hatred. His whole body had been tense, his hands curled into angry fists, every muscle taut.

She wished suddenly that it was dark, that Blue Crow were there beside her.

She heard the sound of Lee's footsteps in the hallway and then he was there, his broad shoulders filling the doorway.

From the corner of her eye, she saw him limp toward the table and lower himself into a chair. The white T-shirt he wore made his skin seem darker, his hair blacker.

She took a deep breath, plastered a smile on her face and poured him a cup of coffee.

"I fixed waffles," she said. "Do you want syrup or jelly?"

"Syrup."

She moved around the kitchen, getting the syrup and refilling his coffee cup before she sat down.

They ate in silence. Kelly was acutely aware of Lee's every move. She saw his grimace when he reached for his coffee cup with his right hand, inadvertently jarring his injured arm. She felt the heat of his gaze when his eyes met hers, felt the electricity that arced between them.

He wanted her.

And, heaven help her, in spite of everything, she wanted him.

Chapter Twenty-One

ꕥ

The silence stretched between them, awkward, uncomfortable, absolute.

Shaken by the intensity of his gaze and her own reaction to it, she dropped her fork. It clattered loudly as it hit the table.

And then that stark silence took over once again.

Kelly searched her mind for some safe topic of conversation, but it was as if she'd lost the power of thought, of speech.

She tried not to notice the way the thin white cotton molded itself to Lee's chest, tried to ignore the way her heart was slamming against her ribs.

And then he moved. She watched his length unfold from the chair. She noticed his limp, the way his faded jeans hugged his long legs.

He rounded the table and it was suddenly hard for her to breathe. Mesmerized, she stared up at him, her gaze trapped by his dark brooding one.

It was a mistake, Lee thought as he bent down and slanted his mouth over Kelly's. A big mistake. But he could no more keep himself from kissing her than he could refuse his next breath.

Her lips were soft, yielding. He ran his tongue over her lower lip, the tastes of coffee and syrup and woman mingling on his tongue as he boldly explored her mouth.

Heat shot through him, bright fingers of flame that burned away his resolve. His hands closed over her arms and he groaned low in his throat as he drew her to her feet, then wrapped his good arm around her, pressing her sweet feminine curves against his aching flesh.

And all the while, a part of him waited for her to reject him, to call him a dirty redskin and push him away.

But Kelly had no such thoughts. Rising on tiptoe, she wound her arms around Lee's neck and molded her body to his. Her eyelids fluttered down as the wonder of his touch spiraled through her. Like a leaf uncurling beneath the kiss of the sun, desire unfolded deep in the core of her being, growing, expanding, watered by the sound of her name on his lips, nurtured by their mutual need.

She pressed against him, wanting to be closer, closer, wanting to taste and touch every inch of his heated flesh.

She felt him take an unsteady step backward, heard him groan softly as he reached blindly for the table.

Her first thought was that he was rejecting her, repulsed by her boldness, and then she realized that he was in pain.

"Kelly, I've got to sit down."

She quickly drew away, her passion fading as concern took its place.

"Let me help you back to bed," she said, reaching for his hand.

To bed. He had a sudden image of Kelly lying beneath him, her lustrous brown hair spread across the pillow, her sky-blue eyes hazy with desire. Hard on the heels of that image came the memory of the beating he'd endured after Melinda's betrayal.

But this wasn't Melinda.

It was Kelly. Kelly holding his hand. Kelly looking up at him, her expressive eyes reflecting compassion and concern.

He grimaced as a twinge of pain ran the length of his leg.

"Come on," Kelly said, slipping her arm around his waist. "You should rest."

He let her help him down the hall to his room. He sat on the edge of the bed, his head bowed, as he waited for the pain in his thigh to subside. He was aware of Kelly waiting close by and then she was standing in front of him, cradling his head against her breasts as she lightly stroked his hair.

Her touch was infinitely gentle, caring. He felt the sting of tears behind his eyes and knew if she didn't leave off mothering him, he'd make a complete fool of himself. But, try as he might, he couldn't bring himself to push her away. No woman had comforted him so tenderly since his grandmother died almost ten years ago.

Jaw clenched, his hands fisted at his sides, he closed his eyes and gave himself over to her touch. Just another minute or two, he thought, and he'd send her away.

But there was magic in the warmth of her hands as she stroked his hair and then began to gently massage his neck and shoulders.

Hesitantly he lifted his hands to her waist, then let his palms slide over her buttocks and down the length of her thighs. Her hands stilled on his shoulders.

Immediately, Lee pulled away from her. And then he felt her hands on his head, drawing his face to her breasts once more.

"Kelly..."

"Hmmm?"

"Do you know what you're doing?"

"Yes."

"Are you sure?"

His breath penetrated her shirt, warm and inviting. She slid her fingers through his hair.

"Kelly?"

"I'm sure."

Afraid he was making the biggest mistake of his life, he tilted his head up so he could see her face.

"I won't stop this time," he warned. "Whatever starts between us, I'll finish."

"It's already started, Lee," she murmured, and knew there would be no turning back this time.

His eyes glowed like the burning embers of a fire as he drew her down on the bed beside him, his arms wrapping around her as he kissed her. And kissed her, his tongue delving deep into her mouth. It surprised her that a kiss could arouse her so quickly.

He fell back on the bed, drawing her down on top of him, his hands tracing lazy circles over her back while his lips moved over her face and neck, slowly tantalizing her until she was on fire with need.

Her hands sought to know him and he let her explore to her heart's content, learning the shape of him, the texture of his skin.

Somehow their clothing disappeared and she learned, to her delight, the sensual pleasure of bare skin against bare skin. She saw the admiration in Lee's eyes when he looked at her and was pleased that he found her desirable, that her untutored hands could bring him pleasure. She felt a keen, unreasoning jealousy because he had known other women, because she was not his first lover. Unbidden came the memory of Melinda. Had Melinda been his first love?

She fought down the bitterness that threatened to overwhelm her and began to kiss him hungrily, fiercely determined to wipe the memory of every other woman from his mind.

She heard him groan low in his throat and then he was tucking her beneath him, his legs parting hers.

He whispered her name, his hands tangled in her hair, as his body became one with hers.

And Kelly knew there would never be another man in her life. For as long as she lived, she would belong to Lee Roan Horse.

Kelly studied the face of the man lying beside her. He had fallen asleep soon after they made love, his arm wrapped around her shoulder. She would have gotten up, had she been able, but when she tried to slip out of bed, he had stirred, whispering, "Don't go," and all thought of getting up had left her mind.

A rumbling in her stomach told her it was well past noon. She should get up, take a shower, get dressed. Though she had enjoyed their love-making, she wasn't sure what was expected of her now. Would he expect to take her to bed at his whim, or was it something to be done once and forgotten?

She wished suddenly that she'd had more experience with this sort of thing. She gazed at Lee again, felt her heart stir at the beauty of the man. He had been a tender lover, making her feel beautiful, cherished, being certain he pleasured her before he sought his own release. And when it was over, he had held her close, stroking her hair, whispering endearments in her ear, holding her until she fell asleep in his arms, peacefully, blissfully content.

His eyelashes were thick, like tiny black fans against his bronze cheeks. His lips were well-shaped, firm. She stifled the impulse to run her finger over his lower lip, afraid she would wake him. She let her gaze wander over his broad shoulders, over his heavily muscled arms.

She would have been happy to sit there staring at him for the rest of the day, she thought, but she felt him stir, stretch and then he was awake, his dark eyes gazing into hers.

A slow flush crept into Kelly's cheeks as her eyes met his. Feeling suddenly awkward and more than a little shy, she looked away, only to feel his finger beneath her chin, turning her face to his again.

"It's all up to you, Kelly," he said quietly.

"What do you mean?"

"Where we go from here." He took a deep breath. "It can be the end, or it can be the beginning. It's up to you."

"What do you want?"

"I want you."

Kelly licked her lips. Her heart was beating wildly in her breast, her whole body was yearning to know him again. But before she could answer his question, there was something she had to know.

"Why did you come here, Lee?"

A shadow passed across his face. "What do you mean?"

"You know what I mean. Why are you really here?"

A hundred lies crowded his mind, but he couldn't utter a single one. Even knowing that the truth would bring her pain, he couldn't lie to her, not now.

A muscle twitched in his jaw. For a moment his gaze slid away from her face and then, slowly and deliberately, his eyes met hers.

"You know why."

Kelly sat up, clutching the sheet to her breasts. "I want to hear you say it."

"I came for the gold." The gold, he thought. It was the answer to every question. It was a way to escape from his past into a future where anything was possible. "The gold's here somewhere and it's mine."

Kelly shook her head. "You're wrong. It's mine. Blue Crow gave it to me."

Lee's eyes narrowed ominously. "What do you mean?"

"Just what I said."

"Then you do know where it is?"

Kelly's heart seemed to stop. "He never told me."

It wasn't a lie, she thought. Blue Crow hadn't told her where the gold was, she'd found it with the help of her grandfather's map. She was glad now that she'd burned it.

She slid out of bed, taking the sheet with her, careful to keep her gaze averted. She didn't want to look at Lee, didn't want to remember how right it had felt to be in his arms. She'd been a fool to think he cared for her when all he cared about was the gold. But then, deep in her heart, hadn't she known that all along?

"Kelly."

His voice called to her, but she refused to look at him.

"I think you'd better leave," she said, and biting back the urge to cry, she swept out of the room, quietly but firmly closing the door behind her.

Chapter Twenty-Two

ꟳ

Lee swore under his breath as he watched Kelly leave the room. He should have lied to her, he thought, and then, too late, he realized that he had lied to her. It wasn't the gold he wanted. It was Kelly.

He sat there for an hour, thinking of the brief interlude they had shared. He'd had his share of women, maybe more than his share, but except for Melinda, none of them had meant more than a means of physical relief. He'd made them no promises and expected none in return.

But Kelly was different. For the first time in his life, he'd known the difference between mere sexual gratification and love. She had offered herself to him freely, openly, soothing old hurts with the touch of her hand, vanquishing old ghosts with the gift of her love.

And he loved her.

Another oath escaped his lips. She'd never believe that now, not after what he'd said, never believe that she meant more to him than the gold.

The gold.

Lee stood up and began to pace the room as a niggling fear began to prey on his mind. Whoever else knew about the gold was getting tired of waiting. They'd tried to kill him once and they would try again.

His hands clenched as a new thought occurred to him. He'd assumed the gunmen had been after him, but now that he thought about it, he realized it had been Kelly they were after. With her out of the way, the ranch would be sold to the highest bidder. He pondered the matter while he showered, then dressed in a pair of faded blue jeans and a black T-shirt.

Who else knew about the gold, he wondered as he stamped into his boots. Who else knew about it and wanted it bad enough to kill a woman for it?

Leaving the bedroom, he went into the kitchen in search of Kelly, but she wasn't there. The parlor, too, was empty. Turning back down the hall, he went to her bedroom and knocked on the door.

"Kelly? Kelly, you in there?"

Frowning, he put his hand on the knob. The door opened with a faint squeak, but the room was empty.

Where the hell was she?

He checked the bathroom, then went out to the barn. The horses whickered softly at his arrival, but there was no sign of Kelly.

He stood with his good shoulder braced against the barn door, wondering where she'd gone. He hadn't meant to hurt her, but then, he hadn't meant to fall in love with her, either.

Damn.

He was heading back to the house when something made him walk around to the back. He felt a sudden coldness in the area of his heart when he saw it, a faint scuff mark in the dirt beneath Kelly's window.

Squatting on his heels, Lee examined the print. It had been made by a man's hard-soled shoe.

Rising, he checked the ground for sign. Someone had tried to erase their tracks by using a leafy branch, but that, too, had left a trail of sorts.

Lee followed it until it disappeared at the edge of the woods beyond the pond.

He muttered an oath as he noticed a single set of hoofprints heading away from the ranch.

Kelly struggled in her captor's grasp, but he had arms that felt as solid as steel and all her twisting and biting was in vain. All it earned her was a hard slap to the side of her face.

They'd been riding for almost two hours when her captor drew rein near the foot of the mountain.

He dismounted, then pulled Kelly roughly from the back of the horse. Pushing her to the ground, he tied her hands behind her back.

Kelly stared up at her captor, her stomach churning with fear. His eyes were pale, almost colorless. Lank, stringy brown hair fell over his forehead.

"What do you want?" she asked, her voice trembling uncontrollably.

"I want to know where the gold is," the man answered curtly. "You can make it easy on yourself and tell me now, or we can do it the hard way and you can tell me later. Either way, you will tell me what I want to know."

"I don't know about any gold," Kelly said.

"The hard way, then," the man said with a smile, and Kelly had the awful feeling that he would have been disappointed if she'd told him what he wanted to know without an argument.

She started to plead with him, but before she could form the words, he hunkered down on his heels and slapped her, hard, twice.

Kelly's head reeled back, the salty taste of blood filling her mouth.

"The gold," the man said. "Where is it?"

"I don't—"

He slapped her again, harder this time, and then he sighed.

"We're wasting time," he muttered to himself, and rising to his feet, he gathered a handful of dry twigs and lit a small fire.

Kelly watched the flames lick at the dry tinder, her stomach muscles tightening with fear as the man pulled a jackknife from his pants pocket.

He looked at her, his pale eyes speculative as he opened the knife and held the blade over the tiny dancing flames. When the metal was glowing, her abductor knelt beside her.

"Remember what your daddy always said when he was going to spank you?" he drawled. "Well, this is gonna hurt you a lot more than it hurts me."

Kelly stared in horror as he lifted the blade, holding it close to her left cheek. She could feel the heat radiating from the blade.

"Don't," she whimpered. "Please, don't."

"Just tell me what I want to know and I'll let you go."

Tears welled in Kelly's eyes. He was lying. As soon as she told him what he wanted to know, he would kill her. She read the knowledge in his unblinking gaze.

He waggled the knife in front of her face. "Last chance, girl."

Kelly closed her eyes, her body shaking with fear. She could feel the heat drawing closer. She held her breath, waiting for the pain she could not begin to imagine. But it never came.

She gave a startled cry when she felt a hand on her arm.

"Tekihila."

"Blue Crow!" Tears of relief streamed down her cheeks as he cut her hands free and drew her into his arms.

"All is well, *tekihila,*" he murmured soothingly.

"What…? Where…?" She glanced over his shoulder, shuddered as she saw the man's body lying face down a few feet away. "Is he…?"

"Han. He will not hurt you again."

Trembling violently, she collapsed in Blue Crow's arms. He rocked her gently, his voice washing over her, soothing her while she cried, until nervous exhaustion overcame her and she tumbled into sleep's healing embrace.

And that was how Lee found them when he rode up a few minutes later.

He took in the scene at a glance, the body lying face down in the dirt, Kelly being rocked in the arms of a warrior clad in buckskin leggings and moccasins. A golden eagle hung from a leather thong around the Indian's neck.

Lee shivered as he met the warrior's gaze. Looking into the Indian's face was like looking in a mirror.

"Blue Crow," Lee murmured.

"*Han.*"

Lee shook his head. It wasn't possible. But he couldn't deny the proof of his own eyes. "Is she all right?"

Blue Crow nodded. He tightened his hold on Kelly.

"What happened?"

"The *wasichu* threatened her life."

"And you killed him?"

"*Han.*"

"Good." Dismounting, Lee searched the dead man's pockets. There was no identification of any kind, only a set of car keys. "I'll get rid of the body."

Blue Crow nodded, his dark eyes thoughtful as he watched Lee place the dead man across the back of his horse, then swing up behind it.

Lee stared at Blue Crow and knew he was looking at a man who embodied everything he himself had always yearned to be. Blue Crow was a warrior, indomitable, courageous, filled with a calm self-assurance that came from being at peace with one's self. Physically they looked very much alike, Lee thought ruefully, but that was where the comparison ended.

Blue Crow smiled under Lee's scrutiny. "Can you not believe the truth of your own eyes?"

"It's hard," Lee admitted. "Damn hard. Can you take Kelly home?"

"Han," The smile faded from Blue Crow's face and his expression turned hard. "Be warned, Roan Horse. I will avenge any harm that comes to Kelly because of you."

"You think I'd hurt her?"

Blue Crow didn't answer, but his dark eyes continued to bore into Lee's.

"I thought you were here to guard the gold," Lee muttered.

"I will do that, as well. You have strayed far from the teachings of the People, Lee Roan Horse, far from the true path. You will not find the peace of mind you seek in a bag of gold."

"How do you know what I'm after?"

"I know your heart," Blue Crow replied confidently. "And I say again, you will live to regret it if you hurt Kelly in any way."

"I hear you," Lee said, his voice terse. He sent a last look at Kelly, still sleeping in Blue Crow's arms and then he reined his horse east, toward a deep chasm. He would dump the body there and cover it with rocks.

"Is he gone?"

"Han."

Kelly sat up, her gaze seeking Blue Crow's face. "You don't think Lee would hurt me, do you?"

Blue Crow hesitated a moment and then shook his head. "No, he will not hurt you, *tekihila."* His arm tightened around her waist. "Not in the way you mean."

"I don't understand."

"I think you are destined to be together, though it will be hard for Roan Horse to admit that he needs you. He has spent his whole life alone, relying on no one but himself. He has not learned how to share his life, or his heart."

"You're wrong. He only wants the gold. He told me so."

"Sometimes a man does not know his own heart."

"It doesn't matter. I told him to leave and I meant it." Kelly stared at Blue Crow. His silence made her uneasy. "You think I was wrong?"

"You must do what you think is right, *tekihila*. I cannot tell you how to live your life."

"But you think I'm wrong?" Kelly insisted.

"It may be right, for you."

Kelly sighed with exasperation. "Please, Blue Crow, just tell me what you think."

"I think you cannot fight your destiny."

"And you think Lee is my destiny?"

"*I* think you are his."

"I don't believe that."

"What do you believe in, *skuya?"*

"I don't know."

"Search your heart, *tekihila."*

"I believe in you," Kelly murmured, laying her head on his shoulder. "I believe we were destined to be together."

"Ah, beloved, if only it could be so." His hand stroked her hair, the curve of her cheek and then, reluctantly, he stood up, drawing her up beside him. "Come, I will take you home."

"All right." Kelly looked at him, and then frowned. "It's daytime."

He cocked an eyebrow in her direction.

"I thought you stayed in the cave during the day."

He nodded, comprehending her question. "I heard you call me, *tekihila."*

"And you came."

"*Han.* As I will always come to you, *wastelakapi."*

Blue Crow saw Kelly safely into the house. He took her into his arms and held her for a long moment. For a hundred years, he had waited for her. A hundred years of darkness and loneliness. Had he ignored the urging of his heart to go to her, had he arrived only a few moments later, she might have been badly hurt, perhaps killed. The thought was like a knife in his heart.

Closing his eyes, he pressed his cheek to the top of her head. Breathing deeply, he inhaled the fresh clean scent of her hair, her skin. Her breasts were warm and soft against his bare chest, the touch of her fingers gently kneading the muscles in his back aroused thoughts he should not have, desires he could not fulfill.

"I must go, *tekihila,*" he murmured, his words thick with longing.

"You'll come back tonight, won't you?"

"If you need me."

"I'll always need you."

He looked at her through eyes filled with pain. "I think, if you look deep in your heart, you will find that it is Roan Horse you want."

A guilty flush heated Kelly's cheeks. He knew, she thought, he knew that Lee had made love to her.

A faint smile touched Blue Crow's lips. "It is all right, *tekihila*. I knew you could not be mine."

He placed his hand over her mouth, stilling her protest. "He is coming. Think carefully before you send him away," he said quietly, and then he was gone.

Lee knocked on the front door, then shoved his hands in his back pockets while he waited for Kelly to answer. Maybe she was right. Maybe it was time he got the hell out of here, or at least away from her. She could keep her damn gold. He'd leave Cedar Flats, go to California, see the ocean…

All his good intentions fled the instant she opened the door. "What do you want?"

"I came to get my things."

Kelly took a step back, allowing him entrance to the house.

"What did you do with...with that man?"

"You've got your secrets," Lee replied curtly. "I've got mine."

"If you buried him on my property, it is my business."

"You're better off not knowing anything about it, Kelly. If anybody comes around asking questions, you can honestly say you don't know."

She didn't like it, but she was in no mood to argue.

"Dammit, Kelly, I don't like leaving you here alone."

"You mean you don't like leaving the gold," Kelly retorted bitterly. "Besides, I'm not alone."

"You mean Blue Crow?"

"Yes."

"What's between you two, anyway?"

"That's none of your business."

"He's a ghost!"

"He loves me."

Lee cursed softly, hating the surge of jealousy that swept through him. Jealous! he thought irritably. He was jealous of a hundred-year-old ghost. It was ridiculous. But he couldn't forget how content Kelly had looked in Blue Crow's arms, or the trusting way she'd held onto the ancient warrior, even in her sleep.

"I'm sure you'll be very happy together," Lee muttered.

"What are you going to do now?"

"What the hell do you care?"

"I don't." But she did care. That was what hurt. She cared more than she wanted to admit.

Lee crossed the floor and went down the hallway to his room. He could hear Kelly's footsteps behind him.

"What's the matter?" he called over his shoulder, his tone caustic. "Afraid to leave me alone for fear I'll steal the family silver?"

"We don't have any silver."

He swore again, anger and jealousy and a deep sense of loss ripping through him, tearing at his insides like the claws of a mountain lion. He wouldn't have been surprised to see his life's blood spreading over the floor.

The first thing he saw when he walked into the guest room was the bed, the blankets thrown back, the sheets rumpled from their lovemaking earlier that day.

Lee shook his head ruefully. How had a day that started so good ended up so damn bad?

He turned to find Kelly staring at him from the doorway, a single tear glistening on her cheek.

"What's wrong?" he asked gruffly.

She shook her head, helpless to admit that she didn't want him to go, that, as much as she loved Blue Crow, she was also in love with Lee.

"Kelly, I... Dammit, I'm..." He ran a hand through his hair. "I'm sorry, Kelly. I didn't want to hurt you."

With an effort, she gathered the shreds of her dignity around her. "You didn't."

"Liar."

His voice was soft, caressing. Another tear slid down her cheek.

"Kelly..."

"Go on, go if you're going."

Lee took a deep breath. Maybe it was time for truth, time to take a risk.

He took a step toward her, one hand outstretched in a silent plea. "I don't want to leave you."

Hope unfurled deep within Kelly, painful in its intensity. "I don't want you to go," she said, and placed her hand in his.

Slowly, Lee's long fingers closed over hers. "It's not because of the gold, Kelly," he said. "Maybe it was never the gold."

"I want to believe you. I do believe you, but…"

"But you don't trust me?"

"Trust has to be earned, Lee."

A smile turned up one corner of his mouth. "You're not gonna make this easy for me, are you?"

"Nothing worthwhile is ever easy."

"I wouldn't know," Lee said, a twinge of bitterness evident in his tone. "I've never had anything worthwhile. Until now."

"So," Kelly asked, her voice shaky. "Where do we go from here?"

"I don't know." Lee gazed into the blue tranquility of her eyes and felt as if he were drowning in sunshine. "I love you, Kelly," he whispered fervently. "I've never been in love before and it scares the hell out of me."

"Lee…"

He pressed a finger to her lips to quiet her. "I love you, Kelly," he said again, surprised to discover how easily the words came to him now.

And then, very gently, he sealed his vow with a kiss.

For a moment they stood close in each other's arms and then Lee drew back and gazed into Kelly's face.

"About the gold…"

She went rigid in his arms, the softness leaving her face, the dreamy expression melting from her eyes. "What about it?"

"Kelly, hear me out."

"I'm listening."

"You need to get rid of it."

"What do you mean?"

"I mean you need to cash it in and put the money in the bank."

"Why?"

"Because it's too dangerous to have it here on the ranch."

"How do you know it's here?"

"Because Blue Crow is here."

"The gold's been safe here for over a hundred years."

"It isn't just the gold, Kelly. You aren't safe here, either."

"What do you mean? That man who...who...he's dead, isn't he?"

"Maybe he wasn't alone."

Maybe you're working with him. The disloyal thought jumped to the forefront of Kelly's mind. Maybe all Lee's talk about loving her was just a ruse, a way to make her lower her guard and tell him where the gold was hidden.

As if reading her mind, Lee removed his arms from her waist and took a step backward.

"Do whatever you want with the gold," he said tersely. "It's none of my business."

She flushed guiltily. "Lee..."

"This isn't gonna work, Kelly."

She stared up at him, not knowing what to say.

Lee drew in a deep breath and let it out in a soul-deep sigh. "You don't have to say anything. I can see the doubts in your eyes, Kelly. You're wondering if I'm lying about loving you, if it's just some kind of cheap trick to get my hands on the gold."

"No, I—"

"You're a terrible liar, Kelly. I can see the truth in your face and I don't blame you. I haven't given you any reason to trust me."

She was too numb for tears. The joy she'd felt only moments before was gone, leaving the bitter taste of ashes in her mouth. But oh, he was being so unfair! She'd only known him for a few weeks. And how could he blame her for being just a little suspicious when, only hours ago, he had boldly admitted that he'd come to the ranch to find the gold?

"You're being unfair!" she exclaimed, her anger rising.

"Unfair about what?"

"Everything. It's all happening so fast. One minute you tell me you want the gold and the next you say you don't want the gold, that you love me. I don't know what to believe."

"Believe this," he murmured, and, sweeping her into his arms, he kissed her long and hard, kissed her until the world was spinning out of control, until her blood flowed like liquid honey, until she ached with a fierce need that made her sob his name.

Lee gazed deep into Kelly's eyes and then, with a softly muttered oath, he tore his lips from hers, grabbed his gear and left the house.

From the window, Kelly watched him bolt across the yard to the barn. Ten minutes later, he emerged carrying a gunny sack.

Heart numb, she watched him slide behind the wheel of his battered truck and roar out of the yard.

She had a terrible feeling that he wouldn't be back.

Chapter Twenty-Three

℘

Kelly took a long hot shower, scrubbed herself from head to foot twice, then pulled on a pair of jeans and an old sweater.

Sitting in front of the fireplace, she tried to sort out her feelings for Blue Crow, for Lee, but to no avail. She'd never believed it was possible to be in love with two men at the same time. Realistically, she supposed she wasn't in love with two men, since one of them was a ghost…

Right or wrong, flesh or fantasy, she was in love with Blue Crow. He was everything a man should be, kind, honest, loyal, trustworthy, gentle, tender…

And then there was Lee. He wasn't honest or trustworthy. She doubted his loyalty. But he could be tender, so tender. Even now, she yearned to be in his arms again, to hear the husky rasp of his voice whispering her name, to feel his arms enfolding her, to know the touch of his lips on hers, trailing fire…

She had never dreamed that loving a man could be so fulfilling. Being in Lee's arms, his body united with hers, had been almost spiritual.

"And all he wanted was the gold."

She spoke the words aloud, hardly recognizing the sound of her own voice, she sounded so empty, so bitter.

Maybe he was telling the truth.

She tried not to listen to the little voice of her conscience. He had lied to her from the beginning. He never wanted to buy the ranch, he'd only wanted to steal the gold.

He said he loved you.

"Another lie!"

How do you know?

"Stop it! Just stop it!" She put her hands over her ears in a ridiculous effort to shut out the voice in her head. How would she ever know if he truly loved her, or if all he wanted was the gold? A lot of men married women they didn't love to obtain wealth, or power, or position. Lee'd been poor all his life. He believed the Triple M belonged to his people, that the gold should rightfully be his.

With a sigh, she buried her face in her hands. "What should I do?" she asked the empty room. "What should I do?"

"Follow your heart, *tekihila."*

"Blue Crow." She sniffed back a tear as she lifted her head.

"Do not weep, *skuya."*

"I can't help it. I don't know what to do. Lee said he loved me, but I'm afraid to believe him. What if he only wants the gold? What if…?" Kelly shrugged. "He hasn't asked me, but what if we got married and then he took the gold and left me?"

"What would you miss the most, *tekihila?* The man, or the yellow iron?"

"The man, of course."

"Then that is your answer."

"Lee thinks I should exchange the gold for cash and put it in the bank so no one else can touch it," Kelly remarked.

"Perhaps that would be wise."

"I guess so." Kelly gazed into Blue Crow's eyes. "What will happen to you when the gold is gone?"

Blue Crow shrugged. "I will follow *Wanagi Tacaku,* the spirit path, to *Wanagi Yata,* the place of souls."

"No!"

"Do you not think it is time?"

"But…what will I do without you?"

"You will no longer need me, *tekihila."*

With a wordless cry of protest, Kelly wrapped her arms around Blue Crow and hugged him close. She could not bear the thought of never seeing him again.

She felt his arms go around her, felt his lips move in her hair as he murmured her name over and over again.

"Please don't leave me," she whispered.

"Would you have my soul trapped forever in the cave, *wastelakapi?* Have I not wandered this part of the earth long enough?"

Kelly bit down on her lip. Selfishly, she had thought only of herself, of how much she would miss him when he was gone. Now, she thought how lonely he must have been all these years, caught between two worlds, belonging to neither. Kelly had always had a strong belief in an afterlife; now it occurred to her that he might have family waiting for him on the other side.

"Will you stay with me tonight?" she asked, her voice muffled against his chest.

"If you wish."

"I do."

Wordlessly, Kelly took him by the hand and led him to her room. After shutting the door, she drew him down beside her on the bed, sighed as his arms enfolded her.

She tried not to cry, but she couldn't stop the tears.

She clung to him all night long, memorizing the sight of his face, his touch and taste and smell. She whispered his name, vowing that she loved him, that even death would not dim her love.

He held her until she fell asleep in his arms, held her until dawn began to chase the stars from the sky.

Covering her, he placed a kiss on her cheek. *"Ohinniyan, tekihila,"* he murmured. "Forever, my love."

* * * * *

Kelly rose early in the morning, her mind made up. She would take the gold from the cave, cash it in, deposit the money in the bank and then take a long vacation.

A long cruise, she thought. Perhaps a few weeks away from the ranch, away from Lee, would help her to see things more clearly.

It was still dark outside when she went to the barn and saddled Dusty. The yard seemed empty without Lee's truck.

Dusty balked at being saddled before breakfast, but Kelly was too impatient to wait. It would take several trips to haul the gold down the mountain. It would be so much easier if she had someone to help her, someone to drive her car to the foot of the mountain so she wouldn't have to make the long ride from the cave to the Triple M on horseback. And where would she hide the first bags of gold while she went back for the rest?

Frowning, she urged Dusty into a lope. Having a fortune in gold was turning out to be more of a curse than a blessing. It had come between her and Lee; when it was gone, she would lose Blue Crow, as well. What good was money if you had no one to share it with?

Black clouds were gathering overhead when she reached the cave.

Taking a deep breath, she ducked inside, feeling for the lantern beside the entrance.

Holding the lantern high, she made her way toward the back of the cave. Toward Blue Crow's body.

It was there, on the shelf. Unable to help herself, she drew the blanket from his face and placed her fingertips on his cheek. The first time she had touched him, his skin had felt supple and warm. Now, it felt cool, hard.

Frightened without knowing why, she replaced the blanket, then began to fill a burlap bag with handfuls of gold nuggets.

She didn't realize she was crying until she felt the dampness on her hands.

She didn't look at Blue Crow's body as she dragged the heavy burlap bag out of the cave to where Dusty stood cropping a patch of yellow grass.

Grunting softly, she lifted the sack onto the gelding's back and secured it in place.

A faint sound from behind drew her attention and she whirled around, her heart hammering with anticipation.

But it wasn't Blue Crow.

"Lee!"

"Kelly."

Her gaze moved over him, her curiosity at his appearance quickly turning to fear when she saw the gun shoved in the waistband of his jeans. "What…what are you doing here?"

"What do you think?"

She didn't want to put it in words. He'd wanted the gold all the time and now, it seemed, he'd come to take it.

Oddly enough, it no longer mattered. She thought of Blue Crow and suddenly she wasn't afraid anymore. If she couldn't be with him in this life, perhaps they could be together in the next.

"Go on, take the gold," Kelly said. "I don't want it." A faint smile played over her lips. "I guess I won't need it where I'm going."

Lee frowned at her. "What the hell are you talking about?"

He took a step forward and then, to her astonishment, he staggered forward and fell face down at her feet.

She saw the other man then and the sight of his cold yellow eyes sent shards of fear slicing through every fiber of her being.

Eyes like a coyote. In the back of her mind, she heard Blue Crow's voice warning her about a man with yellow eyes.

"Back off," the man said. "That's better. Now, turn around."

Kelly did as she was told. Behind her, she could hear muffled footsteps, the clink of metal, and then she felt a man's hand on her ankle, followed by the touch of cold steel. Looking down, she saw that he had shackled her feet.

"What are you doing?" The question escaped her lips before she could stop it.

The man looked at her as if she weren't very bright. "Just fixin' it so's you don't try to run off afore I'm through with ya."

Kelly glanced at Lee, still lying on the ground, and saw that his ankles were also shackled. While she watched, the man took Lee's gun and shoved it into the waistband of his trousers.

The man kicked Lee in the ribs, hard. "Come on, Injun, we're wasting time."

Lee groaned softly. He rolled over, one hand massaging the back of his neck. The chains around his ankle rattled, drawing his gaze.

"What the hell," he muttered. He looked at Kelly and then, very slowly, glanced over his shoulder.

"Get up, Injun," the man said. "We've got a lot of gold to move and we're wasting daylight."

"Who the hell are you?"

"Get up, Injun."

Keeping one eye on the pistol in the man's hand, Lee climbed to his feet and stood beside Kelly. "What now?"

"The two of you are gonna haul that gold down here." He jerked his head to the side. "My truck's waiting."

Lee glanced down the hill. A tan pickup was parked below.

The man grinned at the look of comprehension spreading over Lee's face. "My partner was a lousy shot," he remarked affably. "I'm not. Now, get movin'."

Lee followed Kelly into the cave, his mind racing. He had to distract the man long enough for Kelly to make a run for it. Run for it, he mused bleakly. She couldn't run with those damn shackles. Somehow, he'd have to overpower the man.

But their captor wasn't taking any chances. He kept well out of arm's reach. The gun in his hand never wavered.

It took a dozen trips down the hill to load the gold into the pickup. Kelly and Lee were both sweating profusely as they made their way up the hill the last time.

It was now or never, Lee thought. The last of the gold had been loaded into the truck. All that was left was for the man to shoot the two of them and leave their bodies in the cave.

Kelly tripped on a root and sprawled face down in the dirt. For a moment, she stayed as she was, too numb with fear to move or think.

She was going to die. Somehow, she hadn't felt any fear when she thought Lee was going to kill her, but now, facing death at the hands of this stranger, she was suddenly terrified.

She lifted her head to find Lee standing beside her. He was about to offer her a hand up when the yellow-eyed man struck him across the side of the face with the butt of his pistol.

Lee reeled backward, thrown off balance by the shackles on his feet.

Kelly scrambled to her knees, then gained her feet, her eyes widening as she saw the ugly gash on Lee's cheek. The blood trickling down his cheek seemed very red.

The gunman walked up behind Lee. "Put your hands behind your back," he said curtly, and when Lee hesitated, he hit him across the side of the head with the barrel of the pistol. "Come on, redskin," the man said impatiently, "I've got places to go and things to do."

Kelly felt a sudden overwhelming sense of hopelessness as she watched the yellow-eyed man lash Lee's hands together.

"Let's go," the man said, and gave Lee a shove toward the entrance to the cave.

Kelly followed Lee, the urge to scream rising in her throat. She was going to die. Where she had once counted her future in years, she now had only minutes.

She tried to pray, tried to force her thoughts away from the bloody images that were filling her mind. images of herself and Lee lying in pools of blood, their bodies left to rot, or to be torn apart by scavengers.

And then they were inside the cave and she knew time had run out.

The man stood with his back to the entrance of the cave, the gun in his hand seeming to grow larger with every passing moment.

She wished she'd had time to tell Lee she loved him, that she could have seen Blue Crow one last time, and then there was no more time for thought.

The gun was pointed at her chest, the man's finger was curling around the trigger…

She screamed as Lee elbowed her aside, the shrill echo of her cry rising above the sound of the gunshot to echo off the walls of the cave.

And then everything happened in slow motion.

She saw Lee fall, his shirt front covered with blood.

She saw the gunman's face turn deathly pale as the body on the shelf rose to its feet and walked toward him. But it was not the body Kelly had seen when she lifted the blanket. This was a skeleton draped in hanging shreds of rotting flesh.

A wordless cry was torn from the gunman's throat as the walking corpse took the gun from his hand.

Was it only her imagination, or did the man look grateful when the skeleton put the gun to his chest and pulled the trigger?

She blinked in horror and the corpse was gone.

A low moan drew her attention to Lee. With a wordless cry, she dropped to her knees beside him and cradled his head in her lap.

She pressed her hand over his chest in an effort to make the wound stop bleeding.

"Oh God, Lee," she murmured as she freed his hands. "What can I do?"

"Nothing, Kelly." His voice was faint. "I didn't come here…to take the gold…"

"Don't talk. You've got to save your energy." She grabbed the scarf from her hair and pressed it over the wound in his chest. "I'll go get help. You'll be fine."

"No. Too late. I came…to help you…take…gold to town."

She nodded, the tears running down her cheeks. "I know, I know."

"Believe me."

"I do, I do." She stared at his chest, at the dark stain that was spreading ever wider. *Oh God, please don't let him die, not now…please, I'll be so good…*

"Kelly…" He pressed his hand over hers. "Love…you…"

"I love you."

She whispered the words past her tears, but he didn't hear them.

With a sob, she kissed him, willing him to know with his last breath that she loved him.

She held tight to his hand, watching the shallow rise and fall of his chest. A moment later, a long shuddering sigh wracked his body and then he lay still.

It was over, she thought, and then she felt a warm breath whisper past her cheek, felt a hand in her hair.

"Tekihila?"

Kelly opened her eyes, expecting to see Blue Crow kneeling beside her. Instead, she found herself gazing into Lee's deep black eyes.

She stared into his face, unable to speak.

"Tekihila, are you hurt?"

"Lee?"

"Roan Horse is gone."

"What do you mean?"

"Do you not know me, *wastelakapi?"*

"Blue Crow?"

"Han."

"No." She shook her head. "No, it can't be."

Taking her hands in his, he sat up, then slipped his arm around her shoulders.

"How?" Kelly asked.

Blue Crow shook his head. How could he explain what he himself did not understand? Still, he owed it to her to try.

"I watched his spirit leave his body," Blue Crow said, a note of awe in his voice, "and before I had time to think of what I was doing, I willed myself to take his place." He shook his head again, still unable to believe what had happened. "I cannot explain it, *tekihila.* My spirit lives in his body and yet a part of Roan Horse remains."

"No." Kelly shook her head. "No, it can't be."

"It is true, *wastelakapi."*

Kelly stood up, needing a moment to be alone. It was all so incredible.

From the corner of her eye, she watched Lee…or was it Blue Crow?…stand up. He moved toward the stranger's body and searched the man's pockets until he found the key to the shackles. Removing the chains from his feet, Blue Crow turned toward her, a question in his eyes.

At her nod, he knelt to remove the shackles from her feet. Tossing the leg irons aside, he gazed up at her. His eyes were as black as ebony, soul-deep and filled with love.

"A hundred years I waited for you, *wastelakapi.* Will you now deny me?"

"It is you," Kelly murmured, her voice filled with wonder.

She glanced toward the shelf where Blue Crow's body had lain. Nothing remained but the faded Hudson's Bay blanket.

Blue Crow stood up and took her hands in his. "Will you be my woman, *tekihila?* Will you share your life with me here and in the hereafter?"

"I will," Kelly replied breathlessly, and then he was kissing her, his lips warm with the promise of a thousand tomorrows.

Epilogue

ℰ𝒪

Kelly sat on the top rail of the corral, watching Blue Crow put a young filly through its paces.

Three years had passed since the strange happenings in the cave. They had been the happiest three years of Kelly's life.

The first few days after the shooting, she hadn't known how to feel. She had been torn between the need to grieve for Lee and the need to rejoice that Blue Crow was alive, truly alive. And then she would remember that Blue Crow was alive only because Lee had sacrificed his life to save hers and she wanted to cry all over again.

Most confusing of all had been watching Blue Crow. Sometimes, when she gazed into his fathomless black eyes, she saw Lee staring back at her and she had come to believe that what Blue Crow said was true, that a part of Lee's spirit had remained with them.

The morning after the shooting, they had gone back and buried the man in the cave. His driver's license identified him as Lucas Trask, age 31, unmarried. That same afternoon, they had taken the gold into Coleville and cashed it in.

A huge weight seemed to fall from Kelly's shoulders as they deposited the money in the bank. While they were opening the account, Kelly overheard one of the tellers remarking that Harry Renford had quit his job without giving notice and left town.

A week after the shooting, she had married Blue Crow in a simple ceremony, witnessed only by the minister and his wife.

For a time, she had worried about the two bodies buried on her property, but no one had come around asking after their whereabouts. Kelly couldn't help wondering if Harry Renford had been mixed up in the plot to steal the gold, if that wasn't why he had suddenly left town.

Kelly let her gaze wander over the ranch. The corrals were filled with horses now. Cattle grazed in the pasture behind the house. Chickens scratched in the dirt, a cat lay sprawled in the sun, a shaggy black dog slept in the shade under the porch.

In the last three years, they had remodeled the house, installing all new appliances, as well as wall-to-wall carpet in the living room and bedrooms. At the end of last year, they had added on a nursery for the baby that would be born in the summer.

And still they had more money than they could spend. At Blue Crow's suggestion, they had started a scholarship fund to help send underprivileged Lakota kids to college. It gave Kelly a deep sense of satisfaction, knowing that a large share of the treasure that Blue Crow had guarded for a hundred years was being used to help his people.

Kelly smiled as Blue Crow walked toward her. Reaching up, he lifted her gently to the ground. As always, whether they were apart an hour or a day, they could not keep from touching each other.

She went into his arms readily, her head resting against his chest, and knew she would ask no more of the future than to spend the rest of her life in this man's arms.

She felt Blue Crow's hand slide between them to rest on her stomach, now swollen with Blue Crow's child. It was a boy, of that she had no doubt, and his name would be Lee Roan Horse.

"Ohinniyan, wastelakapi," Blue Crow murmured.

"Forever, beloved," Kelly replied, and hand in hand they followed the path toward home.

Also by Madeline Baker

ꕥ

eBooks:

Apache Flame

Dakota Dreams

Hawk's Woman

Heart of the Hunter

Lakota Love Song

Love's Serenade

Shadows Through Time

Under Apache Skies

Wolf Shadow

Print Books:

Apache Flame

Hawk's Woman

Lakota Love Song

Shadows Through Time

Wolf Shadow

About the Author

ജ

Madeline Baker started writing simply for the fun of it. Now she is the award-winning author of more than thirty historical romance books and one of the most popular writers of Native American romance. She lives in California, where she was born and raised.

Madeline welcomes comments from readers. You can find her website and email address on her author bio page at www.ellorascave.com.

Tell Us What You Think

We appreciate hearing reader opinions about our books. You can email us at Comments@EllorasCave.com.

Why an electronic book?

We live in the Information Age—an exciting time in the history of human civilization, in which technology rules supreme and continues to progress in leaps and bounds every minute of every day. For a multitude of reasons, more and more avid literary fans are opting to purchase e-books instead of paper books. The question from those not yet initiated into the world of electronic reading is simply: *Why?*

1. ***Price.*** An electronic title at Ellora's Cave Publishing and Cerridwen Press runs anywhere from 40% to 75% less than the cover price of the exact same title in paperback format. Why? Basic mathematics and cost. It is less expensive to publish an e-book (no paper and printing, no warehousing and shipping) than it is to publish a paperback, so the savings are passed along to the consumer.
2. ***Space.*** Running out of room in your house for your books? That is one worry you will never have with electronic books. For a low one-time cost, you can purchase a handheld device specifically designed for e-reading. Many e-readers have large, convenient screens for viewing. Better yet, hundreds of titles can be stored within your new library—on a single microchip. There are a variety of e-readers from different manufacturers. You can also read e-books on your PC or laptop computer. (Please note that Ellora's Cave does not endorse any specific brands.

You can check our websites at www.ellorascave.com or www.cerridwenpress.com for information we make available to new consumers.)

3. ***Mobility.*** Because your new e-library consists of only a microchip within a small, easily transportable e-reader, your entire cache of books can be taken with you wherever you go.
4. ***Personal Viewing Preferences.*** Are the words you are currently reading too small? Too large? Too... ANNOYING? Paperback books cannot be modified according to personal preferences, but e-books can.
5. ***Instant Gratification.*** Is it the middle of the night and all the bookstores near you are closed? Are you tired of waiting days, sometimes weeks, for bookstores to ship the novels you bought? Ellora's Cave Publishing sells instantaneous downloads twenty-four hours a day, seven days a week, every day of the year. Our webstore is never closed. Our e-book delivery system is 100% automated, meaning your order is filled as soon as you pay for it.

Those are a few of the top reasons why electronic books are replacing paperbacks for many avid readers.

As always, Ellora's Cave and Cerridwen Press welcome your questions and comments. We invite you to email us at Comments@ellorascave.com or write to us directly at Ellora's Cave Publishing Inc., 1056 Home Avenue, Akron, OH 44310-3502.

ELLORA'S CAVE
ROMANTICA PUBLISHING

Made in the USA
Lexington, KY
12 December 2011